MARINE G: SBS

CHINA SEAS

MARINE G: SBS

CHINA SEAS

David Monnery

First published in Great Britain 1996
22 Books, Invicta House, Sir Thomas Longley Road,
Rochester, Kent

A CIP catalogue record for this book is available
from the British Library

ISBN 1 898125 63 5

10 9 8 7 6 5 4 3 2 1

Typeset by Hewer Text Composition Services, Edinburgh
Printed in Great Britain by Cox and Wyman Limited, Reading

1

The metallic clang of the grappling hooks on the stern rail was lost in the rumble of the oil-tanker's engines and the swish of her passage through the ocean swell. For the seven young Vietnamese in the stolen speedboat the next few moments spent trying to position themselves alongside the inviting bamboo ladders were anxious ones. However, no enquiring silhouette appeared on the deck above them, and eventually a combination of luck and judgement produced the desired juxtaposition. Two of the youths began rapidly climbing the fifty-foot wall of the tanker's stern.

At the top they paused briefly, eyes raised above the parapet, before slipping across the rails in unison. Having drawn their shiny new guns, they scoured the dimly lit poop deck for a few moments and then signalled down to the speedboat for reinforcements.

Another four men clambered over the rail, grins breaking out on their faces now that the hard part was over. The leader took them off in search of a route up to the bridge, walking on his toes the way *ninjas* do in the movies.

They came to an auspicious-looking door in the superstructure, and filed inside, the sound of their collective breathing suddenly audible. A metal stairway beckoned, but before they could start up, someone else started down, half running, to judge by the clattering urgency of the footfalls. The leader had no time to think, no time to do anything but see the surprised face, raise the pistol and pull the trigger.

The noise sounded deafening in the enclosed space, and seemed to echo wildly, like a ricocheting bullet. The sailor, a Malay or Filipino, collapsed on to his back and then slid down the stairs, landing at their feet with a bullet hole in his forehead and a glassy stare of incomprehension.

For a moment the leader looked as stunned as the other youths by his accuracy of shot, but he quickly recovered, flexing the gun and flashing an arrogant grin at his followers before leading the way up the stairs.

On the bridge of the Liberian-flagged *Antares* Captain Martin Lansing had just been told that there was a speedboat hanging off his starboard stern, and had immediately assumed the worst. One of the world's black spots for modern piracy, the Singapore Straits rivalled the north-east coastline of Brazil and the anchorages of West Africa, and in recent years no ship, no matter how large, could be considered safe from attack. The shot was only dimly audible on the bridge, and in other circumstances might well have been mistaken for something else. Here and now, however, it simply removed any lingering doubts.

'Get out a distress call,' Lansing told Sánchez, his Mexican radio officer.

He could see the distant lights of Singapore off the starboard bow, still shining brightly at two in the morning. Maybe the mayday signal would elicit a practical response, but Lansing didn't feel too optimistic. In Hong Kong a couple of months earlier an old friend had recounted the story of another ship in this situation, whose captain had been told: 'Sorry, we'd love to help, but we don't actually have anything to help you with.'

Lansing kept a revolver in the adjoining cabin, but he had no intention of using it. The latest guidelines advised no resistance, and with good reason – once armed pirates were aboard your ship there was no way to fight them. The last captain to try had been shot in the head, along with two of his crew. Merchant seamen were not soldiers.

He should caution the rest of his crew, Lansing suddenly realized, but before he could act on the thought the first of the hijackers appeared in the bridge doorway, revolver in hand. At the same moment Sánchez emerged from the adjoining radio room, and Lansing caught a glimpse of a smile on the man's face before the sight of the intruders wiped it away.

Almost thirty-five miles to the east of the *Antares*, and about eight miles north of the Indonesian island of Batam, an innocent-looking sampan rocked to and fro in the waters of the strait. Several items of clothing hung on the line which had been raised above the craft's covered section, but from a distance it was not possible to read the labels, most of which bore the exotic brand names of C&A and Marks & Spencer. Nor was it obvious to a casual glance that the sampan boasted an impressive array of communications equipment and an engine capable of propelling the craft at an almost unseemly twenty-five knots.

The boat's occupants, though, were clearly neither Chinese nor Malay.

'They've received a distress call,' Lieutenant Robert Cafell shouted out through the covered section's open doorway.

'Where?' Captain Callum Marker and Corporal Stuart Finn asked in unison. Both men were sitting on the foredeck, along with the fourth member of the team, Corporal Ian Dubery.

There was a short pause.

'In the Phillip Channel,' Cafell replied, disgust in his voice.

'Fuck,' Finn said. 'Four fucking nights and the locals get all the fun.'

'So it goes,' Marker muttered, though he felt equally disappointed. In the week since the Special Boat Squadron team had arrived in Singapore they had seen enough bureaucratic in-fighting to last them a lifetime, but precious little in the way of real action. Marker suspected that the team's current position, way out at the eastern end of the pirates' normal range of operations, had been chosen as a means of minimizing their chances of active involvement. Malaysia and Singapore had been fully independent for several decades now, but the colonial past was far from forgotten, and a lingering resentment of the white races persisted. He could understand the reasons why, but that didn't make it any less irritating to be on the receiving end. They had, after all, been invited out East to share their expertise.

It was the usual international cock-up. The SBS team's official host was the new computerized piracy centre in Kuala Lumpur, Malaysia, but this centre was financed internationally, and each donor expected a say in how the money was spent. Marker knew this particular crack-down was being funded for the most part by the shipowners' International Maritime Federation, the International Chamber of Commerce's Maritime Bureau and a bevy of shipping insurance companies, Lloyd's of London prominent among them.

The operation itself was being conducted in a stretch of ocean where the maritime boundaries of three nations – and three national egos – rubbed up against each other in one of the world's busiest shipping channels. One of these nations – Indonesia – had been neither invited to nor informed of the exercise now in progress. There was a very simple reason for this – the Indonesian naval forces in the area were known to have turned a blind eye to the recent epidemic of piracy, and were suspected of worse – of being actively involved.

So the flotilla of craft strung out along the Straits was manned by the Singapore Maritime Police, the Singapore naval defence forces, their Malaysian equivalents and, representing world order in general and the interests of Western financial concerns in particular, Britain's SBS.

And up until a few moments ago the whole business had looked and felt like one of those well-intentioned ideas whose time had not yet come. Now it seemed as if someone had finally swum into the waiting net.

'What now, boss?' Cafell asked from inside the covered section.

'Just keep listening,' Marker told him. 'They might come our way.'

'Yeah, and Arsenal might start playing attractive football,' Finn said sourly.

Marker smiled. The younger man was probably right. If the pirates' home base was hidden somewhere out in the western reaches of the Riau Islands, then they would have presumably boarded the *Antares* a couple of hours earlier. It looked like another quiet night for the SBS team.

On the tanker's bridge three of the Vietnamese were holding guns on Lansing, Sánchez and two other members of the crew whom they had collected *en route*. The other four hijackers had gone to secure the remainder of the eleven-man crew in their sleeping quarters. Most ominously, the leader, whose grasp of English was less than adequate, had refused to allow anyone near the controls. When Lansing had explained that the ship must either be stopped or guided, the leader had simply ignored him. One of the pirates had actually giggled, like a small boy with a secret to savour.

By Lansing's estimation they had less than an hour to spare before the *Antares* ploughed into one of the eastern islands of the Riau Archipelago and disgorged enough oil to wipe out half the local ecology. Since the fully loaded ship would need almost half that time to reach a dead halt the situation was rapidly becoming serious. And the recent guidelines' instruction to play for time once the distress signal had been sent was seeming less and less appropriate.

One of the hijackers burst back on to the bridge, and fired several indecipherable sentences at the leader. The latter, apparently satisfied, turned to Lansing. 'Crew all prisoners,' he said. 'Now, show safe.' He waved the gun to reinforce his demand, and Lansing noticed for the first time that the safety-catch was off.

'It's in my cabin – this way,' he said, starting slowly for the door. Guidelines for dealing with pirates were all very well, but this lot were not much beyond adolescence. Even the leader, who sported a wispy goatee, seemed barely out of his teens. Lansing found himself wishing that there was something of value inside the safe.

So, apparently, did the pirates' leader. After rummaging among the worthless papers it contained, he jerked round angrily, raising the revolver and pushing the barrel to within a few inches of Lansing's nose. 'Safe,' he repeated.

'This is the safe,' Lansing told him.

'Gems,' the man said. 'Gems.'

'There are no gems. This is an oil-tanker.'

'You . . .' the man began, but his vocabulary didn't include the words he needed, and as his hand began to shake with frustration the gun went off, sending a bullet through the centre of the tanker captain's brain.

There was a moment of silent surprise, and then the Vietnamese cursed, swung a foot at the crumpled corpse, and abruptly started back towards the bridge. How was this possible? he asked himself. The information had seemed so precise, and up until this moment everything had gone so perfectly. It felt almost like a betrayal, but if that was the case he couldn't begin to imagine why.

Back on the bridge the three crewmen eyed his return with frightened eyes, but he was more concerned with the growing doubt he saw in the faces of his followers. This was not what he had promised them.

'Look!' one of his men suddenly shouted, pointing through the starboard window.

In the distance two pinpoints of light seemed to be converging on the tanker.

The bastards had sent a distress call. The leader coldly turned his revolver on the Mexican and pulled the trigger. The two other crewmen started to plead – but to no avail. One witness would be one too many.

On the customized sampan Finn had just come to relieve Cafell in the 'radio room' when the container ship made its first appearance on the radar screen. It was probably heading for Singapore, one last port of call before sailing west with another load of assorted high-tech treasure. The SBS team had watched a steady stream of such ships pass through the Straits during the past few days and nights, and most of those travelling west seemed appreciably lower in the water than those travelling east. It was a sign of the times.

Once they had established eye contact, this particular ship proved no exception, for the white superstructure and dark funnel, set alongside each other to aft, seemed almost dwarfed by the row upon row of piled containers on the long forward deck. Somewhere between ten and fifteen thousand tonnes, it was travelling at around twenty knots and visibly slowing as it entered the mouth of the Straits.

It was also about to receive company. No other craft was visible to the naked eye, but the flickering trace on the radar scanner could only be a small boat rapidly closing on the container ship. Either that, Finn thought, or he'd just tracked the biggest, fastest flying fish the world had ever seen. Or Dawn French was out windsurfing.

'Boss,' he called out softly, 'come and have a look at this.'

Marker stood at his shoulder for a moment, watching the screen. 'What's happening with the other lot?' he asked quietly.

'They're in pursuit. In a northerly direction. Probably headed back towards Singapore.'

'Two attacks in one night seems like a bit too much of a coincidence,' Marker murmured, as much to himself as to Finn.

The young Londoner raised an eyebrow. 'Meaning?'

Marker shrugged. 'Don't know. But the first attack certainly worked as a diversion, even if it wasn't intended as one . . .'

'Shall I let our gallant allies in on the secret?' Finn asked.

'No,' Marker said. The two dots on the radar screen had now merged into one. 'If the first attack *was* a diversion, then Long John Silver out there will be listening in to make sure it's worked. Let's foster his illusions for a while.'

On the bridge of the container ship *Ocean Carousel* Captain Spiros Lamrakis was staring out along the length of his fully loaded ship, and wondering what was happening further into the Straits. His radio operator had picked up the distress call from the *Antares*, and handed it on to the captain more as a matter of interest than of practical value. Even if there had been any assistance they could offer the beleaguered tanker, both men knew that they were too far away to offer it. 'There but for fortune,' the American had said, leaving Lamrakis with a sense of relief which was only vaguely tinged with guilt.

It was like airline crashes, he thought, staring out at the dark sea. Each time there was one, he felt a little safer flying. Lightning usually had the decency to wait a while before it struck again in the same place.

He turned his mind back to the topic which had been occupying it before the distress call – his sixteen-year-old son. He suspected it would have been hard enough for a father who lived at home to influence the boy's behaviour for the better, let alone a father who spent more than half each year at sea. But as her latest letter made clear, his wife was rapidly reaching the end of her patience with the boy, and Lamrakis had the distinct feeling that he had to either come up with something brilliant or accept a permanent rift in the family.

He wondered if the captain of the tanker up ahead had a son.

Unknown to Lamrakis, the *Ocean Carousel* had already been boarded by more than a dozen armed men. These were not the children of unwanted Vietnamese migrants, sucked into violent crime by vicious discrimination and the collapse of their parents' world. These were professionals: members of the Indonesian armed forces by day, pirates by night. They had access to the most modern weaponry and equipment, intelligence of sailings and cargoes which would have made Francis Drake green with envy, and a territorial base which could not be violated by the forces of international law and order without risking a major war.

And as Lamrakis would soon discover, they were not interested in small pickings. These pirates had not come simply to steal his cargo – they had come to steal his ship too.

Aboard the sampan the SBS men were taking turns keeping the nightscope on the distant container ship. At first it seemed as if the rendezvous with the smaller vessel might have been innocent after all, for there was no change in the ship's course or speed, no sign that anything untoward had occurred. Perhaps, Marker mused, the container ship's captain was new to these waters, and had asked for a pilot. But in that case the small boat had come from the wrong direction . . .

'She's turning to port,' Finn announced.

'She's heading for the Riau Channel,' Cafell said, looking enquiringly at Marker.

'In that case . . .' Marker began.

'I'm picking up a message from command,' Dubery interrupted him from inside the covered section.

The other three waited, their eyes on the distant silhouette of the container ship.

'They're alerting the land forces on Singapore,' Dubery reported. 'And they've just boarded the tanker. Several of the crew are dead. The op's being abandoned for the night.'

'Acknowledge,' Marker told him, 'and tell them we're on our way in.' He smiled grimly at the other two. 'Just in case anyone's listening in,' he explained. 'Now let's get this thing moving. Rob, take the wheel. Keep the island between us and them. Finn, take lookout. I'll start thinking up excuses for being in Indonesian waters with a souped-up sampan.'

'Practising for the Olympics,' Finn suggested. 'Sampan foursomes.'

'Looking for Michael Palin?' Cafell offered.

Marker sighed. 'You know what I like about working with Ian?' he asked the other two. 'He sometimes has nothing to say.'

'Yes, boss,' Cafell said with a grin.

'I'm hurt now,' Finn muttered.

Marker smiled and sat back with his hands behind his head. The four of them made a good team: Cafell with his cheerful practicality and navigational skills, Dubery with his dependability and boat-handling, Finn . . . well, Finn was clever, he was curious, and as far as Marker could tell he wasn't afraid of anyone or anything.

They had first worked together the previous summer. Marker and Cafell had been sent to the Turks and Caicos Islands in the West Indies to investigate possible drug smuggling and the disappearance of a retired SBS officer. They had ended up uncovering a trade in spare parts for transplant surgery, a trail of blood which originated in a Haitian prison orphanage and ended on the operating tables of a chain of Florida hospitals. As the investigation had proceeded, reinforcements had been deemed necessary, and Dubery and Finn had been flown out from England. The four-man team had put a stop to the trade, and most of the principals were now either dead or behind bars in the US. All except the head honcho, who had managed to distance himself from the whole business.

This time they had been sent out as a four-man package, with orders that bordered on the downright vague. They were to offer the benefits of their experience to those in charge of the current campaign against piracy in South-East Asian waters. They were to assist in an operational capacity if the relevant authorities invited them to. No time limit had been set to their sojourn in the area, but completed expense sheets were expected in Poole on a fortnightly basis. Stamping out international piracy was all very well, but the Royal Marine Corps still had to keep within its budget.

Marker smiled to himself, and stared out across the black waters at the blacker line of land a mile or so off their port bow. Bintan Island was Indonesian, and the moment they entered the Riau Channel between Bintan and Batam there could be no disputing whose waters they were in. At best they could claim to be lost, and look like fools. 'Brits in Anti-Pirate Op Lose Their Way' – he could see the headlines.

Whatever. But if they wanted to catch these bastards, then they could hardly be deterred by the risk of losing face. And if the pirates didn't give a toss for maritime boundaries, how could they? With any luck they could get the photographic proof they needed and head back to Singapore, leaving the Indonesian authorities to learn of the visit later, from the evidence collected against their own armed forces. The sampan *looked* innocent enough. When it was travelling at less than five knots, that was.

The container ship was about a mile ahead of them, still moving at around fifteen knots. There were a few dim lights off the port bow now.

'Tanjung Uban,' Finn said, as if reading Marker's thoughts. 'Sounds like an anagram, but it's a small town.'

The strait they were entering was about five miles wide, but a smaller island in mid-channel effectively reduced the width to a couple of miles on either side. The container ship seemed to be making for the eastern channel, which would take it within a mile or so of the lights.

'It's three-thirty,' Marker said. 'You'd think they'd want to get wherever it is they're going before dawn.'

'Why?' Finn wanted to know. 'This is Indonesia. We can't send search planes into Indonesian airspace, can we?'

'Maybe not, but this isn't like bits of Siberia used to be. There are tourists all over the place – on beaches, out in boats, snorkelling, fishing. And where tourists can go, so can intelligence agents. These guys can't be berthing stolen ships in plain view. Not ships this size. Someone would notice.'

'There are hundreds of islands in this chain,' Cafell said from the wheel, 'and only a few of them are inhabited. It shouldn't be that hard to find a secluded anchorage.'

'Maybe,' Marker conceded. 'But secluded and secure are two different things. These are not cowboys we're dealing with.'

'I reckon there must be well over a thousand containers on that ship,' Finn said. 'Say they're all full of home computers from Hong Kong, maybe a hundred per container, something like five hundred quid each. That's fifty thousand per container, which adds up to . . .'

'Fifty million for the cargo,' Cafell said. 'Plus whatever they can get for the ship.'

'With a repaint, a new name and some forged papers they can probably pick up another fifty-million-pound cargo,' Marker said. 'It's been done.'

'Christ,' Finn muttered. 'This piracy business is beginning to sound attractive. Maybe it's what we were all trained for.'

'I couldn't take the stress,' Marker murmured. Nor the ethics, he told himself. Errol Flynn and Hollywood notwithstanding, olden-day pirates hadn't been noted for their chivalry, and some of their modern descendants seemed to specialize in brutality for its own sake. Over the past twenty years many of the crowded boats fleeing Vietnam had been attacked by Thai pirates who seemed more interested in murder and rape than good old-fashioned theft.

The bunch who had seized the container ship were in a different league, of course. Marker had no doubt they would kill to protect themselves, but there would be nothing personal in it. He remembered Brando telling the man in *The Godfather* that it was simply a matter of business. Sometimes Marker found that proposition even more horrifying than casual sadism, but it was always a hard call.

They were in the eastern channel now, the island in mid-strait a dark hump to starboard, the desultory lights of sleeping Tanjung Uban falling behind to port. Marker wondered how long it would be before their Malaysian and Singaporean allies missed them and hoped that, in the excitement of their chase, it would be a while. The last thing they needed was a flurry of suspicious-sounding messages on the radio.

'It's clouding over, boss,' Finn observed.

It was. There was going to be another Sumatra, Marker realized. This region was prone to experience three or four of these violent pre-dawn thunder-storms each month, but this would be the second in four nights. The first had occurred on their first night out, and had been exhilarating, almost fright-ening, in its intensity. Now that Finn had pointed it out, Marker could feel the tension building in the air.

'We'd better open the gap a little,' he said. Even in waters like these they had a good chance of tracking the container ship by radar, while an inconvenient burst of lightning could reveal the sampan in what looked suspiciously like pursuit.

He had hardly got the words out before the first fork of lightning ripped earthwards, burying itself in the island off to starboard. A blast of thunder followed almost instantaneously, and the rain seemed to take its cue from that. Like most tropical storms it shifted from odd drops to a fully-fledged Niagara in about four seconds.

They seemed to be encased in a wall of dark water, which every now and then would burst with light and reverberate with noise. For the next half hour both container ship and land kept vanishing from view, but the blip on the radar moved steadily south-south-east down the centre of the strait. Dawn was not much more than ninety minutes away when the *son et lumière* finally abated, and the rain slackened to a mere downpour. While Marker and Finn bailed water from the foredeck, Dubery took the wheel and Cafell bent over his charts to pinpoint their exact location.

'I reckon that's Nginang,' he said, gesturing towards a scarcely visible shape in the murk off to starboard.

'They're changing course,' Dubery announced. 'To the west.'

Marker appeared at Cafell's shoulder. 'Which way?' he asked.

Cafell held the torch with one hand as he traced the

container ship's direction with the other. 'They're heading into this,' he said, indicating the small, island-dotted sea which lay between the larger masses of Batam and Rempang. 'Their base must be in there – there's no other reason they would risk a ship that size in waters like these.'

Marker walked back to the doorway. The rain was relenting now. 'Close up a little,' he told Dubery. 'We don't want to lose them.'

The rain stopped as suddenly as it had begun, and the clouds seemed to slide away across the sky like a huge roof, revealing an ever-larger canvas of stars. The container ship was clearly visible now, a jet-black square against the rounded ridge of an island. In the relative silence that followed the storm the SBS men could just detect the dull rumble of the engines across the black water.

'It's turning again,' Dubery announced. 'And slowing.'

'I'll bet their base is down that channel,' Cafell said, struggling to read the map by the light of the stars.

'Keep us on this course,' Marker told Dubery. 'And let's keep talk to a minimum from now on.'

The sampan chugged across the water. It seemed to be making a hell of a noise, but logic told Marker the engines of the container ship would provide an adequate cover. There was more chance of their being seen than heard, particularly since dawn was not far over the horizon.

The container ship was slowly disappearing now, turning into the mouth of a half-mile-wide channel between two densely forested shorelines. There seemed to be a hint of light emerging from the channel, and as the sampan drew parallel with the opening the sources became apparent. About half a mile to the south a jetty poked out into the water, and behind it the jungle had been cleared to make room for several barracks-like buildings. Some fifty yards offshore a small warship rode at anchor – an Indonesian Navy Sabola-class patrol boat.

In the centre of the stream the huge and still lightless bulk of the container ship had come to a dead halt, dwarfing both the warship and the channel. Its metal ladder was in the process of being lowered, and even at this distance the SBS men could hear the metallic clunk as it locked itself down.

Several smaller boats, most of which looked like speedboats, were tied up at the jetty.

They had found the pirates' lair.

2

Aboard the *Ocean Carousel* Captain Lamrakis and his first mate had just been escorted down to the cabin where the rest of the crew were being held. Leaving the first mate to fend off the inevitable torrent of questions, Lamrakis placed his back against a spare patch of wall and let himself sink to the floor.

His hours on the bridge with the smiling Indonesian had been nerve-racking. The hazards posed by the ship's new course had been bad, but a growing realization of the hijack leader's utter indifference to the lives of the captive crew had been much worse. No threats had been made – Lamrakis would probably have felt better if they had – but no promises of eventual safety had been offered either, and, much as he wanted to, he found it hard to believe that such an omission could be accidental. Standing on the bridge of his ship as the storm raged around it, he had suddenly sensed, with appalling clarity, that he would never see his wife or son again.

Maybe he was wrong. Sitting there, surrounded by faces as fearful as his own, he could only hope so. The problem was – putting himself in the hijackers' position – he could see no good reason for letting himself or his crew go free.

*   *   *

As the sampan pulled around a forested headland the pirates' base disappeared from view.

'Find us a place to hide,' Marker told Cafell, whose map was becoming easier to read with each minute.

'Do you want hot showers, or will cold do?'

'On this island,' Marker added, jerking his thumb to the left.

'It's Rempang,' Cafell muttered.

'Looks inviting,' Finn said ironically. 'Anyone seen *King Kong*?' he added as an afterthought.

'Which one?' Marker asked. His knowledge of films was about as extensive as Cafell's of naval history. Or Finn's of trivia.

'Not the Jessica Lange one,' Finn said. 'We had that question in the pub quiz a few weeks back.'

'What are you two jabbering on about?' Cafell asked.

'Nothing,' Finn said. 'But when you go ashore, and you find a lot of hysterical natives staring up at a huge gate in a huge wall, don't ask them to open it for you.'

'I'll try and remember that,' Cafell said. 'Now, if we can get back to the real world, this is a big island, about twenty miles long and nearly ten miles wide. But there should be a nice little bay about a quarter of a mile ahead. On the map it looks almost enclosed, which will make it a nice hidey-hole. But you can never . . .'

They all turned at the sound of an engine starting up behind them.

'One of the speedboats,' said Marker. 'Get some speed up,' he barked at Dubery. 'They'll never hear us over that racket.'

The sampan surged forward in search of Cafell's bay,

with Marker keeping an anxious look over the stern. There was a fifty-fifty chance the speedboat would take off in the opposite direction. If it didn't, there was a much better than even chance that the surface of the sea would still be offering evidence of their passage.

'Cut the speed,' Marker shouted at Dubery, just as the mouth of the bay came into sight. The sampan took the turn on the nautical equivalent of two wheels, and seconds later was decelerating to a stop in the relatively still waters of a palm-fringed cove straight from the holiday brochures. The only sour note was provided by prominent signs on both the small stretches of beach. None of the SBS men read Bahasa, but they didn't need to – the signs came with their own English translation. This was military property, and trespassers invited the death sentence.

As Dubery cut the engine the sound of the speedboat became audible. At first it seemed to swell, as if the craft was coming in their direction, but then it definitely began to fade. Then suddenly it cut out altogether, leaving only the sounds of the jungle and the sea.

'Standing sentry,' Marker said. 'We'll probably hear another one heading down to the other end of the channel before long. Between them they'll keep any unwelcome boats away from the area.'

'And us here,' Finn said.

'Until dark,' Marker agreed. 'But since we're exactly where we want to be that doesn't really matter, does it?'

Cafell and Finn looked at each other in mock disbelief.

'But first off, I think we'd better hide ourselves a little better. If we could get the sampan in front of those trees over there, or even better, right underneath the branches, it would probably escape a casual glance.'

'For all we know, the pirates use these beaches for their sandcastle competitions,' Finn said.

'Let's hope so,' Marker replied, 'because then there'll be a path from here to their base.' He grinned at them. 'Well, don't just stand there, you two. Let's get in the water and give this tub a push. Ian, keep watch – land and sea.'

The other three stripped down to their shorts, lowered themselves into the warm, chest-deep water and began manhandling the sampan towards the cover of the overhanging trees. Marker was reminded of Bogart in *The African Queen*, pulling the boat through the reed marshes and getting covered with leeches. In Florida the previous summer he and Cafell had seen the boat which had been used in the movie, tied up outside a Holiday Inn to amuse the tourists.

Feeling something brush against his left leg, Marker immediately assumed the worst. But weren't leeches freshwater creatures? He realized he didn't know. Ignoring the clinging sensation, he pushed against the sampan with his shoulder and silently invoked his almost daily resolution to learn something about the natural world before he died.

The water was deep enough under the trees for a shallow draught, and once the three men had manoeuvred the boat into position it was virtually invisible to anything but the most determined scrutiny. Back on deck Marker found that the object on his leg was a particularly sticky lump of seaweed.

The four of them gathered on the foredeck for a conference. In the branches above, two small parrots were staring down at them – green with red tail feathers and a prominent blue spot on their heads, they looked as though they'd bruised themselves head-butting. Through the fronds which hid the sampan the early-morning light was turning the waters of the bay from black to a deep blue-green. In the distance a speedboat engine started up, as if to remind them of why they were there.

'So where do we go from here?' Marker asked, swatting at a mosquito on his bare arm. 'Suggestions?'

'Breakfast sounds good,' Finn offered.

'And after we've enjoyed our Shredded Wheat?'

'I suppose we have to pay the bad guys a visit.'

'Yeah, we need some pictures,' Cafell agreed. 'A few shots of the freighter next to that Indonesian patrol boat and we should have the cat among the pigeons.'

'Doesn't sound too difficult, provided you don't get us lost in the jungle,' Finn remarked.

'Yeah, but it's not enough,' Marker said quietly. 'This place is obviously only a transhipment point. Say the kickbacks go right to the top of the military in this area – what's to stop them picking out a few scapegoats and simply finding some other convenient place to bring the ships? We'll cause them a bit of aggro, but we'll be no nearer finding out who's fingering the cargoes at the beginning or who's disposing of them at the end.'

'So what do we need to do?' asked Dubery.

'This lot have to be in contact with both the fingerers and the disposers. Maybe we can find some clues in one of the buildings down there.'

'Like a telephone pad with the top sheet ripped off, but you can still read the imprint on the sheet below?' Finn asked.

Marker grinned. 'I was thinking more of records. Military units tend to keep them – out of habit if they can't think of a better reason.'

'That sounds like a night job,' Cafell said.

'Yeah, and first we need to know the lie of the land. So we'll set up an OP this morning, take our snaps, and then go in tonight.'

'What about our hosts in Singapore?'

'With any luck they'll notice that another ship has gone missing, assume we're on the job, and keep quiet about it. I don't think it's worth the risk of using the radio.' He looked round at the other three. 'Any other brilliant ideas? Any strong objections?'

The others shook their heads, faces suddenly serious, as each confronted the possibility of combat before sunrise.

An hour later, with the sun making its presence felt behind the forested ridge, the four men waded across to the nearest beach and headed off into the thick vegetation. They were all wearing light camouflage fatigues, matching floppy hats, jungle boots and streaks of camouflage cream across their faces, necks, hands and arms. Each man carried a holstered Browning High Power 9mm pistol and a cradled Heckler & Koch MP5SD silenced sub-machine-gun. Finn was also carrying the Nikon and its assorted lenses, Dubery the digging tools, and Cafell and Marker the team's supply of food and water.

Progress was slow, and made slower by the need for frequent listening halts. The four men would stand motionless, ears straining for any sounds with a human source, but there would be only the never-ending racket of the jungle, and, pervading everything, the drone of mosquitoes massing for another attack.

By Cafell's reckoning they had less than a mile to travel, but half that distance took them the better part of an hour, so it was with some relief that they found the first evidence of human presence – a telegraph pole silhouetted against the sky. Ten minutes later they reached the dirt road which ran beneath the wires, and crouched for several minutes in the foliage beside it. Amounting to little more than a swath of deep ruts between the trees, the 'road' seemed both unused and unusable.

'It's not on the map,' Cafell announced.

'It's probably just a supply road for the base,' Marker said. 'Or maybe just a by-product of putting in the telephone.'

'If we get into the base, can I call my mum?' Finn asked.

'Why spoil her day?' Cafell murmured.

'Come on,' Marker said, standing up. 'At this rate we won't get there until Christmas.'

They walked cautiously up the slowly climbing road for a hundred yards or so, stopped and listened to the relentless cacophony all around them, then off again. After four such advances a distant low humming noise had added itself to the hubbub of nature. It sounded like a generator.

They resumed their journey, taking care to keep within the shadows on the left side of the road. The sun was now occasionally visible through the trees, the sky above them blue and cloudless. Both temperature and humidity seemed to be rising exponentially.

The long uphill stretch was coming to an end, and

Finn was sent forward to reconnoitre. He edged the last few yards to the crest on his stomach, and found himself only twenty yards from the ruins of some sort of temple. Beyond this the forested land fell steeply away towards the sea channel, where the container ship rode at anchor in mid-stream. Beyond it another thickly vegetated slope rose towards the sun. The jetty and barrack-type buildings below were hidden from view by the trees, but the gleaming sides of oil tanks and a water-tower were visible.

A few yards beyond the ruin their road took a sharp turn to the right, angling down the slope towards a probable hairpin, leaving the telegraph poles to take the more direct route to the shore, plunging down through the trees.

Finn's attention was caught by the activity on the container ship.

'They're giving it a complete face-lift,' he explained on rejoining the others. 'The name on the stern is *Ocean Carousel* but the local Rolf Harris is busy painting something else beginning with "BO" on the starboard bow. And there are about twenty men with brushes hard at work changing the colour of the funnel from red to green.' He rummaged in his bergen for the camera. 'Back in a minute,' he added, and was gone again.

A few minutes later he returned. 'Rolf's adding a "T",' he said. 'My money's on "Botulism".'

'You got some pictures?' Marker asked.

'Yeah, but nothing with the patrol boat. If it's still there it's out of sight behind the ruin.'

'What ruin?'

'There's a kind of temple just over the top.'

'It was probably a mosque,' Cafell said. 'This used to

26

be an important part of the world – there were lots of wealthy sultanates on these islands. And bits of Ming pottery are still being washed up on the beaches from Chinese trading junks wrecked hundreds of years ago. I bet you lot didn't know Marco Polo came to Bintan.'

'The inventor of the mint?' Finn murmured.

Marker sighed. 'What's the best way down?' he asked Finn.

'Good question.' The younger man explained about the telegraph poles. 'That would be the most direct route, but it would take us right into the base, which won't be much use when it comes to taking photos that tie everything together. We could head straight through the jungle and end up fifty yards or so to the north, but I reckon the best bet would be to carry on down the road to where it turns and take to the jungle then. It looks like there's a small headland about a hundred and fifty yards south of the jetty which would be perfect for getting pictures.'

'Sounds a bit on the visible side,' Cafell said.

'Maybe,' Finn agreed. 'It's impossible to tell from up here.'

'Let's give it a try,' Marker decided. 'But just in case . . .' He looked from man to man. 'Our main aim is to get in and out with no one the wiser. Our second best is simply to get out and away. If we run into trouble don't hesitate to use whatever force is necessary – these are not nice people. If we get split up we'll use Rob's mosque as the first fall-back position, and the boat as the second. Clear?'

The others nodded.

They resumed their journey, working their way round the back of the half-overgrown ruin to avoid the open crest and rejoining the dirt track on its descent. The noises of human activity grew louder: the clatter of something being closed or dropped, a distant shout, laughter in reply. An outboard motor started up, swelled in volume, then faded into the south. They reached the expected hairpin and took what seemed a suspiciously easy route through the jungle towards the unseen shoreline. The glitter of an abandoned gum wrapper offered unwelcome evidence that the path had been recently used.

They approached the headland with great care, but, for the moment at least, it seemed devoid of human occupancy. On the far side, facing away from the invisible base, there was a small, sandy beach, but the rest of the shoreline was rocky, with trees and bushes jostling each other for room right down to the edge of the water. Once ensconced inside the mass of tightly woven vegetation, the four men had the advantages of both shade and concealment. They also had as good a view of the base and channel as they could have hoped for.

Marker divided up the hours of daylight into shifts, and took the first watch with Finn while Cafell and Dubery got some sleep. In the channel the container ship's face-lift was proceeding apace, with the funnel now showing more green than red, and the new name *Botany Bay* glistening on the starboard bow. Halfway through the morning the Liberian flag in the stern was taken down and a Panamanian flag hoisted in its place. Finn kept himself busy capturing on film this and other facets of the transformation.

Marker wondered whether a ship of this class and name already existed or whether the pirates had simply thought up a fictional identity. Probably the former, he decided – it was much easier to forge existing documents than start from scratch. At some point in the next few months the owners of the original *Botany Bay* would receive an anxious call from a shipping agent, enquiring about the non-arrival of a valuable cargo.

The hours dragged by, the temperature continued to rise. The sky grew increasingly overcast, taking the humidity towards Turkish-bath levels. Not for the first time, Marker wondered how people coped with living their whole lives in such a climate. He decided he would rather live in Greenland than at equatorial sea level.

He smiled to himself. Ten days ago he had been overjoyed to hear that he was heading out East once more. Since the job in Florida and the succeeding period of leave he had tried to settle, with less than complete success, back into the well-worn routines of an SBS instructor. It wasn't that he didn't enjoy the job – he did – and he didn't think he was still suffering fall-out from his failed marriage. Penny was gone and that was that. He had to accept it, had to carry whatever it was he had managed to learn from the whole episode into his next relationship – always assuming there would be one.

No, the restlessness which seemed to be afflicting him had only one source – himself. He wondered whether it could be in his genes, since his mother and father, both professional actors, had spent their lives moving from rep to rep, and until he was fourteen he had had no permanent home. Boarding-school terms were followed by summer seasons at a seaside resort or Christmas seasons in whichever provincial town the pantomime was playing. His stay in the house in Highgate, which finally became a home when TV replaced the theatre as his parents' primary source of income, lasted only four years. The Marines and SBS had been a sort of emotional home since he turned eighteen – too much so in the end as far as his marriage was concerned. Penny had demanded he choose between that home and the one he shared with her, and he had tried to convince himself that no such choice had to be made. Ironically, now that she was gone, the work seemed less emotionally fulfilling than it had when she was still there.

At the same time, he was damned if he knew what else he could do with his life. The sea was where he had always wanted to work, and the sea took you away from other homes.

Marker sighed, resisted the temptation to wipe his camouflaged brow with his camouflaged forearm, and turned the Nikon's zoom lens on the container ship. It was impossible to tell whether the men swarming over it were navy or civilian – they were certainly not wearing uniforms. He wondered where the ship's crew were. Perhaps still on board, or perhaps in the buildings facing the jetty. Only one man had come out of these since their observation had begun, and he had been in uniform. Not a naval one, though. Not unless sailors wore khaki in this corner of the world.

He had definitely been Chinese, but then so were eighty per cent of the population of Singapore.

The patrol boat was still rocking gently at anchor between the jetty and the container ship, apparently bereft of a crew. They had to be the men painting the funnel, Marker decided. Why import civilians, after all? He wondered what sort of percentage this naval unit was receiving for its work. A mere twelve hours' worth probably: the ship would sail as soon as it got dark. The evening breeze would even help to dry the paint.

But where would it be sailing to? He was hoping that there would be some clue to the destination in one of the buildings, but Finn's remark about the notepad by the telephone had probably been depressingly apt.

Of course, once they got back to Singapore – which they should do well before dawn – an international search would be set in motion. The trouble was, there were so many different routes the rechristened ship could take from here: south or east through the Indonesian archipelago towards Australia or the Philippines respectively, north towards Thailand, Vietnam or China. The bastards might even have the nerve to sail past Singapore and up the Malacca Strait towards the west. And the moment they found out a search was underway – as they were bound to – it would be another secluded cove, another coat of paint, another name.

If only he'd had the forethought to bring one of those tracking devices they'd used in the Caribbean.

He turned the glasses on the base buildings. There were only three: the whole set-up had either been constructed for a very specific and limited purpose – shore support for just the one patrol boat, perhaps – or it had been custom-built for piracy. There couldn't be more than a dozen men permanently stationed ashore, and there would only be one admin office, maybe no more than a desk. A search shouldn't take very long.

'Boss,' Finn said softly at his side. 'I've been thinking.'
'Yeah?'

'There's no way we're going to be able to track these bastards, is there?'

'It doesn't look like it.'

Finn's face split into a grin. 'Well, I was just looking at those barrels on the jetty and, well, you remember *Monkey Business*? The Marx Brothers?'

Marker raised an eyebrow. 'Are you suggesting we try stowing away on the damn ship?'

Finn tried to shrug in the confined space. 'Yeah. Not all of us. Maybe one or two. Can't think of a better way to find out where it's going.'

Marker let the idea sink in.

'Rob will probably know the layout better than its captain,' Finn added, 'so we shouldn't have any trouble finding somewhere to hide.'

Maybe, Marker thought. But they wouldn't be eating in the galley with the crew, and there was no knowing how long it would be before the ship put into another port. At least five days, he guessed, and the team was carrying about eight man-days' worth of emergency rations. Still, there was no way he would consider sending just one man into such a situation. Two men might get hungrier, but they would be just as easy to hide, and they could offer each other both practical and emotional support. Not to mention the chance to sleep.

'I've heard worse ideas,' he told Finn. 'We'll talk it over when we wake up the others.'

Another hour went by, during which time the men on the container ship completed the repainting of the funnel and the day grew even hotter. Marker resisted the temptation to consume more of their water supply – any stowaways would need it. At noon he woke the other two, and the four men huddled together in the confined space to consider Finn's suggestion.

Cafell and Dubery were both enthusiastic; almost too much so, Marker thought. 'OK,' he said, 'I agree that a couple of us wouldn't have much trouble getting aboard once it gets dark, and Rob thinks there are a thousand places to hide on the ship once we get there, so maybe the odds aren't that bad. But I don't want anyone thinking this is going to be a picnic. Whoever goes, they're going to be out of contact with the rest of the world until the ship docks again, and they'll probably go hungry in the process. And there's always the chance something will go wrong and they'll be discovered while the ship is at sea, in which case there's a good chance they'll walk the plank.'

'We know all that, boss,' Finn said. 'So who gets to go?'

'You and me,' Marker said. The two single men, he thought.

'No chance,' Cafell said. 'Neither of you has any idea what the inside of that ship looks like . . .'

'Can't you make us a model this afternoon?' Finn asked with a grin. Cafell's obsession with mapping and model-making was almost legendary in the Royal Marine Corps.

Marker had been afraid Cafell would put forward this argument, mostly because it was unanswerable. If Cafell went then Marker, as the other officer, would have to stay behind. Finn and Dubery might be resourceful young men, but he wasn't about to leave them in such a situation, a long way from friendly territory and with the base offices still to be searched.

He really had no choice, but somehow that didn't

make the decision any easier. 'OK,' he said. 'Rob's indispensable, and it was Finn's idea. You're both elected. But I want this clear – no heroics. You'll find out where the ship's going when you get there. I don't want you searching the bridge for clues, looking for the original crew, or trying to take the boat back for its owners.'

'Boss . . .' Cafell began, looking hurt.

'Can we organize quizzes?' Finn asked.

Marker and Finn spent the afternoon hours napping uneasily in the heat, while Cafell and Dubery kept watch on the base and ship. As dusk approached, the traffic between the two increased and an air of expectancy seemed to enliven the men on the distant jetty, leaving the watchers increasingly afraid that the *Botany Bay* might sail so close to sundown as to make a surreptitious boarding impossible. But soon after five the noisy arrival of a previously unseen motor boat suggested another explanation for the Indonesians' impatience. The fourteen passengers on this boat were all young women, and they didn't have the appearance of a travelling choir.

'Friday night,' Cafell muttered to himself, as the women were escorted towards the buildings by their grinning hosts. He wondered what Ellen was doing back in Poole, and involuntarily found himself remembering their lovemaking the night before his departure. For the first time, he felt a slight shiver of apprehension about their plans for the evening.

Half an hour later he woke Marker and Finn, and reported on what he and Dubery had seen.

'Lucky dogs,' Finn said.

It would be dark in less than an hour. Marker told Cafell and Finn to get their gear together, and make sure everything was watertight for the swim ahead. Since there didn't seem much chance of winning a pitched battle, they reluctantly decided to leave the MP5s behind, and rely on the Brownings for any localized crisis. They would take all the team's food and water, and hope to eke it out for the week they would probably need.

As the minutes crawled by, even the idler mosquitoes came out to bite, and darkness fell slowly across the channel. There was no sign of human presence forward of the superstructure on the container ship, and only a few lights showing from the bridge deck and the accommodation portholes far below. The navy patrol boat was in darkness, the jetty empty save for a man and woman who had emerged hand in hand a few minutes earlier, both naked to the waist. An occasional flaring light in the cabin of the motor boat suggested a cigarette smoker. The sounds of Western pop music came drifting across from the direction of the buildings.

A slight breeze was now blowing, but the air still seemed almost unbearably sultry, and the dark channel looked more cool and inviting than at any time that day. Slightly before seven o'clock, Cafell and Finn shook hands with the other two and slipped into the water. The bow anchor chain was about two hundred yards away, and they swam slowly towards it, making no more than a ripple on the surface.

Marker watched through the nightscope as the two heads bobbed into view beside the chain, and as Cafell, with an agility which belied his size, clambered monkey-like up towards the anchor stowage. There were no shouts from the other boats or the shore, only a sudden increase in the volume of the music as Finn followed his partner up the chain. Then the rope snaked up towards the rail, and the hook which Cafell had improvised from a twisted piece of root caught first time. Marker thought he heard the faintest of thuds as wood struck metal, but there was no sign that anyone else had. The two men shimmied up in quick succession, visible through the nightscope but not to the naked eye. As Finn disappeared over the rail Marker thought he caught a glimpse of a thumbs up flashed in their direction.

'They're on,' he told Dubery, who had been concentrating his attention on the jetty area.

'Just in time,' Dubery said. 'It looks like the crew have had their fun,' he added in a faintly disapproving tone.

Marker turned his own glasses in the same direction. About a dozen men were making their way down to the jetty, all but two of them ethnic Chinese. Several still had women in tow. As the first batch of men disappeared from view behind the jetty an outboard motor sprang into life, and a few seconds later one of the smaller boats curved out across the channel towards the bottom of the container ship's steps. As the disembarkees climbed up towards the deck the boat returned for their comrades, leaving only a small group of women chatting to each other by the side of the water. A few seconds later a male voice from the direction of the buildings called out, causing one of the women to say something which made her friends laugh. An angrier shout followed, and the women started walking slowly back up the path.

The ship's steps were now being lifted, and the

steady hum of her engines was competing with the onshore music and the rasp of the anchor-raising machinery. Fifteen minutes more and another group of men emerged, two of them still struggling with their trousers. They also dropped off the jetty and out of sight for a few moments, before a sleek speedboat emerged into view and roared away down the channel.

'Advance lookout,' Marker murmured.

Five minutes later the container ship itself was underway, inching its huge bulk south towards the open sea, bearing a new identity, the same £50-million cargo, two crews and a couple of stowaways.

Marker and Dubery watched it recede from view, until only the top of the funnel was visible above a distant headland.

'How long should we wait before the recce, boss?' asked Dubery.

'I guess we let them wear themselves out in pleasure,' Marker said drily. 'The man who delivered the girls is still on his boat, so maybe he's expecting to take them back to wherever they came from tonight. Maybe parties break up early in Indonesia.' He paused. 'But there doesn't seem much point in hanging around out here. I think it's time we worked our way back around to the other side. Find somewhere for you to park yourself while I do my impersonation of a cat burglar . . .'

'Hey, boss, I don't want to be parked somewhere . . .' Dubery began indignantly.

'Bad choice of words,' Marker admitted. 'But I'm doing this alone. One of us has to get back home, or Rob and Finn are even further out on a limb than they think they are. Right?'

Dubery thought about it. 'Aye,' he agreed reluctantly.

'Not to mention getting the sampan back to its rightful owner. Now let's get going. And let's be extra-careful – there's no telling how many fucking couples we may trip over in the dark.'

On board the *Botany Bay* Cafell and Finn had found a temporary home in a deep, canyon-like space between rows of stacked containers. Sometime in the early hours, once the ship's routine had been established and half its crew were asleep, they planned to start exploring the superstructure, which loomed above the mountain of containers some two hundred yards aft. For now they could do little but sit and wait. The narrow line of sky above was overcast, depriving them of the chance to employ their celestial navigation skills, but since both men were carrying a compass that didn't much matter. The ship had followed the channel south to regain the open sea, and then shifted course to the south-east. This might indicate a destination elsewhere in the thousand-mile-long Indonesian archipelago, or simply betoken a reluctance to risk the ship being seen in the Singapore Straits, even wearing its new disguise. Either way, by morning the two SBS men would have a much clearer idea of where fate and the pirates were taking them.

In the stores cabin on the first floor of the ship's superstructure Spiros Lamrakis listened as one of his crew members beat a fist against the locked door. Since their incarceration some eighteen hours earlier no one had seen either a morsel of food or a drop of water. The lack of any toilet facilities and the terrible heat had turned the cabin into a fetid hell-hole, and several of the men were already in severe distress.

The knocking on the door subsided, as much from a dearth of hope as a failure of energy. No one had come to answer on the other occasions, and Lamrakis knew in his heart that no one would come this time either. His ship had been taken by men without scruples or compassion.

Having retraced their original route to the crest of the hill, Marker and Dubery crouched down inside the ruined mosque. Even in the darkness Marker could make out the shards of ceramic tile which littered the ground, and the older he got, the more sadness such evidence of things vanished seemed to evoke in him. He supposed it was just mortality tapping him on the shoulder.

The sound of partying was still wafting up the hill from the base below, and there was no reason to suppose there would be much change in the next few hours. The sooner they got back to Singapore the better, he thought. There was no point in hanging around.

Marker said as much to Dubery, who nodded, wished his boss luck, and watched him disappear into the tunnel through the trees which accompanied the telegraph poles down the slope. For a few seconds he could hear Marker's progress, but then there were only the sounds of jungle, generator and distant music. Dubery settled down in the shadows, conscious of that sense of inner peace which always seemed to accompany his being alone. He sometimes wondered why, when he was so used to feeling like this, he had ever got married, ever joined the team-oriented SBS.

The answer, of course, was simple. He loved Helen, and he loved the SBS. Almost as much as he loved being alone in situations like this, surrounded by the natural world. He had only returned from a week's leave with his family in the Outer Hebrides ten days before, and had still been working his way through the usual period of readjustment to life in Poole when the orders came through for the trip to Singapore. He supposed the latter was a fascinating city, but exploring crowded streets could never compete with the excitement of being out in a strange boat in unfamiliar waters. Or crouching in a ruined mosque on an island he had never heard of, with geckos scurrying across the walls and monkeys screaming somewhere in the distance. Though he could have done without the mosquitoes.

A quarter of a mile away, Marker was edging an eye around the side of a tree. Across about ten yards of open ground the water-tower rose into the overcast night sky. Through its girder support he could see the oil storage tanks, the empty jetty and the patrol boat, which, bereft of comparison with the container ship, seemed larger than it had. To the right of the tower, beyond a stretch of open grass worn down by sport of some kind, was the first of the buildings. It was about forty feet long by twenty wide, and raised off the ground on breeze-blocks. No one was visible through the open door, but the occasional shout of merriment was clearly audible.

As he watched, a woman – or girl, more like it – emerged in the doorway, lit a cigarette, and sat herself down on the concrete steps. She was wearing just a T-shirt and knickers, and in the dim light the dark sockets of her eyes seemed to fill her face.

It didn't seem likely that this building housed any administrative functions – the furthest building, which contained the telephone connection, seemed the obvious bet – but he had to be sure. After doing his best to imprint the overall geography of the base on his mind, Marker slipped back into the darkness of the trees and started working his way round to the back of the building. Five minutes later he had found a vantage point on the slope from which he could see through several of the screened windows.

It was a dormitory barracks, and there seemed to be movement of one sort or another on most of the visible beds. In the middle of the floor one naked girl was rummaging through a pile of cassettes next to a stereo system, a look almost of wonder on her face.

Marker moved on towards the next building, the largest of the three. As he had suspected, it contained the base kitchen, canteen and recreation room. In the latter another naked girl was being fucked on the table-tennis table, her body arched back, her feet hanging above the floor. The man had not even bothered to remove his trousers, and the look of intense concentration on his face made a striking contrast with the vacant expression on hers. She could have been an inflatable doll, Marker thought. From both his point of view and hers.

He wondered if this party took place every Friday, or only after a successful act of piracy. If the unit here was getting even a half-decent cut of the proceeds, he supposed it could afford a boatload of girls every night.

He moved on towards the third building. This was in darkness, and he had no choice but to put his face up against the two back windows. A room full of stores greeted his gaze at the first, but he found what he was looking for at the second – a large office with a single desk and a table piled with papers. On the far wall the only door hung open.

Marker edged silently along the side of the building, the MP5 cradled in his arms, and slid an eye around its corner. Two men were sitting on the jetty with their backs to him, the smoke from their cigarettes curling up above their heads, but no one else was in sight. Marker waited a few seconds more to be sure, then slipped the five paces along the front of the low building, up the steps and in through the open door.

He waited for a few seconds behind the door jamb, letting his eyes grow accustomed to the faint yellow glow which bathed the room, and then moved across to the table with the piles of paper. It took only a minute to realize that the party responsible had never heard of filing. Each stack contained a bewildering array of store requisitions, food invoices, fuel records, even newspapers. It would take days to go through them all. Wasted days, most likely.

He tried the top and the drawers of the desk, and found more of the same. Looking round, he noticed something else, and his heart sank. A waste bin containing long strips of paper sat beneath a covered machine. It was a shredder, he realized, and pulled off the cover to confirm his suspicions.

That seemed to be that. They had been shredding something, and the piles on the table proved it wasn't base records.

And then he noticed the fax machine half buried by the papers on the desk. It was one of those new ones which Finn had been raving about in the Singapore shopping arcade. And two sheets were still sitting in its tray.

Both were written in Bahasa. The top one was short and sweet, but Marker had no idea what it was about. The other contained five words he understood – 'Ocean', 'Carousel', 'Hong', 'Kong' and 'Singapore' – and a lot more which he didn't. But those five were enough to make him extremely curious about the rest. He took one of the base invoices and began making copies of both fax messages, just as Gerry and the Pacemakers' 'Ferry Across the Mersey' began playing somewhere outside. Marker inwardly shook his head at the absurdity of it all – faxes, shredders, thirty-year-old British pop, all sharing space on a little tropical island in the back of beyond. They probably had *Baywatch* on the rec room TV. Like an actor friend of his dad's had once said: shrink the world and you shrink people.

His copying finished, he was taking one last look around when footsteps suddenly sounded on the path outside. With no time to find a hiding place, he simply sank to his haunches, his back against the wall, the dull sheen of the MP5 all but covered by his arms. Two figures appeared in the doorway, a man and a woman.

Be still, Marker told himself, his mind going back years to a theatre in Cleethorpes, and his mother trying to teach him how to be a tree. 'You have to believe you are a tree,' she had said. 'Think like one . . . And don't breathe so loud. Let your lungs do it for you.'

The couple were halfway across the room now, the man half pulling the girl towards the door which led into the storeroom, oblivious to Marker's presence. He had a brief glimpse of the girl's face in the amber light – she was no more than sixteen, and looked both angry and frightened. A few seconds after the two of them had disappeared from view a heavy slap was audible above the distant music, followed by the sound of tearing cloth and a whimper from the girl.

Marker stood up slowly, aching to intervene but knowing he could not. Cafell and Finn's safety might well rest on his making an undetected exit. And there was always the crew of the *Ocean Carousel* to consider.

The man said something sharply, and the girl whimpered again. Marker walked quietly round the edge of the office, keeping to the deepest shadows, and reached the frame of the open door. Fifty yards or so to his left a couple were dancing on the grass outside the dormitory barracks, swaying gently in each other's arms to Procul Harum's 'A Whiter Shade of Pale'. He watched them for several seconds longer than he needed to, struck by the unlikely poignancy of the scene, then slipped out of the door, down the steps, and along the front of the building. Once out of sight he paused for a moment, listening for any indication that he had been seen, then continued on his way, following the line of telegraph poles up the steep slope to the ruined mosque, where Dubery was waiting. The relief on the younger man's face was eloquent enough, but no actual words were spoken until they were almost halfway back to the sampan.

'Any joy, boss?' the Scot asked in a whisper.

'Maybe. I don't know,' Marker told him. 'I found a couple of faxes,' he added, and the expression on Dubery's face almost made him laugh out loud.

3

Cafell explained what their options were. 'We can bury ourselves right at the bottom of the ship,' he said, 'either in the steering-gear chamber or the paint store. I don't fancy a week in the chemical storeroom – there's no knowing what fumes we'd be breathing.'

'None of it sounds exactly inviting,' Finn remarked.

'It isn't,' Cafell agreed, 'and there's a chance we'd get locked in down there. But it's unlikely we'll be found.'

'Try me with another option.'

'We could look for an empty cabin above decks, but the risk of running into someone would be a lot higher.'

'What about the cargo holds?' Finn asked.

'A good place to get trapped.'

'What about staying where we are?'

'Fine, until we run into a typhoon, and then we'll just get washed overboard by the first wave.'

'Jesus Christ, who came up with this stupid idea?'

'I thought you did.'

'Yeah. OK, well, I don't mind taking the odd risk for a bit of extra comfort. This bunch don't know the ship very well, do they? We should be able to lock ourselves in somewhere, and if anyone rattles the door we can slip out while they're off looking for a key.'

'Slip out to where?' Cafell asked. He was beginning to wonder whether they should stay where they were. The two-hundred-yard journey aft, whether down the open walkways by the rails or across two hundred yards of unevenly stacked containers, seemed anything but an appealing prospect, particularly if there was a moon.

'And at least we'll have a fighting chance of getting off the damn boat if we're at deck level,' Finn went on. 'If we're found in the paint store there's no way out.'

'Maybe we *could* stay here,' Cafell said thoughtfully.

'Where did the typhoon go?' Finn wanted to know.

Cafell studied the side of the container they were leaning against. 'We have rope. If the worst came to the worst we could tie ourselves in.'

'Oh Jesus, I saw that film,' Finn said.

It was a little after four in the morning when Marker and Dubery brought the sampan home to the Marine Police HQ in Queenstown, and both men slept through most of the half-hour taxi ride which brought them into the heart of Singapore. In the command centre overlooking Marina Bay they found Commodore Xiao Guo-feng, the Singaporean who had been chosen as the overall coordinator of the multinational operation, and Tanaka Sukiman, the Malay from the Kuala Lumpur Anti-Piracy Centre. Both men looked tired, and were doubtless wondering why the British SBS commander had radioed ahead to request this meeting with just the two of them at such an unfortunate hour.

They were also much too polite to demand an explanation. 'We've ordered coffee,' Sukiman announced, and the words were no sooner out of his mouth than a knock on the door heralded its arrival. Marker and Dubery, who had not eaten for almost twenty-four hours, fell on the accompanying pastries.

'How did things turn out yesterday?' Marker asked, after taking a gulp of the strong black coffee.

Xiao grimaced. 'It was just a Vietnamese street gang with ideas above their station, he said bitterly. 'Another ten minutes and the tanker would have grounded itself on a reef, with heaven knows what consequences. As it is, there are four crewmen to bury, including the captain, and another two men are still critical in hospital.' He shook his head in disbelief. 'Just children,' he said.

'Did you catch them?' Marker asked.

'They caught themselves. Our boats followed them in towards the harbour, and they tried to shake off the pursuit by cutting through the construction area for the new terminal on Pulau Brani. Their boat must have been travelling at around fifty knots when it hit the concrete piling. There was one survivor, and half his bones are broken. They'll probably have to carry him to the scaffold.'

Sukiman put down his coffee and smiled at the two Brits. 'Now, can you tell us why you wanted this meeting? And where you have been for the last twenty-four hours.'

Marker told them about the patrol boat base on Batam, the new identity for the *Ocean Carousel*, the decision to put two of his men on board the container ship, the searching of the base. 'These are the pictures we took,' he said, taking the two rolls from his pocket, 'and this is my copy of the two faxes.' He passed the bedraggled sheet of paper to Sukiman.

'I do not understand Bahasa very well,' the Malay said after a few seconds, 'but one thing is clear – the longer message originated here in Singapore.'

'That's what I thought,' Marker said, 'and that's why I wanted this meeting. I hope neither of you will take offence at what I'm about to say ... but I've done two tours of duty in Hong Kong, mostly on drug interception exercises, and I have a pretty good idea how long the reach of the Triads is. If they're involved in this, and it seems likely to me that they are, then the less people there are in the know the better. For one thing, my two men will be sitting ducks if the pirates find out they're on board. For another, we need to get a hold of whoever sent that fax before he finds out we're looking for him, or any incriminating evidence will wind up in a shredder.'

Xiao looked at the table, but when he raised his face there was no resentment. 'There is certainly Triad activity here in Singapore,' he said, 'both legitimate and criminal. Up until a year or so ago I would have said the growth in their power was mostly a reflection of the recent influx from Hong Kong, but there doesn't seem much doubt that lately there have been a growing number of Singaporean Chinese who have been persuaded to join their ranks. Still, I would be surprised to find that any of the officers involved in this operation had Triad connections.' He shrugged. 'But of course I understand your concern. No one outside this room need know the whereabouts of your men, and as for the other matter ... well, if we end up moving against one of the Triad factions we shall need to mobilize a considerable force, and we shall just have to hope that we can keep the target secret until the last possible moment.'

'That sounds fine,' Marker said. He liked both the serious Xiao and the cheerful Sukiman.

'I'll get these translated,' Xiao said, picking up the copy of the fax messages, 'and get an accurate fix on the source. Let's just hope it wasn't a backstreet copy shop.' He paused in the doorway. 'Shall we meet back here at ten? I should have something to tell you by then.'

Rosalie Kai took one look at the packed MTR cars and wished she had followed her instincts and waited for a tram. They might be slower than the subway, but they offered two priceless compensations: distracting views and breathable air.

Where were all these people going on a Saturday morning? As she was half carried into the car by the crush, she remembered the images of a half-empty subway she had seen on TV the previous night. They had been part of a scaremongering piece about the imminent Beijing take-over, and, for those condemned to a life of MTR commuting, had made 1997 seem almost inviting.

She fought her way through to a more human-sized space. It was only for five stops, after all. Through a gap in the crush she noticed a seated woman holding a copy of the English-language *South China Morning Post* in front of her face like a shield, its banner headline proclaiming some fresh hold-up in the new airport negotiations. The other main item followed up the previous morning's story of the hijacking off Singapore – the news of Bellamy's death had obviously arrived too late for the final morning editions.

The train stopped at North Point, and a new influx of passengers worsened the scrimmage. Rosalie thought back over the report she had heard on the radio: nothing definite had been mentioned about the cause of death, other than that the police were still trying to ascertain what it had been. Which might or might not be suspicious. Was she reading her own personal history into this?

She had seen Douglas Bellamy occasionally over the years – their operational areas had inevitably overlapped at times – but she couldn't remember speaking to him since her father's funeral, almost twenty years ago. She had first met him soon after his arrival in Hong Kong. He had been in his early twenties, fresh down from Oxford, and like most of the newcomers from England he had wangled an invitation to the Bohannan house in Shek O, where her British policeman father had lived what looked like the ideal colonial life with his exotically beautiful Chinese wife and his lovely young Eurasian daughter in his beautiful family mansion full of exotic things. She had asked the young Bellamy about England – she had asked them all about England in those days – and he had not yet been in Hong Kong long enough to forget what the old country was really like. She could still remember the strange mixture of elation and disappointment she had felt.

Now he was dead. At forty-two, according to the radio.

The train was entering Wan Chai station, and she fought her way back through the crush towards the door, twice feeling fingers scrabbling across her breasts. This daily assault usually made her angry, but today she found herself feeling pity for anyone who sought pleasure in such a pathetic manner.

Outside on Hennessy Road the traffic seemed almost grid-locked, the cream and blue double-decker buses stranded like elephants among the honking cars and taxis. She began walking briskly west down the urban canyon and, as happened on most mornings, felt her spirits lifted by the exhilaration of Hong Kong's skyline. The city might be hell to live in, but there was something magnificent about it just the same. She would miss it if she ever left.

At the intersection with Arsenal Street she turned right, and walked across the road to the front entrance of the Royal Hong Kong Police Building. The lift carried her up to the open-plan office of the Organized and Serious Crimes Group. Her partner, Li Zai-Shuo, was already at work on his side of the desk they shared. Ten yards away, among the area of desks occupied by the Narcotics Section, two red-faced English officers were involved in a quiet but unmistakably forceful exchange of views.

'What's going on?' she asked Li.

He gave her a characteristically ironic smile. 'They're already taking sides over Bellamy,' he said in Cantonese.

She sat down. 'What's the latest?' she asked in the same language.

'What do you know?'

'Only what was on the radio – nothing.'

'Well, the first take was that he killed himself but tried to make it look like an accident. His gun-cleaning stuff was on the desk where he supposedly shot himself.'

'And the second?'

Li shrugged. 'The talk is that he was in hock to several of the Triads. Gambling debts.'

Rosalie gathered her hair into the scrunchy she kept at work, feeling sick at heart. 'And what are Dempster and Crabbe arguing about?' she asked, though she could guess the answer.

'Whether he was very stupid and a little corrupt or very corrupt and a little stupid,' Li said acerbically. My money's on suicide – the Triads don't usually kill people who owe them money, especially not policemen who have other things to offer.' He stopped suddenly, as if suddenly aware of whom he was talking to. 'I'm sorry,' he said simply.

'Forget it,' she said. He hadn't said anything that she hadn't already thought.

'Want some coffee?' he asked, getting to his feet.

She nodded, and watched him thread his way across the office to the machine. Seven years ago, when she had first been assigned a desk here, the ratio of English faces to Chinese had been roughly two to one. Now it was the reverse. A couple more years and the faces would all be either Chinese or, like hers, oriental enough to pass muster. And all the conversations would be in Cantonese or Mandarin.

'Who's in charge of the Bellamy case?' she asked Li when he returned.

'Ormond's taken it on himself,' he answered. 'Where do you want to start this morning?'

She took a sip of coffee to hide the sudden surge of emotion. George Ormond had been one of the junior officers involved in her father's case, and, quite unreasonably, she had never quite forgiven him for it. He didn't seem to like her much either. Perhaps he sensed her resentment, perhaps in his mind she was tarred by her father's brush.

'Rosalie?' Li asked patiently.

'Sorry. I don't know . . . Have we had any luck with the Zhou family?'

'The old woman's still denying that she knew anything about the babies. The husband and younger son are still missing, maybe drowned, maybe hiding out. The older son not only denies any knowledge, he's talking about suing the family of the speedboat owner.'

Kai half choked on her coffee. 'He's what?'

Li grinned. 'The speedboat was to blame, apparently.'

'And since the fourteen babies were drowned I suppose we should charge the dead driver with murder?'

'I'm sure that'll occur to the Zhous' lawyer.'

'Our simple sampan-dwelling family have a lawyer already?'

'Zhang Zi-yang.'

'Of course.' Zhang worked for several of the Triad factions. 'Have we got any of the Zhou family on our books?

'Both the sons have been in custody for juvenile offences, but nothing serious, and nothing lately. There are about seven cousins though, and at least three brothers-in-law – it's a big family. I was going to run through the whole clan this morning, see if I can find some kind of lever.'

'You do that.' It didn't sound promising, but the chances of getting anything out of the Zhou family had always been remote. 'I've got to do the rounds of the newspaper offices.'

'In person?'

'I want to make sure they all get it right.'

'Have you got the appeal with you?'

Rosalie pulled it out of her briefcase and passed it across. The photograph of the dead babies, stacked like sardines in the narrow space beneath the false deck, was attached by paper-clip to a single sheet.

'A barbaric trade,' Li read softly. 'These fourteen children died when a smuggler's boat collided with a speedboat. At first it was thought that they had all drowned, but post-mortems proved that four had already died of suffocation. It is not only the smugglers who are responsible for these deaths, and for the whole barbaric trade in infants, but also the purchasers for whom the children are intended. Please, help us put a stop to such cruelty. If you have any information which would be useful to the police contact Inspector Rosalie Kai on 860-2000 ext 141. Caller anonymity will be respected.' He looked up at her. 'Are you sure it's a good idea to include your real name?'

'I think it makes it more personal.'

'You could use a false name.'

'I could, but . . .' She shrugged. At that moment she really didn't care.

She got up and made her way to the women's toilet. As usual it was empty, since the number of women working in the OSCG could still be counted on one hand. She washed her hands and stared at herself in the mirror, wondering if other people saw what she did. There were the Chinese bones, the wider English eyes, her mother's nose and her father's chin. She was tall by Hong Kong standards; bigger-breasted too. She remembered the first time she had realized that wherever she went she would always be something of an outsider.

Enough, she told herself. So the baby-smuggling investigation was probably going nowhere – there was no point in expecting miracles. So Doug Bellamy had gone the same way as her father – it was all water under the bridge, as he had been fond of saying. So Hong Kong was a gold earring waiting for Beijing's vacuum cleaner, as the cartoon in the *Post* had claimed that morning. Life went on, more or less.

Back at their desk Li was busy on his computer. She slipped the appeal back into her briefcase, checked that she had the envelope full of copies, raised a hand in farewell and left the office.

The first few hours of daylight had passed without incident for the two SBS stowaways aboard the container ship. The vessel was ploughing through the slight swell at a steady fifteen knots, the sun shining hazily down through a thin layer of high cloud. By Cafell's reckoning their heading was a few degrees north of north-east, which would take the ship into the South China Sea.

'This is interesting,' Finn said, waving the guidebook which he had found in Cafell's bergen. 'You know the Japs did all sorts of nasties after taking Singapore: bayoneted wounded prisoners in their beds, tortured any Chinese they didn't like the look of, shipped out the lucky ones to build the Burma Railway . . .'

'Bunch of real sweeties,' Cafell agreed.

'Well, the interesting bit is that the two Jap divisions responsible came from Hiroshima and Nagasaki.'

Cafell grunted. 'Was that why they drew the short straw in 1945?'

'Doesn't say. Either that or poetic justice.'

'I don't know. I don't think anyone deserved that.'

'It shortened the war.'

'Not according to my dad. When he was on NATO exercises in the fifties, some Americans he talked to told him there were two reasons why they'd dropped the atom bombs, and shortening the war wasn't one of them, since they already knew the Japanese were going to surrender. The first reason was just curiosity – they'd built the things and wanted to see the effect on a real target. The second was that they wanted the Japanese to surrender quickly – before the Russians got a stake in the occupation, the way they had in Germany and Korea.'

Finn shook his head. 'I think I was happier believing the official story,' he said, looking down to where the container ends framed a narrow rectangle of green sea and blue-white sky. 'We made the right decision staying here,' he added. 'This corridor even generates its own breeze.'

'Wait till the sun's directly overhead,' Cafell said cheerfully.

'It'll only be on us for an hour or so.' Finn's eyes caught the piece of paper on which Cafell had been making his calculations. 'So where are we headed?'

'Could be anywhere in the South China Sea. Probably not Vietnam, though. The Philippines, Hong Kong, Taiwan . . . even China.'

'And how far away are we?'

'At this speed about four days from Manila, five from Hong Kong, six from Taiwan.'

'Christ. And there's no reason in all that time for any of the crew to check up here? That seems weird.'

'Not really. A freight-train driver doesn't check his train every few miles – he just takes it for granted the load will still be there when he gets wherever it is he's going. The crew of a ship like this hardly ever needs to go forward, let alone up among the containers.' Cafell sighed. 'The main enemy on this trip is going to be boredom.'

At ten o'clock Marker was back at the command centre, staring out at the jungle of skyscrapers which loomed above the mouth of the Singapore River. Reckoning that there was no need for both of them to make the meeting, he had left Dubery at the hotel, still catching up on lost sleep.

Sukiman arrived next, and Xiao almost bounced through the door behind him, his face a study in barely restrained excitement. 'We have found the source,' Xiao said, perching on the edge of his desk. 'The fax was sent from a warehouse on the Panjang Road, on the edge of Chinatown. It belongs to two brothers, Wu Ka-shing and Wu Hou-sheng. They have an import-export business which was established about two years ago, soon after the older brother arrived from Hong Kong. The younger one followed a few months later. An old friend in the OSCG told me the Wus were investigated pretty thoroughly a year or so ago, and came up clean. He also gave me the names of several other companies they control. And listen to this – one of them spent most of last week cornering the market in industrial detergent!'

Sukiman's face was blank. 'I am sorry . . .'

'The tanker,' Marker said. 'If the oil had spilled they would have cleaned up. In more ways than one.'

Sukiman understood. 'And if our pirates on Batam knew the *Antares* was going to be hijacked it could only be because they set it up . . .'

'The Vietnamese survivor says their leader, a man named Bao, was given all the information about how and when, and told that the tanker was carrying gems in its safe. He says Bao claimed that it was his own idea to confuse things by letting the tanker drift, but the survivor didn't think so, even at the time.' Xiao sighed. 'He also says the captain was shot by accident – Bao was waving the gun in his face and it went off.'

'Oh Christ,' Marker murmured. 'Is there any evidence the Wu brothers are Triad-connected?'

'We'd have to check that out with the police in Hong Kong, and in the circumstances . . .'

'Point taken,' Marker said. The RHKP had earned its nickname: 'the best force that money could buy'.

'I've also been doing a little judicious checking on the current state of play as regards the Triads,' Xiao said. 'No one seems quite sure what's going on, except to say that this seems to be a period of transition. Whether that's good news or bad news depends on who you listen to. One school of thought believes that the loss of their Hong Kong base will inevitably weaken the Triads; another believes that an enforced relocation will actually strengthen them, and that Beijing's gain will be everyone else's loss.'

Marker suddenly remembered something. 'Did the intelligence of the sailing and cargo come from Hong Kong?' he asked.

'It's impossible to tell,' Sukiman said. 'It seems the likely bet.'

'What was the cargo?' Marker asked, realizing he still didn't know.

'Mostly electronic goods,' Sukiman told him. 'From China – the Shenzhen free enterprise zone just across the border with Hong Kong. Probably US $60 million worth.'

'We may find out more about the source of the intelligence when we pay our visit to the Wu brothers,' Xiao said, pulling himself upright.

'And when will we be doing that?' Marker asked.

Xiao smiled at him. 'I suppose you could come along as an observer. We are waiting until this evening, because on a Saturday night people expect to see police on the streets.'

Xiao arranged for Marker to be driven back to the city centre, but halfway there the Englishman decided a stroll would do him more good than sitting around in an air-conditioned hotel. He got the driver to drop him off outside the Tajong Pagar metro station, and started walking up Maxwell Road towards the heart of the local Chinatown.

He had been to Singapore nearly ten years before, but only briefly, as part of the South-East Asia tour he had taken during his first term of duty in Hong Kong. Much of its remaining charm had vanished since then, for street after street of two and three-storey housing had been bulldozed to make way for shining high-rise blocks. An attempt at damage limitation had been made in recent years, with mixed success. The famous Raffles Hotel, for example, had been renovated with great care, but something had definitely been lost in the new blend of colonial elegance and modern shopping mall.

It was the way the world was going, Marker supposed. Singapore just seemed an extreme example of the phoney-Canute syndrome – all determination on the surface, utter submission to market forces whenever it mattered. The same government which had banned chewing gum, and which enforced huge fines for littering and jaywalking, had sanctioned what locals called the 'architectural holocaust'.

Chinatown, though now living in the shadow of the financial centre's skyscrapers, had remained relatively unscathed, and most of its streets were still lined with low-rise baroque-style shop-houses, complete with weathered shutters and, in many cases, striking ornamentation. At the first crossroads Marker reached a triangular area of pavement that had been sequestered for one of the traditional Sunday morning songbird competitions, and in each of thirty or more bamboo cages a bird was either singing its heart out or receiving its final instructions from a proud owner. Every now and then one of the birds would stop and cock its head, as if seeking inspiration from its fellow competitors.

After a few minutes he walked on, down a street full of shops selling intricate paper models, mostly of houses and cars. These, Marker knew, were burnt at funerals, in the expectation that they would improve the quality of the afterlife.

Rosalie Kai had explained that to him on their way up Hong Kong's Ladder Street, almost three years before. He had thought about her quite a lot since their arrival in Singapore, and now that Hong Kong seemed likely to be his and Dubery's next port of call . . .

He could see her very clearly in his mind: the Western eyes in the Chinese face, and the way they somehow managed to reflect both a fiercely independent spirit and an almost painful vulnerability. She had been the only other woman he had felt really drawn to during his time with Penny, and at times he had felt almost certain that she was also attracted to him. But the timing could hardly have been worse, for he had known in his bones that any sexual involvement with her would torpedo any last chance he and Penny had of holding their marriage together.

Rosalie had seemed happy for them to be friends. They had told each other the stories of their lives, gone to the Chinese theatre and to movies, and she had shown him parts of Hong Kong which few English servicemen saw. They had made each other laugh, had fun together. For a couple of weeks, or so it seemed to Marker in retrospect, each had provided the other with an escape from the rest of their lives.

He had given her his English address, but neither of them had written.

Walking up South Bridge Road, past the gaudy splendour of the Hindu Sri Mariamman Temple, he wondered how the past three years had treated her, what she was planning to do when Beijing lowered the boom on Hong Kong, and how she would react to seeing him again.

For the next two hours Rosalie criss-crossed the city, visiting editorial offices and cajoling editors into providing front-page space for the photograph and text. Most were struck by the picture, but still needed persuading that their readers wanted something like that to look at over their Sunday breakfast. She needed to be considerably more charming than she felt, and was blackmailed into accepting two dinner invitations.

She would enjoy cancelling them later, she thought,

as she enjoyed her takeaway *dim sum* lunch in Kowloon Park. The birds in the adjacent aviary kept up a non-stop racket, and the noise of the traffic on Nathan Road was only slightly dulled, but the open space still offered some respite from the clamour of the city, and there were few more peaceful sights than the graceful white minarets and dome of the mosque which occupied the park's south-eastern corner. Almost for the first time that day, she felt able to cope with her own emotions.

It was all so long ago. The winter of 1977. She had been the one to find the body, and looking back she supposed the shock had stayed with her through the weeks that followed. At first she had assumed he was innocent, driven to suicide by a campaign of false accusations, but the cumulative evidence of his involvement in organized crime soon became overwhelming, even for a thirteen-year-old desperate to believe otherwise. The Independent Commission Against Corruption, of which, ironically, he had always spoken so highly, uncovered bank accounts in Singapore and Taiwan which contained over a million pounds, and as the investigation proceeded it became apparent that her father, then chief of the RHKP Narcotics Division, had been a key player in the Triad-controlled drug trade. But though the suicide verdict began to look increasingly shaky, there didn't seem to be much mileage for anyone in reopening the case as a murder. Ronald Bohannan was dead, and it seemed best to let things lie. Almost as an afterthought the investigators discovered a string of apartments he had owned. Each contained a mistress, the youngest of whom was fourteen, a year older than Rosalie.

The family's old life disintegrated. The hitherto

endless stream of English visitors to the house in Shek O had long since dried up, and now Rosalie's mother, drawn back into the Chinese community from which her husband had plucked her, decided to remarry. Rosalie went with her to the new luxury apartment downtown, but her stepfather, Kai Bin-yan, made no attempt to know his new stepdaughter, or even to hide his prejudice against mixed-blood children. With the money from the house in Shek O her mother sent her to England, where she enjoyed three miserable years of public school before returning to Hong Kong. There she attended college and lived alone, seeing her mother as little as possible. At the end of three years she surprised even herself by applying to join the RHKP.

Whatever her motives, which seemed as emotionally charged as they were unclear, she soon discovered a fascination for the work. Initial success, moreover, came as quickly as she could have hoped. As the British withdrawal grew ever nearer the RHKP had entered a major period of transition, providing a rare window of opportunity for non-whites wishing to fill those ranks previously reserved for the British. Some of her father's old friends had even offered help, but she had firmly refused them. If she was to enjoy any professional success then it had to be achieved honestly, in each and every aspect of her life as a police officer.

And it had been, she thought, staring across the park. There had been enough offers. She could have been well on the way to her own first million by now.

She smiled to herself, and decided to walk down to the ferry rather than search for a cab. It was Saturday, after all.

An hour later she was back at the desk, asking Li if there was any news.

'Nothing exciting. They didn't find anything in his desk at Marine, and his wife's still refusing to accept that he ever went gambling, let alone owed the Triads a life's ransom. Speaking of which, I've tied two members of the Zhou clan to the Blue Dragon Triad, which might open up a new line of investigation.'

'Good,' she said absent-mindedly, still thinking about Doug Bellamy's wife. Another woman who had been deceived, who had let herself be deceived. As for accepting the truth, well, that took years.

The phone call telling Marker that the operation had been brought forward came shortly before five o'clock; the car to collect him arrived in front of the hotel not much more than five minutes later. He had been planning to take Dubery along for the ride, but the Scot, presumably thinking he had at least an hour to spare, had left a note saying he had gone for a walk.

The car sped across Anderson Bridge and along the bay shore, the sinking sun flashing between the buildings to the right. They turned right on to Keppel Road, passing the main railway station on one side and the cranes of old Empire Dock on the other, and drove towards the deepening silhouette of the World Trade Centre. Here they pulled into the car park, where about a dozen cars were lined up in two rows, like the starters in a Grand Prix. The two lead vehicles had adapted front ends, presumably to save their drivers the trouble of opening gates by hand. Marker was ushered across to one of the cars near the rear, which contained both Xiao Guo-feng and the police chief in charge of the raid, one

Wang Jing-hua, who seemed less than ecstatic about the Englishman's presence. A few moments later they were on the move.

'Only a few of the men know where we're going,' Xiao confided to Marker.

'I hope that includes the ones at the front,' Marker murmured, causing Xiao to grin at him. Wang seemed less amused.

'This is the layout,' Xiao said, handing Marker a photocopied sketch map of the target area. 'There are new warehouses all along the south side of the Padang Road,' he added. 'The Wu brothers have the one main building, several outbuildings including the garage, and a line of offices on the side furthest from the road.'

'And beyond them?'

'A disused railway line, some derelict docks and the sea.'

'How far's that?'

Xiao shrugged. 'Maybe two hundred yards. The Marine Police will have a couple of launches standing by.' He turned to look Marker in the eye. 'You're only here as an observer,' he reminded him.

'I know. But I expect a front seat.'

Wang said something to Xiao in Chinese, and there wasn't much chance of mistaking the disapproval in his tone. Not that it was going to matter much, Marker thought, looking out of the window. The light was fading with its usual tropical swiftness: another fifteen minutes and it wouldn't matter which row he was sitting in.

There were industrial premises on both sides of the road now, and occasional views of the sea beyond. 'This is it,' Xiao said, and through the windscreen

Marker had a fleeting glimpse of the front-armoured cars swinging off the highway. Seconds later their car was passing through the demolished gates, and ducking between parked lorries to follow the prearranged course towards the rear of the modern warehouse.

Two cars were already disgorging officers, but there was no sign of life inside the buildings. After waiting behind their cars for several moments the armed policemen were ordered forward, and in a series of leap-frogging manoeuvres they reached the doors. Throwing these open failed to evoke a response from within, and after another pause first one, then two, men slipped inside, SMGs at the ready. A minute or so later Xiao and Marker heard a single shot from deep inside the building, and a few minutes after that the police chief emerged, a self-satisfied look on his face. He said a few words to Xiao and turned away, ignoring Marker completely.

'I've been invited inside,' Xiao said apologetically.

'Have fun,' Marker said. He waited until the two men had disappeared through the door and climbed out into the evening air, thinking that Dubery wasn't missing much – all the fun was happening inside the building. He had only a yard strewn with cars for company, most of them with their doors still hanging open. Even the two policemen he had seen at the far end of the building had suddenly vanished.

It was almost fully dark now. He leaned against the car, intertwined fingers supporting his chin on the roof, wondering how Cafell and Finn were getting on.

It was then that he caught the hint of movement in the shadows some fifty yards to his left. The dark figure descended the last few rungs of the ladder, stood motionless for a moment, and then scurried a couple of steps in the general direction of the sea before disappearing into the gloom.

Marker went after him, keeping his pace to not much more than a brisk walk, his ears straining for sounds of the other man's progress. He walked cautiously between two outhouses and found himself facing a breeze-block wall some ten feet high. A slight sound jerked his head around, and he caught a glimpse of something disappearing behind the wall some thirty yards to his left. The man was over.

Looking up, Marker could see the razor wire atop the wall, and couldn't believe his quarry had simply climbed over it. He made for the spot where the man had disappeared and found that a ladder had been set into the wall at this point, presumably as an emergency exit. At the top there was a hinged section of razor wire, easy to pass through, impossible to distinguish from the other side.

Pausing for a second, he could see the man half walking, half running across an area of industrial wasteland. Derelict cranes loomed beyond him, dark shapes against the shining sea. He seemed to be carrying a bag of some kind.

Marker dropped to the ground, skipped across a pair of rusted rails, and broke into a jog. He was about fifty yards behind when the man suddenly turned, saw him, and took off like a startled rabbit. Marker upped his own pace, but the man was fast, and for a couple of minutes the gap between them seemed not to narrow.

They were close to the sea now, the smell of salt strong on the breeze. Cranes towered above them, the distant lights of downtown Singapore twinkling through the girders. The ground was littered with industrial rubbish, which made running in the dark a perilous business.

They were now almost surrounded by water, Marker realized. He slowed down and started moving diagonally to his left, closing the only avenue of escape. Faced with the same realization, the man in front of him opened fire, spitting light and sound to no apparent effect. In reply Marker fired once, into the air, just to let the other man know he was armed.

For what seemed like a long time, but was probably no more than a few seconds, neither man moved, and then suddenly both became aware of the lights approaching them – one of the police launches was heading in to investigate the gunfire.

The man turned and began running again, towards the sea this time. Marker went after him slowly, then picked up his pace when he realized that it was unlikely the man still believed he could escape – he obviously had something else in mind, like getting rid of the briefcase.

He was still thirty yards away when he saw the bag arc into the air, and heard the faint splash as it hit the water. A few seconds later he saw the man walking towards him, hands above his head, the gun nowhere to be seen. He was Chinese, probably in his late twenties, with long hair in a pony-tail, silver dragon earrings and a sleazy smile.

The launch was bathing them both in the glare of its searchlight, and Marker gestured his prisoner back towards the waterfront. He was about to ask the police to turn their light on the waters of the harbour when he caught sight of the briefcase, bobbing in the water not ten feet away from the side of the launch.

It was shortly after eight o'clock on the Saturday evening, some forty-four hours after the crew's initial incarceration, that the door to their A-deck prison finally swung open. In the cabin the stench was now almost unbearable, and several men were suffering severely from lack of water. Lamrakis pushed himself forward, willing his brain to come up with the right words to deal with their nose-holding captors, but his almost apologetic request for water was simply ignored. 'Out' was the only word spoken in reply, and that was rendered almost redundant by the jerk of the sub-machine-gun which accompanied it.

Lamrakis started to protest, and the barrel of the gun was rammed into his stomach, almost causing him to retch with the pain.

The prisoners filed out, some walking without too much difficulty, others only able to move with the support of a friend. They climbed one flight of stairs to the boat deck, then another.

'In,' the man told them, gesturing towards the lifeboat. A feeling of relief almost threatened to overwhelm Lamrakis. They were getting off the ship, away from these apologies for humankind. He knew without looking that there would be no food or water in the lifeboat, but they could always drink rain.

He helped the more stricken members of his crew clamber aboard, and then, as the lifeboat was slowly lowered towards the waiting sea, he began working out their position from the few stars visible between the clouds. He had one last glimpse of grinning faces looking down, and tried consciously to commit each and every one to memory.

Searching for some explanation as to why the ship had stopped, Cafell had moved along the wall of containers to a position just above the walkway, from which he could see back along the length of the ship. Even with the naked eye he could see the lifeboat riding the swell, and with the veiled nightscope he could make out fifteen or so occupants – the original crew.

By Cafell's reckoning the ship had only just left Indonesian waters, and that fact presumably explained the timing of the crew's release. If they were discovered drifting in the international waters of the South China Sea then any suspicions of Indonesian involvement would remain only that – suspicions.

Still, at least the crew were alive, and would probably be picked up without too much delay in such a busy sea lane.

The lifeboat was beginning to recede as the container ship got back underway. Cafell took another look through the nightscope, and almost lost his hold as the brilliant light blazed in the eyepiece. A split second later the crash of the explosion rolled over him.

In the nightscope there was now nothing but the open sea. Cafell pulled himself back from the edge of the deck and sat with his back against a container, breath rasping from his lungs, his mind in shock.

After soaking in the bath for almost half an hour, Rosalie put on a kimono and searched the fridge for something edible. At the back she found a yoghurt container half full of week-old chicken lo mein, which seemed to smell OK. She heated it up in the microwave and took the plate out on to the balcony of her three-room flat. The lights of Kowloon danced in the waters of the harbour, but for once the night city failed to raise her spirits, and after wolfing down the food she went back inside and curled up on the futon in front of the TV. A British cop show was on, the one with Helen Mirren as the woman inspector. Rosalie had seen this story before, but she watched it anyway, fascinated by the dreadful emptiness of the culture it portrayed.

It had been a bad day in more ways than one. The past had come back to haunt her, and the present had offered no compensation. When first assigned to the baby-smuggling investigation she had been more than a little resentful of the implied gender-typing. Anything to do with babies – put a woman in charge. But after a few days on the case such considerations had come to seem irrelevant. This was one crime which enraged her.

The combination of ingrained prejudice and China's one-baby-per-family law made the scale of the trade possible. For many parents a daughter was simply not good enough, and they were quite prepared to sell a female first-born, hoping for a son at the second attempt. This was bad enough, but the callousness of those involved in the transport and sale of the babies was almost beyond belief. As someone at the office had said, the smugglers worked on the same principles as banana-shippers – a certain number of boxes always had to be written off.

Maybe the newspaper appeal would turn up something, but tonight she found it hard to dredge up any optimism. They might catch a few of the people who were hired to ferry the babies across the thirty miles which separated Chinese waters from the buyers in Hong Kong, and a few others, like the Zhous, might even meet their just deserts in some other way, but as long as China maintained the one-child policy, and as long as boys were considered more valuable than girls, the trade would continue in one form or another. After all, she thought cynically, matching supply with demand was Hong Kong's *raison d'être*.

She turned off the TV and sat gazing at the empty screen, thinking that she was in danger of giving up on her fellow human beings.

4

Rosalie arrived at the RHKP building on Arsenal Street soon after seven the following morning. There were only about a dozen people in the OSCG office, and most of those were working on the Bellamy case. According to Pao Xin-xin, a long-time acquaintance from police college days, the heavy money was now on suicide. The problem was going to be getting the dead man's well-connected family to accept the shame implicit in such a scenario. Not surprisingly, they preferred the notion that the policeman had been killed by enemies he had made in the line of duty.

Kai walked over to the coffee machine and found, as usual, that the consumer of the last cup had failed to set up another pot. She did so, and sat on the edge of the table reading the papers while the water filtered its way through. The appeal was prominently featured on the front page of six of the seven papers she had given it to, and even in the seventh it shared page three with news of a local film star's tragic romance.

She took the coffee back to her desk and sat looking at the phone, willing it to ring.

It obliged.

She picked up the receiver. 'Inspector Kai.'

'Do you like babies?' a man asked in Cantonese.

'Yes,' she said. It didn't seem like the time or place for qualifications.

'Then would you like to have mine?' the man asked.

She sighed. 'Wasting police time is a criminal offence,' she said. 'Now get off the line.' She hung up, wondering how many more would come up with variations on the same theme.

The phone rang again, and she picked it up half expecting to hear the same caller. But this one was a woman.

'I have some information,' she said in Cantonese. Her story took some telling, but the gist of it seemed to be that the baby in the neighbouring flat didn't look like either its mother or father. It also cried all the time, as if it was homesick. And while it was true that the mother had looked pregnant before the baby's arrival a month before, she could easily have stuffed a sweater under her clothes to fool people.

Kai thanked the woman and replaced the receiver, marvelling at the human gift for wishful thinking. She felt less generous after two near-identical calls, and almost relished the fifth call, which was essentially a reprise of the first. The sixth caller took issue with her English first name and suggested that she cut her losses and make use of the full British passport with which she had no doubt been issued.

She started on her second cup of coffee, wondering if the entire exercise was going to prove a disagreeable waste of time.

The seventh caller offered some sort of answer. 'You would be wise to cease this line of enquiry,' an educated male voice told her in English.

'And why might that be?' she asked, failing to keep the sarcasm out of her voice.

'The crime rate has been soaring in Quarry Bay recently,' he said conversationally. 'Someone broke into one of the flats in your block only a few days ago.'

She felt the hairs standing up on her arm, but said nothing. The caller seemed to grunt with amusement before he hung up.

She put down the receiver and sat staring into space, wondering why she had expected the offer of a bribe, yet had not even considered the possibility of a threat.

The taxi carried Marker and Dubery at a leisurely pace down the almost empty Connaught Road. It was barely nine o'clock, but a few young men were already playing cricket on the Padang. Beyond the wide expanse of mown grass the pale green dome of the Supreme Court and the Corinthian columns of City Hall provided the perfect colonial backdrop.

As the taxi swung left over Anderson Bridge Marker studied the huge Merlion – half mermaid, half lion – which guarded the mouth of the Singapore River, and wondered once again what had persuaded the city to burden itself with such a ludicrous symbol. The river itself was almost clear of traffic; like much else in the last few years it had been almost sanitized out of existence. The lighters, barges and sampans which had still been crowding its waters at the time of Marker's last visit were now confined to the bay, while the busy godowns, the warehouses, had been turned into cafés and galleries for the tourists and the local rich.

In Xiao Guo-feng's temporary office at the Marine Police Building on Marina Bay, Xiao and Tanaka

Sukiman were already waiting for the two SBS men. So were a large silver pot of fresh coffee and another plate of gorgeous-looking pastries. Marker's thoughts went back to briefings in Poole, with the mug of tea and obligatory plate of Kit-Kats.

'I'm afraid we haven't found anything useful at the Wu warehouse,' Xiao began, as Sukiman poured the coffee. 'At least, not yet. They have bills of sale for all the goods on the premises, most of which come from Red China. We're checking them out, but at the moment we have no reason to believe that any of the goods are contraband.'

'How did they explain opening fire on your men?' Marker asked.

Xiao grimaced. 'They said they thought we were criminals.' He put down his coffee cup. 'We've only just started going through the paperwork, but as you'd expect, they do a lot of business with Hong Kong. One of our experts is trying to get into their computer records, but she says she's not optimistic. One programme already self-destructed on her. She says the defences are very sophisticated.'

'What do the Wu brothers say?'

'They're complaining about the invasion of privacy.'

'What about my man and his briefcase?'

Xiao grinned. 'You really upset Wang, making him lose face like that. As for the man, well, he's not talking, of course, but it seems likely he's a Triad accountant. The briefcase contained a lot of financial print-outs, most of which seem to be variations on the company's tax returns. So there's a chance we'll get the Wu brothers for tax evasion, even if we can't tie them in to the smuggling.'

Marker felt disappointed. 'Were they questioned about the fax?'

'Oh yes. They agree it looks like it was sent from their office, but they deny any knowledge of sending it. They employ over fifty workers, delivery people are always coming and going, they don't keep their fax machine under constant surveillance, etc., etc.' Xiao ruefully shook his head. 'There's no way we can prove otherwise.'

The four men were silent for a few moments.

'If the information on sailings and cargoes is coming from Hong Kong,' Marker asked, 'why not relay it directly to the base on Rempang? Why put it through Singapore?'

'Family ties could be one reason,' Xiao replied, 'but these days that's not so likely. My guess would be to establish a cut-out between the principals in Hong Kong and their hired guns. Which reminds me, we did pick up one piece of information which might be useful. We put a tap on the Wu phones yesterday morning, and just before the raid the older brother took a call from Hong Kong. It was mostly family talk, but towards the end of the call the man in Hong Kong said that "one of their friends" had killed himself two nights ago, and that there might be a delay in re-establishing access to their usual channels of information. I listened to the tape, and the word "friends" was certainly not being used in any real sense.'

'An informant,' Marker guessed.

'Probably.'

'An English police chief killed himself in Hong Kong on Friday night,' Dubery volunteered. 'It was in this morning's paper.'

'Oh Jesus,' Marker murmured.

Xiao turned to Sukiman. 'Are we going to continue with the operation?' he asked.

Sukiman looked thoughful. 'It looks as if we have discovered the identity of at least one of our enemies. And they have told us there may be a delay before they can resume operations. I think we should suspend ours until we can follow up the leads we have. I shall have to talk to London, and then to the authorities in Hong Kong.' He turned to Marker. 'You have had no news of your colleagues?'

'Not yet. But they've only been at sea for thirty-six hours.'

'I have some information that may be relevant,' the Malay said. 'A lifebuoy from the *Ocean Carousel* was picked up in the South China Sea early this morning by a bulk carrier.' He turned to the large map on the wall. 'Here, about a hundred miles north of Bunguran. Of course, it is possible that this lifebuoy was lost overboard several days ago, before the ship was hijacked, but it seems much more probable that the pirates are trying to convince the world that the ship has sunk.'

Marker agreed. 'Especially if it still had the name *Ocean Carousel* written all over it. On Rempang they were going to great lengths to remove all trace of that name. In fact I think I even saw one man working on the lifebuoys.'

'I did,' Dubery said quietly. 'At least we know they're heading north,' he added.

'Looks like it. I think it's time we reported in,' Marker decided.

Xiao told him he could use the office next door.

It might be half-past two in the morning in Poole, but

Colhoun had told Marker to wake him at any time of day or night with news of Cafell and Finn. He punched out the CO's home number, and imagined it ringing in the country house on the Dorset coast.

'Colhoun,' the familiar voice answered almost immediately.

'Marker, boss.'

'What's happened?' If the CO had been sleeping there was no sign of it in his voice.

Marker brought him up to date. 'Sukiman will be talking to the Foreign Office sometime today,' he concluded, 'but it'll probably take days to get anything off the ground. I'd like to move on to Hong Kong. Rob and Finn already seem headed in that general direction, and it seems pretty clear that at least some of the piracy is organized from there.'

There was a silence while Colhoun thought about it. 'In principle, yes,' he said at last. 'But I want to make sure that you'll get adequate cooperation from the locals, which means calling in a few favours. And I'm going to leave that till morning. Cafell and Finn will be at sea for a few days yet, and people who get woken up at three in the morning – myself excepted, of course – are rarely at their most accommodating. What time is it now in Singapore?'

Marker looked at his watch. 'Nine forty-four,' he said.

'Seven and a half hours' difference. All right, I should have something for you by ten ... seventeen-thirty your time. I'll call you at your hotel at eighteen hundred. In the meantime you can book yourselves on an evening flight.'

* * *

Cafell stood up and arched his back. He and Finn would have to keep up with their exercises, he thought, or both of them would be too stiff to move once they reached their eventual destination.

His companion was asleep, curled up like a baby with an innocent expression on his face. Given their current circumstances it was an almost painful sight.

Cafell found his mind rerunning the terrible sequence yet again: the boat, the jagged flash, the empty sea. For the hundredth time he asked himself what kind of men could do something like that. He knew it was a futile question, but it seemed almost to have a life of its own.

He had helped to kill one man in his military career: one of the guards at the camp in Haiti had died as a result of bullets fired by him and Marker. He had not enjoyed it, either at the time or in retrospect, but he had not had any trouble accepting it either. Even in a bad cause – and that had been a good one – the lottery of combat seemed a very different business from the cold-blooded murder of defenceless people. He knew he could never commit the latter, and he had no idea how anyone else could.

Earlier that month, sitting in the garden at home, his father, a retired Polaris submarine captain, had told him that he still didn't know whether he would have obeyed an order to launch his nuclear missiles against the Soviet Union. 'I would have been responsible for killing fifty million people,' he had said. 'Maybe more. All just getting on with their lives.'

Cafell had been shocked, not so much by the feelings as by his father's admission of them. He had also been strangely pleased, and had told his mother as much. 'I never understood how they could put such a burden on good men,' was all she had said. But then his mother had always been opposed to nuclear power in all its incarnations.

He had been really lucky with parents, he decided. And they would make good grandparents, if he ever had any children.

His thoughts turned to Ellen, as they seemed to do every other minute of the waking day. They had been together more than six months now, though in some ways it seemed only days, in others more like years. It was all so simple and yet so confusing at the same time. They loved each other, liked each other, enjoyed doing many of the same things. That was the simple part. She hadn't said she would only marry him if he quit the SBS, but in his own mind Cafell knew that for him the two were incompatible. Children had a right to a father who was there, and to a father who guarded his own life more jealously than an SBS officer sometimes could.

It had also occurred to him that the SBS was like an extended boyhood adventure, and that the time had come for him to grow up.

At other times, as he watched friends playing musical marriages, he found it hard to believe he would ever give up the life he loved for such a thin chance of lasting happiness.

By the time he had spent a week in this open-air prison he should have all the answers, Cafell told himself. Always assuming that a posse of pirates didn't suddenly swarm over the containers above him, in which case everything else would become somewhat academic.

* * *

By four in the afternoon Rosalie had taken ninety-seven calls, not one of which had offered her and Li any assistance in their investigation. There were only two other detectives in the vast OSCG office, both of them using the excuse of a paperwork backlog to escape an afternoon with their extended families. Rosalie no longer had such a family, but she couldn't help thinking that there had to be better ways of spending a Sunday than sitting at her desk, being variously propositioned, bored and threatened by complete strangers.

Three more calls, she told herself. Then she would put the answering machine on and go out for an expensive meal. Maybe go to a film afterwards – something that would make her laugh.

It was lucky that she was still rummaging around in her desk when the hundred and first call came in.

'My name is Chen,' the voice told the answerphone after a brief pause. The man didn't sound nervous, just somewhat taken aback. 'I am a doctor of traditional medicine in Mongkok,' he went on, 'and I have some information about the business of the children.'

She picked up the receiver. 'I'm Inspector Kai. What can you tell me?'

'Ah,' he said, sounding pleased at hearing a real voice. 'You are there.'

'I was just leaving,' she volunteered. There was something in the man's voice which encouraged trust.

'It is not a long story,' he said, 'but bear with me – I sometimes have trouble keeping things in order these days.'

'Take as long as you want,' she said.

'As I said, I am a traditional doctor, an acupuncturist

and herbalist, but I also prescribe Western medicines for some complaints. I live in Mongkok, just north of Argyle Street. Do you know the area?'

'Yes,' she said. Mongkok was one of Kowloon's poorest areas, a maze of narrow streets and over-crowded apartment blocks. It was also one of the main recruitment areas of the Blue Dragon Triad.

'Yesterday evening some young men came to see me. They wanted me to examine some babies, they said. It wasn't really a request, you understand, but of course I would have gone in any case. They took me to their car – a red one, but I'm afraid I know nothing about cars – and drove me to a warehouse. I couldn't tell you where exactly, because they made me wear a blindfold until I was inside the building. The journey was about twenty minutes, I think. It was a large warehouse, a modern one, and right next to the harbour. We went out of a door, across a dock and into a large boat-house. There were two boats tied up inside, a large black speedboat and an ordinary-looking sampan. I was taken aboard the sampan and shown ten babies, eight of them alive. The two who had died showed all the symptoms of bacterial pneumonia. The others, as far as I could tell from a brief examination, showed no signs of the disease as yet. But some of them probably would in due course, I told the men. They wanted to know how long, and seemed relieved when I suggested it could be a matter of several days. They then drove me back to Mongkok, and of course made it clear that I should not talk about this with anyone.'

'I'm glad you have,' Rosalie said. 'Do you think you would be able to identify the location from the harbour?' she asked.

'I don't think so. So much has changed in the last few years, and I don't often leave home any more. I hardly recognize my own street, let alone others.'

'I know what you mean,' she said.

'But I did see the name of the speedboat,' he added, almost mischievously. 'The *Sea Dragon*.'

'Great,' she said, more enthusiastically than she felt. 'The harbour was probably home to a hundred speedboats bearing the same nomenclature, for in the matter of both boats and people the Chinese showed an irritating lack of imagination when it came to bestowing names.

'And the sampan had three square holes cut in the planking on either side, like windows. I have never seen one like it.'

'Anything else?' she asked.

'Oh yes.' He had been saving the best for last. 'They are coming for me again tonight,' the doctor said. 'They want me to look at some more babies.'

The call came through an hour early.

'Got your tickets?' Colhoun asked.

'Yeah, but for first thing tomorrow morning. It didn't seem like such a good idea to arrive after midnight.'

'What time do you get there?'

'Eleven fifteen.'

'All right. You'll either be met by someone from the Marine Police or someone from the Organized and Serious Crimes Group – the people I spoke to didn't seem too sure which agency was in charge of fighting international piracy.' Colhoun grunted with amusement, disgust or both. 'If you're dealing with the Marine Police tread carefully – Bellamy was one of theirs, and they're probably all feeling a little defensive at the moment. MI6 also know you're coming, but I'm afraid the days of luxury hotels are over – you'll be bunking with 3rd Raiding Squadron on Stonecutters' Island. John Ferguson's expecting you. Any questions?'

'Nope.'

'I'll talk to you again tomorrow. Have a good flight.'

'Thanks, boss,' Marker began to say, but Colhoun had already hung up. He might be garrulous for a Scot, but not for a normal human being.

'Green light?' Dubery asked.

'Yep. Come on, I'll fill you in over a Singapore Sling at the Raffles. And then we'll find a meal to remember through the next few days of standard-issue scran.'

Finn put down the guidebook and rubbed his eyes. There was no longer enough natural light to read by, and the risk of using a torch, though probably minimal, carried too high a potential penalty to ignore. Since Cafell's witnessing of the wilful slaughter of the ship's original crew, neither SBS man had harboured any illusions about the price of discovery.

It was six-thirty – another hour and a half to go before he was supposed to wake Cafell. Finn liked these solitary watches the least, but that was no surprise – he had never really liked being on his own. The company of a few mates or a girl – the company of a few girls, come to that – and he felt alive. Alone, he began asking himself questions which didn't have answers, like what the fuck was he doing a million miles from home stowing away on a ship run by the local sociopaths?

He glanced across at the sleeping Cafell, who always seemed to relish being alone. Marker and Dubery were the same. No party spirit in any of them.

He thought of Stamford Raffles, about whom he'd just been reading in the guidebook. The man had just turned up at the mouth of the Singapore River, thought, hey, this looks like a good place for a city, and five years later there were ten thousand inhabitants. What a world it must have been, Finn thought, when you could do things like that, when one man could make such a difference. Somehow the world had solidified since then, grown harder to put dents in. Or maybe it was like a river, he thought: the wider it got the harder it became for one person to influence the way it flowed.

That was what success had been in Raffles' time – making a difference in the way the river flowed. These days the river took no notice, and nobody had a clue what success was. Famous people moaned on about how terrible fame was, the rich all seemed as miserable as hell, and everyone else wanted to be rich and famous.

Success was having adventures, Finn decided. Adventures like this one, or like the one he'd just had with the teacher in Poole. And he supposed marriage could be an adventure with the right person, though most people seemed really adept at picking the wrong one. Sooner or later he'd have to find a woman to live with, and give up on all that lovely variety.

Later, he decided.

The Fast Patrol Craft rocked gently in the swell, one of five positioned at mile-wide intervals across the broad expanse of water which separated the islands of Hong Kong and Lantau. Further north another two FPCs were covering the narrower Kap Shui Mun channel. There were other ways to reach the Kowloon docks from mainland China, but all the scraps of intelligence they had been able to gather over the last few months suggested that the smugglers would use one of these.

The sun had disappeared about fifteen minutes earlier, leaving the hilly silhouette of Lantau filling the western horizon. The waters around them were filled with craft of various sizes: fishing boats sailing to or from the local banks in the South China Sea, large cargo vessels, pleasure craft, inter-island traffic of one sort or another. The twenty-five-foot-long FPC was linked to the other boats by radio, but like all members of the cordon it was showing no lights and maintaining radio silence until such time as the enemy was identified. In the stern one of the Royal Marines was studying each sampan and speedboat on a northerly course through the night-vision glasses, hoping to match one of them to the rough descriptions Dr Chen had given Rosalie Kai.

There were four of them in the boat, Rosalie and three Marines. For the first hour the Englishmen had treated her to their usual strange mixture of exaggerated courtesy and innuendo-laden flirtation, but since arriving on station they had settled for the self-deprecating humour of professionals, reminding her of Callum Marker.

She hadn't thought about him for a long time, which was probably just as well.

'Your turn, Taff,' one of them said softly, passing the night glasses to the darkest of the three.

'Tea, miss?' the third man asked, holding out a plastic mug with the words 'West Ham' emblazoned on its side. A football team, she supposed.

The tea, already milked and sugared, tasted more like a liquid dessert than a drink. Her father had had a passion for Bird's custard, she remembered. And Heinz treacle puddings, which had arrived in sixty-tin boxes from England.

Marker had liked Sichuan food, as she did.

The radio burst suddenly into speech, and Rosalie thought she heard the faint echo of a shot across the water. 'Gamma calling. Boat answering to the description has just answered our friendly enquiries with hostile fire. We are in pursuit, heading south-south-east.'

Their own boat sprang into motion, the Marine corporal in command barking out orders to the other two above the sound of the engine. They were already skimming the crests of the waves, and Rosalie had little doubt that it was only the strap on her seat which was keeping her on board. They had to be approaching fifty miles an hour, she reckoned, which was definitely the fastest she had ever been on water. One of the Marines in the bow suddenly threw out an arm and yelled something, causing the corporal at the wheel to veer sharply to starboard, and now she could see the smugglers' speedboat careering across the surface towards them, almost on a collision course.

The man at the speedboat's wheel must have realized the same thing, for he veered away to port, forcing the FPC into a tight turn which left them more than a hundred yards in the smugglers' wake. Another FPC

– presumably the one which had made first contact –
was a further fifty yards behind.

'Can we catch them?' Rosalie shouted at the corporal.

'No sweat,' he shouted back.

And they were gaining, slowly perhaps but gaining
nevertheless. There was no way the smugglers could
reach the sanctuary of Chinese waters.

She wondered how the Englishmen intended to board
the smugglers' boat at this speed and in the teeth of
gunfire, but was destined never to find out. A figure
stood up in the stern of the speedboat, apparently
holding something above his head with both arms.
Then, like a basketball player, he lobbed whatever it
was into the air.

'What was it?' the corporal shouted.

'A baby,' she shouted back.

He looked at her with disbelief.

'Slow down – we'll have to let them go,' she shouted,
scanning the dark waters ahead of them for the tell-tale
bundle. A minute later one of the Marines pulled the
baby on board. The smugglers' boat was already almost
out of sight. To Rosalie's surprise, there were tears in
the Englishman's eyes.

She watched the distant boat until it was completely
out of sight, a coldness gripping at her heart. She hoped
to God that Li had enjoyed more success in following
the doctor.

On the other side of Hong Kong Island, on the long,
curving veranda of a large, white villa overlooking Tai
Tam Bay, two men were sitting across a chessboard.
One man was in his early seventies, with greying
hair and a deeply weathered face. His name was Shu

Zhi-fang, and for the last three years he had served as Dragon Head of the Blue Dragon Triad. The other was only just into his thirties; he had longish hair, a flat face which came to life only when he smiled, and the look of a man dedicated to physical fitness. Lu Zhen was the society's chief enforcer, its Number 426, its 'Red Pole'.

The pieces on the board had been set up, but the two men had not yet finished discussing business.

'They have no idea what the police were looking for?' Shu asked, pushing his lower lip forward to blow the smoke from his cigarette straight up towards the rafters. 'No idea what precipitated the raid?'

'None,' Lu said, repressing a cough.

'Well, what are their police sources saying?'

'The police were only brought in to conduct the raid. It was ordered by some task force the authorities in Singapore and Malaysia have put together to combat piracy.'

'So this *is* connected to the *Ocean Carousel*?'

'I don't see how. Wu Ka-shing swears there is no evidence to connect him with our friends in the Riau Islands.'

'A coincidence? Or have the Wu brothers been freelancing?'

'Maybe, but if so they have covered their tracks well. The only thing the Singapore police have been able to pin on them so far is possible tax evasion.'

Shu laughed, scattering smoke across the board. 'The ship is on schedule?'

'It should arrive at Chuntao on Thursday evening.'

Shu took one last contemplative drag on the cigarette.

'Then let's play,' he said, palming two pawns and holding out the closed fists for the younger man to choose.

An hour later, as the headlights of Lu's car climbed the hill behind the villa, Shu lit another cigarette and began walking slowly down the path towards his private beach. Beyond the mouth of the bay an oil-tanker was silhouetted against the night sky, reminding him of the earlier conversation.

He walked along the sand a few feet from the receding tide, and turned up the path which wound diagonally across the cliff to the grassy stretch of hillside overlooking the bay. Just under the trees which ringed the hilltop he reached the stone tomb marking his wife's place of burial.

He stood beside it for several minutes, looking out across the sea as if he were following her gaze, breathing in the fragrance of the trees. He knew she would have disapproved of his decisions in recent years, but that couldn't be helped. It had been easier when she and his predecessor had both still been alive, and the Blue Dragons had been steadily cutting back on the criminal side of their activities.

At the time of his accession Shu had believed that 1997 would change everything. The Communists would purge all traces of genuinely free enterprise from Hong Kong, and the Triads, for historical reasons, would be the first to feel Beijing's whip. In such a situation the Blue Dragons would be left with only two choices – relocation abroad or death.

But there had been one other option. Shu had sought success where all the other Dragon Heads had accepted failure – in forming a working alliance with elements inside the Communist ruling class. Even five years ago it would have been an impossible task, but the creation of the so-called enterprise zones across the border in Guangdong had eventually unleashed a frenzy of greed among Party members and non-Party members alike, and Shu had found the new partners he wanted.

His wife would not have approved, but now there was a good chance he would live out the rest of his days in this villa by the sea. And there would be no need for him to leave her alone on this hillside.

5

In the OSCG office Inspectors Kai and Li were halfway through their first coffee of the morning.

'It was my mistake,' Rosalie admitted, as much to herself as to Li. 'We should have gambled on not losing the doctor.'

Li shook his head. 'Nine times out of ten a loose tail gets shaken, and we agreed yesterday that a close tail would put the doctor at risk. Jen was just lucky – he made about four blind guesses and every one turned out a winner.'

'All for nothing,' she said bitterly. 'If we had tried following the boat . . .'

'You'd have been spotted,' Li said calmly, loosening his tie. 'What's the matter with the air-conditioning this morning?'

'Probably another economy drive.'

'Probably. And anyway, the evening wasn't a complete failure – we know where they bring the kids in, and we have these.' He gestured towards the pile of black and white 8×10s which lay between them.

'They're just foot soldiers.'

Li sighed. 'Yes, but whose? If they're Blue Dragon enforcers, then I think we're in business.'

She sighed as well. 'Sorry. I just keep thinking about

those babies in the boat, and wondering how many of them have come down with bacterial pneumonia.'

'I know . . .'

'Sometimes . . .' She shrugged.

'Sometimes we get lucky,' Li said. 'Which of us is going to ask Halliwell for the round-the-clock on the godown?'

'You do it. I'll probably put his back up somehow, the way I'm feeling this morning.'

'He likes doing you favours.'

'Only because he's hoping for a particular favour in return.'

'Let him hope.'

'Yuk,' she said, making a face. 'Just thinking about those big hairy hands makes my skin crawl.'

Li grinned at her. 'OK, I'll deal with it.'

'I'll get working on the photos. See which of our upstanding citizens they work for.'

The Boeing 727 carrying Marker and Dubery slid gracefully down between the tower blocks and on to the long runway which stretched out into the harbour. For Dubery, who had never landed at Kai Tak before, the plane seemed an awful long time coming to a halt.

The two SBS men were still standing in the passport control queue when they were approached by an old Marine colleague of Marker's, John 'Fergie' Ferguson. He led them through a door marked 'Security,' down several corridors and out through another door into the arrivals lounge.

'So who are you working for these days?' Marker asked, as the blond giant ushered them all into a dark-blue Rover.

'Good question,' Fergie said, twisting his body in the front seat to face them. 'Officially I'm the liaison between the military and the Governor, but lately I seem to have graduated to the role of universal dogsbody. At this moment in time I'm liaising between a couple of ill-dressed commando types and about a dozen different parties, starting with the Marine Police. Which is where we're heading.'

'Sorry we're such a sartorial let-down,' Marker murmured. 'But why a dozen different parties?'

There was a pause while their driver squeezed through a gap between double-decker buses. 'No one tells me anything,' Fergie said, 'but they do drop the odd hint, and I gather your presence here is not entirely unconnected to the demise of a certain Douglas Bellamy.'

'Possibly,' Marker said with a smile.

'Well, there's your explanation. He worked for the Marine Police, and since he was found dead on his boat they handled the initial investigation. The Triad ramifications have brought in the RHKP's Organized Crime group, and then there's something else – which you probably know a lot more about than I do – which has got the Customs people involved. You're going to have your work cut out remembering the names of the people you're working with.'

'Wonderful,' Marker murmured. 'How is the RHKP doing these days?' he asked, remembering all the corruption scandals of the seventies and eighties, and the talks he'd had with Rosalie three years before.

'Business as usual, I guess. There's a lot more Chinese in the officer ranks, but there's still a big gulf between the English at the top, most of whom don't speak a word of Cantonese, and a Chinese rank and file which doesn't speak a lot of English. And of course even the most honest of the Chinese are wondering what 1997 is going to mean for them. Getting a good reference from us is not likely to be a big career plus when Beijing arrives. More like the opposite.'

Marker nodded. They were on Chatham Road now, the skyscrapers of central Kowloon looming through the windscreen. In the back seat Dubery was watching the city go by with a familiar mix of feelings – fascination, estrangement and a sense of disapproval which he found hard to pin down. Singapore had felt the same, and so had Miami the year before. He found himself watching the young women on the pavement, their fathomless faces and taut bodies, hyperconscious of how far he was from home.

In the front seat Marker caught a glimpse of a woman driving in the far lane, and thought for a second it was Rosalie Kai. He smiled inwardly and got Ferguson talking about his last few years in the colony.

It was just after one when they reached the Marine Police HQ on Canton Road. Chief Inspector Charles Skillen was waiting for them in his fifth-floor office, a huge, map-adorned room with large plate-glass windows that offered a panoramic view of the harbour and its junk-filled wharves. Skillen, a solidly built man in his mid-fifties with slightly receding grey hair and a neat moustache, reminded Marker of a long-vanished TV policeman. The name escaped him.

'I should tell you that Doug Bellamy was a friend of mine,' Skillen explained, staring almost belligerently at the two SBS men.

'Understood,' Marker said.

'So how can I help you?'

'For a start, we'd like a run-down on the investigation to date.'

Skillen half turned in his chair to look out of the windows. 'He was found on his yacht, late on Friday night. A man on a nearby boat heard the shot and went to investigate. He found the body. A bullet had pierced the throat and passed up through the brain, killing him instantly. The circumstantial evidence suggested he had been in the act of cleaning his gun.'

Marker waited for Skillen to go on, but the Chief Inspector was staring into space. 'So was it suicide or wasn't it?'

'We're not sure. The forensic evidence is indecisive. He could have killed himself and tried to make it look like an accident. He could have been murdered. It could have been an accident.'

'I imagine his family and friends would prefer an accident,' Marker said as tactfully as he could manage.

Skillen grunted. 'We would have done,' he said. 'But I'm afraid an accidental verdict won't help much now – the investigation has already uncovered enough dirt to blacken anyone's name. Four bank accounts so far, containing over half a million pounds.' He offered a half smile, and Marker could see the hurt in the other man's eyes.

'Is there any indication of who he was getting the money from?'

'Not yet. That end of the investigation is being handled by the OSCG. They're the Triad experts.'

'Did Bellamy have access to intelligence of sailings and cargoes?' Marker asked.

'Is that what you think he was selling? I wasn't aware

that he had that sort of access . . .' Skillen's eyes widened slightly. 'Though come to think of it, a few years ago – five or six, I'd say – he did head up an investigation into corruption among the Customs & Excise staff. Maybe . . .' He looked almost pleased, as if something at last had made sense.

What a farce, Marker thought, as he and Dubery went back down in the lift. This was one of those times he found himself wondering if the British people knew how lucky they were to have a relatively uncorrupt police force. The recently exposed fetish for forging confessions was hardly admirable, but things could be a hell of a lot worse, as most of the world's other police forces seemed keen to demonstrate.

Ferguson was sitting in the lobby, reading the *Hong Kong Standard*. 'So what's next?' he asked.

'Let's get rid of our luggage,' Marker said. 'You can show us the new five-star accommodation on Stonecutters' Island.'

Cafell lowered the binoculars and felt the motion of the sea through his prone body. He reckoned the specks of land on the eastern horizon were parts of Ladd Reef, the most westerly of the Spratly Islands. They were on a course for either Hong Kong or the Pearl River and Canton, and almost halfway there.

It was another blue-sky day, the ship rolling gently in the water like a babe in arms. Cafell remembered Marker once calling the sea his real mother – the boss had no doubt been pissed at the time, but he had meant it just the same.

Cafell pulled himself up and sat with his back against the container, thinking that each of them had their own way of relating to the sea. He supposed most of them were in love with it, one way or another, but that was only a starting-point. There were some, like Ian Dubery, who loved the challenges, others, like Marker, who seemed to find something almost mystical in it all. Cafell could see both points of view, but that was nothing new. Ellen had once called him the most balanced person in the world, and since this had been in the middle of one of their rare rows, he had assumed it was not a compliment.

He made his way back to their niche among the containers, where Finn was staring into space, guidebook in his lap. 'How do you feel about the sea?' he asked.

The young Londoner looked at him with amusement. 'If I'm in it, it feels wet. If I'm not . . .'

'You know what I mean. You must have had some reason for choosing the Marines over the traffic wardens.'

'You think I was drawn to the sea like a magnet by some psychic compulsion?'

Cafell just looked at him.

'OK. But it had nothing to do with the sea. I used to go boating on the River Lea when I was a kid, and, well, it conjured up something. Just freedom probably. You know? You were off the streets, away from all the shit, just floating down the river. And there used to be teams of girls sculling. I used to love watching their thighs go up and down.'

'A religious experience, was it?'

Finn laughed. 'Yeah. But I'm not so sure about the sea. There's hardly any girls out here.'

'Marker thinks it's like a mother.'

'It's old enough. You think how long this lot has

been sloshing around ... Well, according to Darwin anyway. You know there's places in America where they still teach kids the Bible version, that the world's about four thousand years old?'

'How do they explain carbon dating?'

'Easy – God made things so that they started off old.'

Cafell thought about it. 'That's ...'

'Ludicrous?'

'The word I had in mind was "unanswerable".'

'The best lines always are,' Finn said. 'But you know it really pisses me off. Like when people say, "Well, there must be a creator because all of this must have come from somewhere." Why, for fuck's sake? Their imaginations are just too pathetic to cope with the idea that it's been here for ever – there's no beginning, no end. I like that feeling. It's like ...'

'The sea?'

'No, not the fucking sea. What I'm saying is that if there's no beginning and no end then everything's going to happen sooner or later. A monkey will write Shakespeare. A reindeer will write Tolstoy ...'

'A slug will write Jeffrey Archer.'

'I think that's already been done.'

Cafell laughed. 'But what about the sun cooling down?'

'That's just one solar system. And humans'll be long gone by then.'

'Maybe. I read the other day that the Yanks couldn't put a man on the moon now if they wanted to. It's all been cut back. Still,' he added, remembering a recent conversation with his mother, 'there's probably better ways to spend the money.'

'Maybe,' Finn said. 'You know, I've never met a man who didn't think space exploration was a good idea, and I've never met a woman who agreed with it. Why do you think that is?'

Cafell knew what Ellen would say: the same as his mother, that it was a waste of money, that there were enough problems here on earth. Which was true enough. Men tried to solve problems by turning outwards, women by turning inwards. He remembered the Charlie Brown line: there's no problem so big you can't run away from it.

Rosalie accelerated past a tram and then slowed again, looking for Hu Guang-fu's street. A junk moving in full sail across adjacent Belcher Bay held her attention for several seconds, and she almost missed the turning. As a young girl she had often gone sailing with her father, and the graceful junks had always captivated her, but these days she usually found herself wondering what each boat was smuggling.

If this job was souring her ability to enjoy life, she thought, then it was time to find another one.

She parked the car outside the modest apartment block where Hu lived, walked in through the open glass doors and pushed the button for the lift.

Earlier that morning she had checked the 8×10s against the OSCG photo files and come up with a couple of names and a parent organization, the Blue Dragon Triad. The next by-the-book step would have involved cross-referencing men and Triad with the list of current OSCG investigations, but Rosalie was reluctant to follow the book for several reasons. For one thing, she didn't want someone else claiming priority and effectively icing their operation. For a second, her own and others' experience had taught that the success factor in any Triad investigation was in inverse proportion to the number of police officers involved. Apropos of which, she thought most of her British OSCG colleagues were self-serving morons. Talking to Hu Guang-fu would be both more informative and less of a risk.

He opened the door himself, his face breaking into a smile when he saw who it was. 'My wife is out shopping,' he said, as he showed her into a room crowded with the results of a lifetime's compulsive shopping in junk markets. Three bamboo cages of various sizes hung in front of the window, each containing several happy-sounding songbirds.

He cleared a space on the sofa and invited her to sit down. 'I will make some tea, and then you can tell me who it is you want to know about this time.'

She looked round the room, hearing him at work in the kitchen. Hu Guang-fu was a rarity – a member of a defunct Triad. He had been in his early twenties when the Communists, driving south in their final onslaught against the Nationalists, had surrounded the town of Ganzhou in southern Jiangxi province, rounded up the Red Spears, and executed them in the town square. Hu alone had escaped, with the help of the woman who would eventually become his wife.

He was not bitter about the fate of his fellow Red Spears; on the contrary, he had the strong feeling that their reign of terror in Ganzhou had deserved nothing less. But he remained fascinated by the Triads, their history and rituals, and in particular by the way in which essentially criminal fraternities could delude themselves into thinking they still represented something noble. Safely settled in Hong Kong by the time the civil war ended in Communist victory, he had spent the next five years establishing himself, first as a journalist, and then as an academic. By the end of the fifties he had been accepted as the colony's leading expert on the Triads, and as such he had often been called upon to assist the authorities. He had now been retired for several years, but a handful of the RHKP's Chinese officers still made the occasional journey out to Kennedy Town for information, advice and tea.

'I saw your name in the paper on Sunday,' he said, coming back with a cup in either hand. 'The baby-smuggling business. Did you have luck with the appeal?'

'Some. That's . . .'

'In the Golden Triangle they use dead babies to carry heroin,' he said, sitting down.

'They have to be less than two years old for the long sleep to seem natural, and they need to be dead less than eighteen hours for the faces to retain their colour.'

She looked at him. 'How do you live at peace with such knowledge?' she asked.

He smiled. 'There is evil in the world. There always has been. How else would we recognize good?'

She smiled back. 'Right.' At some point in her past the Taoist awareness of relativity she had inherited from her Chinese ancestors had fought a losing battle with the English need for absolutes.

'And my birds are still singing,' he added with a twinkle. 'I take it you've come for more specific information.'

'The Blue Dragons,' she said.

His eyes lit up. 'An interesting group. Now where should I begin? There are more than fifty Triad factions active in Hong Kong at the moment, with upwards of fifty thousand members. Yes, I know you know that,' he said with a grin, 'but I'm setting the scene. These factions are like legitimate businesses, like political parties – their fortunes are constantly rising and falling for a variety of reasons – leadership and luck foremost amongst them.'

He paused, and she resisted the temptation to interrupt.

'There are three basic types of organization at work these days,' he went on. 'There are the traditional Triads, who are doing pretty much what they've always done, with perhaps a little more attention to legitimate business than was once the case. Then there are splinter groups, which have often simply declared independence from a parent organization. These still pay lip-service to the old forms, but basically they're just gangs of thugs who use Triad symbolism as a fashion statement. And then there's the third group, which is composed of both old Triad factions and new splinters. The difference is that these factions have essentially jettisoned the past. They have single designated leaders to decide policy, small executive committees – they worship efficiency, they have no time for morality. Their single-mindedness often reminds me of the Russian Bolsheviks . . .'

'That's ironic.'

'It's more than that. Some of these groups have been extending their operations into the enterprise zones across the border, and the rumour is that a few of them have been doing so in cooperation with the local Communist authorities.'

'The Blue Dragons?' she asked, feeling her pulse quicken.

'I don't know, but I wouldn't be surprised. The Blue Dragons' main recruitment area is Mongkok, and you know what sort of a place that is. For the smart kids the Triad offers the quickest, easiest and most lucrative way out, and from what I've heard the Blue Dragons have a lot of smart kids.'

'What are they into?'

'Ah, that's another interesting thing. They don't touch drugs, or at least they didn't the last I heard. The Dragon Head disapproves – there's a story one of his sons died of an overdose, but I've no idea if it's true. His name is Shu Zhi-fang and he lives in a house on Tai Tam Bay, on that peninsular opposite the Country Park. He must be over seventy by now, but I doubt if he has relinquished any control. His Red Pole is a man named Lu Zhen – very clever, utterly ruthless.'

'If they don't do drugs what do they do?'

'All the usual. Protection, prostitution, and a lot of semi-legal stuff. Computer software copying, Gucci handbags, Rolex watches. So-called "victimless crimes". They also have a lot of legal interests – construction companies, car dealerships, hotels. They've grown a lot since Shu took over a few years ago. Remember what I was saying about fortunes rising and falling? Well, the fortunes of the Blue Dragons have definitely risen.'

She thought for a moment. 'Would a man who has qualms about smuggling drugs get involved in smuggling babies?'

'If the aversion to drugs is just a personal quirk, why not? Involvement in a simple cash trade like that . . .'

'A simple cash trade! What do you mean?'

He smiled and shook his head at her. 'That's what it is. You may not like it, but people across the border want to sell and people here want to buy. It's not like getting involved in smuggling dissidents out, where the Triads' interests and the Chinese authorities' interests are in conflict. With the babies everyone can make some money. And for the Triads there will be an added incentive – all those useful contacts they'll be making across the border in advance of 1997.'

He was right, she thought, as she made her way back down in the lift. She was in danger of becoming a slave to her own rage. But then a picture of the English Marine pulling the spluttering baby out of the water the night before came into her mind, scattering her good resolutions. She drove back towards Central, wondering for the umpteenth time how the father she had loved so much could have spent his professional life wringing profit from such casual barbarism.

The two-mile trip to Stonecutters' Island took only a few minutes in the Navy launch, but it was nice to be out on the water, and to feel the oppressive heat and clamour of the city falling away behind them. The new naval base seemed well provided with home comforts, which presumably tempered the inevitable sense of distance from the real world. Marker found himself feeling nostalgic for HMS *Tamar* and its location at the neon-lit centre of things.

After the two men had been shown to their neat, cabin-like rooms, Marker reported to the base commander, who had already been privately briefed by the Admiralty, and made a phone call to his CO in Poole.

'I think it would be a good idea to get the RAF to have a look for the *Ocean Carousel*, he told Colhoun, 'but I don't want to have to explain myself to any more people than I have to. This town's not what I'd call tight-lipped.'

'I understand,' Colhoun said. 'Just give me your number and I'll get the local head man to call you back.'

Twenty minutes later, Wing Commander David Barton was on the line.

Marker told him what he wanted.

'Do you want to go up yourself?' Barton asked unexpectedly.

'Yeah, that'd be great.'

'We'll expect you Thursday morning then. Don't forget your goggles.'

Marker put down the phone, feeling better than he had for some time. Two and a half more days, and they should at least know where Cafell and Finn were.

Fergie had also been on the phone. 'Chief Inspector Ormond will see you at the OSCG office at nine in the morning,' he told Marker. 'And you can imagine how thrilled he sounded at the prospect.'

'Another friend of Bellamy's?'

'No idea. Anyway, you seem to have the rest of the day off, you lucky buggers. Any ideas?'

'Yeah, lunch, and I don't mean the galley. Can we get a lift back to Kowloon?'

'No probs . . .'

'And how do we get back?'

Fergie ripped the top sheet off a convenient jotting pad and wrote down a number. 'When you've had your fill of the bright lights just call the duty officer and they'll send a boat for you.'

Marker was impressed. 'We must be royalty,' Marker told Dubery. 'Fancy some lunch and sightseeing?'

'Aye, why not?' the Scot said, sounding less than completely convinced.

The afternoon sun was at its hottest, but the shadow of the containers had already reached Cafell's knees – another few minutes and he would be wholly immersed in the relative cool.

He was thinking about Ellen. In fact he seemed to think about little else. Was that just because she was far away? he wondered. Did she occupy all his thinking spaces when he was in England?

He pictured her in the classroom at the Bournemouth school, the way he had seen her through the window a few weeks before when he had arrived early to pick her up. There had been kids all over the place, paint everywhere. Her hair had escaped from its confinement, and she had held it back from her eyes as she leaned over the table to look at a painting.

He saw her in her flat later that same day, remembered the Van Morrison album playing, the Indian bedspread, the look on her face in the candlelight after they had made love.

He had never known anything like this before.

He thought about what she would say if she could see him now, sitting in this space two hundred yards away from a gang of murderers. She would be upset and angry, worried for him and indignant that he could put himself at risk in such a way. She would see it as playing games, but she would also love him for it. Like his maps and models – she loved the fact of them even as she thought them childish. She loved the boy in him, but still wanted him to grow up.

He didn't understand it, but he knew it made sense. Sort of.

Marker and Dubery took the MRT subway under the harbour to Sheung Wan, ate a late *dim sum* lunch in a cheap restaurant on Morrison Street, and then walked east through the secondhand and antique shops on Hollywood Road. Taking his duties as a tourist guide seriously, Marker led Dubery into the smoky, perfume-laden Man Mo Temple, the oldest in Hong Kong. The place was full of locals come to honour one of the two resident gods, of literature and war respectively. Marker explained that the latter, Kuan Ti, served as a protector of pawn shops, policemen, secret societies and the military, and received a look from the younger man which asked 'how the hell did you know that?'

'I've been in here before,' Marker said, answering the unspoken question. Rosalie had said it was nice that the two of them shared a god.

Outside again, they retraced their steps for a hundred yards or so and turned up a long flight of steps which bore the name Ladder Street. 'This was built to help the sedan-chair carriers carry their white bosses home to their houses up on the hill,' Marker explained. 'It used to be lined with opium dens,' he added, thinking that the street, with its overhanging balconies and shuttered windows, still seemed like something out of the nineteenth century.

At the top they turned left along Caine Road, and

after walking for about a mile found themselves passing in front of Government House. Another few minutes and they reached the lower terminus of the Peak Tramway, just in time to catch the next ride up.

Marker had been to the top several times before, but as the two men circled the peak on the mile-long walk he found the views as breathtaking as ever. From the south-western side of the mountain they looked out over the crowded Aberdeen Harbour and the rocky island of Lamma a mile offshore; from the western side they surveyed a wide stretch of ocean strewn with craft and the purple haze of mountainous Lantau. Another corner in the path and the city was spread out below them like a gifted child's Lego fantasy.

As they took the funicular back down Marker asked himself what it was that seemed so unreal about Hong Kong. Was it just that all the different blendings – of Oriental and English, high-tech and medieval, ocean and concrete – felt strange to an Englishman? Or did the Chinese also feel out of place in such a hybrid city?

He supposed he'd have to ask someone Chinese.

It was almost six. Marker stopped at a public phone, took a deep breath and punched out her phone number of three years ago. After four rings the answerphone cut in, and he found himself listening to her voice. It felt strange. The beep went and, realizing he hadn't thought of a message, he instinctively hung up.

'Fancy a drink?' he asked Dubery.

The Scot nodded. 'This is an incredible place,' he said, as much to himself as to Marker.

They found a British-style pub complete with horse brasses, dartboard and a predominantly Chinese clientele, ordered two Tsingtao beers and took a seat in the window. Sitting there, it occurred to Marker that he and Dubery didn't talk to each other very much. Finn and Cafell, on the other hand, were probably both having trouble getting a word in.

'Time to get back?' Dubery suggested after their third beer.

It was gone eight. 'Give me a minute,' Marker said, and walked across to the public phone. He listened to it ring, thinking he wasn't sure whether or not he wanted to talk to her that evening, but then the answerphone engaged and his sense of disappointment was impossible to deny. 'It's Callum Marker,' he said. 'I'm in Hong Kong for a few days, maybe more. I was wondering how you are, whether we could meet up for a drink or a meal. I'll call again tomorrow.'

He replaced the receiver, wondering if he had made a mistake.

It was an unusually sticky evening, and the half-mile walk from her car to the surveillance post overlooking the godown did nothing to make Rosalie feel cooler. At the office she had changed into the short blue dress she kept there for such occasions, and this time it seemed to be working almost too well. The sergeant accompanying her, a man she had never taken to, was playing the part of her client as if he had forgotten it was a part, dragging her along by the arm like a man who couldn't wait. He was still pulling as they started up the stairs of the building which housed the surveillance team, and looked both surprised and indignant when she half shouted at him to let her go.

In the room on the third floor one man was keeping watch, the other sitting with eyes closed in an armchair, dreamily listening to his Walkman. Jackie Cheung's face beamed out from the cassette case on the chair arm.

'Nothing?' she asked the watcher.

He shook his head.

It had just gone seven o'clock. She would hang around till nine, she decided, and then come again in the morning.

The minutes passed as slowly as they always did on surveillance duty. The man with the Walkman offered her a turn with Jackie Cheung but she declined – Chinese pop was like the Chinese food she had eaten in England, a sickly imitation.

She took a turn on watch. The view from the window looked straight across the rusty corrugated roof of the godown to the darkened boat-house, the empty dock and the black waters beyond. Away to the south some of Kowloon's waterside restaurants were bleeding neon across the water, and in the far distance Hong Kong Island split sea and sky with a ribbon of lights. To the right Stonecutters' Island lay mostly in darkness. The Royal Navy had recently moved there from the old HMS *Tamar* base in the heart of Victoria, on the grounds that Beijing should not inherit a fully equipped military garrison in such a sensitive location. And of course the utter hypocrisy of this had been lost on every Englishman in the colony.

Nothing was moving. No cars were drawing up in the alley below, no boats headed in to the dock. Rosalie had the strong sense that this surveillance operation was going to be a waste of time and resources, and felt tempted to call it off there and then. Twelve more hours, she decided.

The Jackie Cheung fan escorted her back to her car,

chatting most of the way about the troubles he was having finding a bigger apartment now that his wife had given birth to twins. She drove back through Kowloon and the Cross-Harbour Tunnel, picked up the print-outs she had ordered by phone at the OSCG offices, and started for home. On impulse she stopped at the Wishful Cottage on Lockhart Road and devoured a plate of deep-fried walnuts in sweet and sour sauce. She had brought Callum Marker here, she remembered.

Back at home she showered and sat on the balcony in her dressing-gown, reading the print-out of the Blue Dragon file by the light of the room behind her. As always, the faces in the photographs reflected little of the barbarism within.

Except perhaps for that of Lu Zhen. He was smiling at the camera, as if he knew the last laugh would be his.

'But it won't,' she murmured. 'It won't.'

6

The following morning Marker and Dubery arrived on Hong Kong Island with almost an hour to spare, and decided to walk the mile or so from their disembarkation point to Wan Chai. But the trip across the harbour had not prepared them for the stickiness of the city streets, and it was with some relief that they finally walked through the revolving doors and into the air-conditioned comfort of the RHKP building.

Chief Inspector Ormond, a bulky Scot with short ginger hair and a reddened face, met them by the lift on the open-plan fifth floor, shook their hands perfunctorily and led them across to where a group of five men were already gathered around a space between desks. 'This is the day shift,' he told the SBS men. 'These are the latest reinforcements,' he told the others. 'OK, let's get started.'

It seemed rather a public place to hold such a meeting, Marker thought.

'If this bunch isn't kosher, then we might as well give up and go home,' Ormond told him, as if he'd read the thought. 'OK?'

'OK,' Marker agreed. He had just seen her walk out of the lift, and now she was walking across the room and dumping her bag on one of the desks. She must have been promoted, he thought. Three years ago she had been working out of the Central Police Station on Hollywood Road, about half a mile up from the Man Mo Temple.

As if aware of his gaze, she suddenly looked round. He smiled at her but she simply raised a hand in acknowledgement of his presence, her face expressionless.

Marker turned his attention back to the matter at hand.

'Bellamy seems to have spent three or four evenings a week in the Macau casinos,' one of the younger Chinese men was saying, 'but most of the time he seems to have come out well on top.'

'That's how he was paid,' someone else muttered.

'Looks like it,' Ormond agreed. 'I think we're going to have to abandon the man-blackmailed-by-debt theory.'

'More like man seduced by greed,' one of the others said bitterly.

'Aye, well,' Ormond muttered. 'So the next question is – which Triad or Triads had him on the payroll? The casinos should have records, and we'll have to go cap in hand to the Portuguese for current ownership info. Plus Bellamy must have kept some sort of receipts, otherwise there wouldn't have been any point in going through the charade of winning money he was already owed. Right? Well, get on your bikes then. I want this business cleared up before 1997, OK?'

The team scattered, leaving Marker, Dubery and Ormond.

'Have a seat,' the Chief Inspector said, 'and tell me what else you want to know.'

'Are you any nearer to deciding whether it was suicide, murder or an accident?' Marker asked.

'Not really. The idea of it being an accident seems a little too pat, but, having said that, we haven't found a motive for either suicide or murder. If he was passing on good information then there was no reason for the Triads to kill him, and as for suicide, well, he had an apparently happy family life, he didn't drink, his doctor said he had no incurable disease, and he had at least half a million salted away for his retirement. As far as we know, he had no reason to think he was about to be caught. Have you reason to think he was?'

'None. We caught him posthumously, so to speak.' Marker told Ormond about the tapped phone call in Singapore. 'They were only talking about him because he was dead.'

Ormond sighed. 'So maybe it was an accident. I don't suppose it matters very much now.' He started tidying the papers on his desk, then abruptly abandoned the task. 'If and when we narrow his paymasters down to a particular Triad,' he asked as he rummaged in his desk for something, 'then what comes next?'

'I don't know,' Marker admitted. 'I have another iron in the fire – nothing that impinges on the Bellamy death,' he added, seeing the sudden flash of indignation in the policeman's eyes. 'I think it's a case of wait and see for the next few days.'

Ormond nodded. 'I'll keep you informed,' he said. 'And I trust you'll be doing some reciprocating when the time comes.'

They all shook hands again, this time with rather more warmth. 'I'll see you downstairs in a few minutes,' Marker told Dubery, and wended his way through the desks to where Rosalie was scrolling through records on her computer screen.

She must have seen his reflection bearing down on her, because she turned and rose to greet him with a hug. There was a smile on her face this time, and he could smell the familiar hint of Shalimar which both she and Penny had always worn.

'This is Inspector Li,' she said, introducing the Chinese man across the desk. 'He is my partner. And this is Callum Marker,' she said, 'an old friend.' The two men shook hands.

'I only heard your message this morning,' she said. These days she received so few calls that she had given up checking the answerphone on a regular basis. 'How about dinner this evening?'

'Fine. Any preferences?'

'Somewhere new,' she said spontaneously. 'Let me think about it. We can meet in the Horse and Groom – remember it? Happy Hour lasts from sunset to midnight these days.' She could tell she was chattering from the look on Li's face.

'OK, what time?'

'Seven?'

'Great,' Marker said. 'I'll let you get on with your work then.' He backed away, feeling like a schoolboy who had just asked for his first date.

She turned back to her screen, ignoring Li's raised eyebrows.

Out in the South China Sea dark clouds were gathering above the *Ocean Carousel*.

'You know something?' Finn said.

'What?'

'If I ever meet the man who wrote "I'd like to get you on a slow boat to China" I'm going to fucking kill him.'

*   *   *

The morning passed slowly and frustratingly for Rosalie and Li. As expected, the dawn stake-out on the Cheung Sha Wan godown had come up empty, and their decision to keep it in place for another twenty-four hours was grounded more in desperation than any real expectation of success. They finally discovered who owned the property that morning, but it took only another hour to establish that the man in question had been dead for six months. Despite a colony-wide search, the sampan described by the doctor had not been found. And none of the hospitals had reported any cases of children with bacterial pneumonia.

Until early that afternoon. Rosalie took the call from the Princess Margaret Hospital in Lai Chi Kok. A woman had brought in a baby that morning, a woman doctor told her, and both were still there. The baby was likely to die in the next few hours.

'If it does, don't tell the mother until I get there,' Rosalie said, without stopping to think how callous she sounded. 'The woman's not the real mother,' she added, as if that made a difference.

The doctor made a noncommittal noise and hung up.

Deciding speed was more important than comfort, Rosalie took a car as far as the Admiralty MTR stop, parked it halfway up a Drake Street kerb, and took the subway. Fifteen minutes later she emerged from the Lai Chi Kok subway and walked briskly up the street to the sprawling public hospital. The doctor, a woman of around her own age, was waiting for her in the paediatric wing. Her face seemed even more drawn than the one Rosalie remembered seeing in the mirror at four o'clock that morning.

'The baby died ten minutes ago,' the doctor said sharply, as if Rosalie was partly to blame. 'The mother – or whoever she is – is still waiting. I think she should be told.'

'Can I talk to you for a minute first?' Rosalie asked. 'Somewhere private.'

'For privacy you need a private hospital,' the doctor said, but she led Rosalie down a corridor and into a small room full of shelves and cabinets, most of which seemed half empty.

Rosalie explained why the police had asked for bacterial pneumonia cases to be reported, and why she needed to talk to the woman. The doctor's face changed, moving from anger into what Rosalie suspected was an equally familiar sense of bitterness. 'I'll take you to her,' she said. 'You can question her after I've given her the bad news.'

The woman was well into her forties, Rosalie thought, too old for a legal adoption. Perhaps she had never been able to have children of her own, or perhaps she had lost those she bore. Whatever the woman's reason for purchasing the baby, the beseeching look on her face as the doctor entered proved it was not a decision she had taken lightly.

'I'm sorry,' the doctor told her. 'Your baby died a few minutes ago.'

The woman stared back, as if hoping that the doctor would reverse the terrible verdict, then abruptly got to her feet.

'This woman is from the police,' the doctor said

gently, 'and she needs to talk to you before you go.'

Rosalie was watching for the flicker of panic in the woman's eyes. 'I know you bought the baby,' she said, 'and I need . . .'

'There will be no one to look after my husband,' the woman said imploringly.

'You will look after him,' Rosalie said. 'You must tell me everything you know here in this room, and that will be the end of it. I promise.'

The woman looked at the doctor, as if seeking confirmation.

'These people sell babies that are ill,' Rosalie said. 'They do not care about anything but money. They have no honour.'

'I know that,' the woman said. 'But what can I tell you? A man came to our door and offered to bring us a baby . . .'

'Where do you live? Which area?'

'Mongkok.'

'And what was the price?'

'Two thousand Hong Kong dollars.'

Rosalie was surprised. 'Excuse me for saying this, but you do not look like a wealthy woman. How did you find so much money?'

'My husband, he was injured at work, paralysed. They paid him compensation, and we decided . . .' She shook her head.

'Did you try to adopt a baby?' Rosalie asked. She couldn't believe the smugglers went round drumming up custom door to door.

'Yes, but the agency says we are too old.'

'Which agency?'

The woman gave her a name and address in Cheung Sha Wan. 'They have other offices in Kowloon and Hong Kong,' the woman volunteered.

I bet they do, Rosalie thought. 'How did you pay?' she asked.

'In cash, when they brought the baby. I knew from the first minute she was not well, but I was afraid to bring her . . . There was something in the newspaper, and I thought they would take the baby away from us.'

Rosalie felt heartsick. After asking the woman a few more questions she escorted her down to the street, put her in a taxi and gave the driver enough money to get her home to Mongkok. The woman looked crushed, but still had the presence of mind not to give the driver an address until Rosalie was out of earshot.

Rosalie walked slowly back towards the MRT station, feeling the weight of the investigation bearing down on her heart. Grief followed rage, despair followed grief, and then she would find another reason for rage. It was like a rollercoaster of negative emotions, and she couldn't seem to get off.

The pleasure she had felt at the prospect of seeing Callum Marker that evening now seemed insubstantial, almost an unwelcome distraction.

Finn woke Cafell soon after four in the afternoon.

'It can't be six . . .' Cafell began indignantly.

'The weather's changed,' Finn told him, and as if to emphasize the point large spots of rain suddenly began to fall.

Cafell looked up. Dark grey clouds were swirling in the rectangle of sky above them, the wind was whipping through the gaps between the containers, and the ship itself was bucking in the rough swell, sending great fountains of spray up and across the loaded deck.

'A spot of drizzle,' Finn shouted. The rain was getting heavier now, the wind still rising, the clouds almost black. 'Still think we should tie ourselves up?'

'Better safe than sorry,' Cafell yelled back. He had no real idea what they were in for, only that it was likely to be bad. 'And we can tie a rope between us,' he added as an afterthought.

'Great,' Finn shouted. 'If we're found dead the head-line will be "SBS Men in Gay Bondage Scandal".'

'I didn't know you cared,' Cafell yelled. He turned with the coil of rope in his hand, saw the man standing there in the rain, mouth open and eyes wide with surprise, and for the first time in his life appreciated the meaning of the expression 'time stood still'.

In an single instant he seemed to take in every detail of the scene, from the stains on the man's T-shirt to the curly black hair plastered across his forehead, from the rivulet of water running down the container behind him to the tattoo on his forearm. He let the rope drop from his own hand, saw the gun snag in the man's waistband, and felt his own grasp the butt of the Browning. There was a flash of detonation, a triple ping as the bullet ricocheted around the walls of their hiding place, and then his own finger was squeezing the trigger, the man jerking back. The dead feet slipped on the wet steel, and the body slid backwards over the edge and into the wave-lashed channel between containers.

For a few seconds Cafell and Finn stood immobilized by shock, the rain streaming down their faces. Then they advanced together to the rim, and stole a glance outwards. Below them the dead man was being buffeted by the water sluicing down the channel; fifty yards away they saw the flicker of a light moving away from them in the direction of the superstructure. There was no other sign of movement.

Cafell pointed at the corpse below and made a lifting gesture. If the pirates found the two of them, he decided, a body here or there wasn't likely to make much difference.

Finn had come to the same conclusion. He went back for the rope, attached it to one of the container handles and swung himself down into the channel. Between waves he tied a harness around the dead man's shoulders, helped lift as Cafell pulled the corpse up, and then climbed back up the re-lowered rope.

There were two bullets in the man's upper trunk, both within inches of the heart. And although he knew it was ridiculous Cafell felt glad that both of them had been responsible for the fatal shots. 'We'll give him to the sea after dark,' he said in Finn's ear.

'If the sea doesn't take him first,' Finn shouted, as the huge ship seemed to hang in the air and a cloud of spray flung itself over them.

As her train pulled into the Mongkok MTR station Rosalie took the sudden decision to visit Dr Chen. After all, she was still wearing the anonymous blouse and trousers she had put on for the early-morning stake-out, so there was no reason for anyone to think she was anything other than a potential patient. She used a public phone to leave a message for Li and started off through the narrow streets towards the doctor's address, wondering what fictional ailment she should claim to have.

The block in which Dr Chen lived was almost visibly crumbling, the lift out of order, the pale-green paint peeling off the stairway walls. She supposed she was breaking an unspoken bargain in coming here – or at least she would be if it hadn't already been broken by their digging out his address and following him on the night of the boat chase. She hoped he would understand, and that he wouldn't use it as a reason to clam up on her.

His two-room flat was at the far end of a dimly lit corridor, and a piece of paper pinned to the door announced his profession. Before knocking she pulled back the thin curtain flapping in the open window and looked out at the fire-escape. In the narrow street below a group of children were playing with a cat, and probably not with the best of intentions. She yelled at them, all five faces turned upwards, and the cat saw its opportunity to escape, hightailing it down the street.

As she raised her hand to rap on the door she heard movement inside the flat. He was in.

She brought her fingers down on the thin wood and waited. No one came. She rapped again, wondering if she had imagined the noise. Or perhaps it had been a cat.

'The doctor is out,' a voice said in Cantonese from the other side of the door.

'When will he be back?' she shouted.

There was a noticeable pause. 'Tomorrow,' the voice decided.

Rosalie reached for the holster in the small of her back and took out the handgun. 'Open the door – police,' she shouted, and remembered in the nick of time to take a large sideways step.

The door seemed almost to explode as a hail of bullets ripped through it. There was a sharp stab of pain, the wet warmth of blood on her face, and for a second she thought she'd been shot.

She backed into the wall a few feet from the door and pulled out the splinter of wood which was still hanging from her cheek.

'I'll make a deal,' the man shouted from inside.

She said nothing. They were on the fourth floor, and to reach either stairs or fire-escape the man had to come out through the door.

Further down the corridor another door opened, and a woman's head poked gingerly out. 'Go and call the police,' Rosalie shouted at her. 'The doctor's been killed,' she added, guessing both that this was the case and that he had been popular with the people he lived among. She had spoken to him for only ten minutes on the telephone, and she had liked him.

The woman ran off towards the stairs, hopefully to do what she'd been told.

Inside the doctor's flat an animated conversation broke out. Either the man was talking to himself or there were two of them.

There was still only the one door.

Should she wait or take the initiative? Silence suddenly descended behind the door, as if a decision had been made.

She decided to give them another option. 'Throw out your guns and then come out with your hands in the air,' she yelled, her voice sounding shriller than she intended. This was a situation which she'd been through in several training simulations, but never in real life. Still, her hands were steady on the gun, and her head felt wonderfully clear, as if the needs of the moment had driven out all the rage and confusion of her visit to the hospital.

'We're coming out,' a voice said, but there was nothing submissive in the tone.

She sank to one knee as the door was pulled back. Two handguns thudded into the threadbare carpet and lay there like unexploded grenades. One thing was certain – neither of these had been responsible for shredding the door.

The first man edged slowly into view, hands above his head. He was not much more than twenty, wearing jeans, Nike T-shirt and bright orange trainers. 'This is all a mistake,' he started to say, and the other man stepped suddenly out behind him, his machine-pistol looking for a target.

She squeezed the trigger, taking the man in the centre of the chest and throwing him backwards. His partner was reaching for one of the guns on the floor, eyes watching her gun swing towards him, and it seemed as if a message from the brain reached the hand at the last possible moment, freezing it in motion, the fingers a few inches from the gleaming butt.

Her finger loosened on the trigger, almost reluctantly. His face broke into a grin, and they stared at each other for a moment, bound by mutual loathing.

'Get back,' she said. 'On the floor, face down.'

She back-heeled the two guns down the corridor like a footballer. Blood was turning the wounded man's blue T-shirt purple, and bloody froth was bubbling between his lips.

The sound of approaching sirens was floating through the open window, and she stood there, shoulder against the wall, until the uniforms arrived. Then, with a heavy heart, she went into the flat.

Dr Chen, a small, thin man with a wispy grey beard, was half lying, half sitting in the cupboard which contained his jars of herbs. His throat was slit, the blood still wet on his shirt front.

Rosalie leaned back against a wall and closed her eyes.

She spent the next two hours answering the questions of the local police and making a formal statement detailing her version of the afternoon's events. Writing down the short history of her dealings with the doctor, she felt close to despair. No doubt the two young men – assuming the injured one survived – would get life for his murder, but securing a conviction against the men who had ordered it seemed a forlorn hope. So try, try and try again, she told herself, echoing her father. Dr Chen had cared enough to put himself at risk, and she would do her best to see he hadn't died in vain.

It was almost seven when she remembered that Marker was waiting for her at the Horse and Groom.

She couldn't see him this evening, not feeling like this.

After leaving the OSCG building that morning the two SBS men had gone their separate ways. Dubery had headed off in search of the silk which Helen had asked for, and Marker had spent the morning strolling round the Central and Wan Chai districts. After lunch he had taken a tram out to Shau Kei Wan, where he had pottered around the market for an hour and then sat by the sea watching the fishing boats go by. Back in

Wan Chai he had scrounged a shower in the YMCA, changed into the shirt he had bought that afternoon, and arrived at the Horse and Groom with half an hour to spare.

He was on his second glass of Merlot when a young and almost obscenely bronzed Australian bartender arrived at his table with a portable phone.

'Callum, I'm sorry, I can't make it this evening,' Rosalie said. 'I'm still working,' she added.

She sounded a million miles away, he thought. 'I'm sorry too,' he said. 'Can we try again tomorrow?'

'I'd love to,' she said, but there didn't seem to be any feeling behind the words.

'Are you OK?' he asked.

'No, but I will be. It's just work. I'll see you tomorrow, same time, same place.'

'OK, but . . .'

There was the click of disconnection. He took the phone back to the bar, and got a sympathetic look in return. 'Can't trust 'em, mate,' the Aussie said. 'Another glass?'

Marker started to say yes and then thought better of it. There was something pathetic about drinking himself into a stupor just because their date had been put off for twenty-four hours.

Outside, the colony was girding its neon loins for another night. He walked west along Lockhart Street, passing the brightly lit RHKP building where she worked, and on into Central. The buildings of HMS *Tamar*, where he had stayed on his last visit, were shrouded in darkness. They were presumably awaiting demolition.

He cut through behind City Hall to the Star Ferry

terminal, and paid the extra dollars to ride on the upper deck of the green and white boat. The gates opened, the crowd bustled aboard, and they were underway almost immediately, heading for Kowloon's wall of light on the other side of the harbour. It always reminded Marker of New York's Staten Island ferry, on which he and Penny had once spent most of a morning mapping out their future together.

Once ashore he made for the bottom of Nathan Road, and then walked briskly northwards up the Golden Mile's tunnel of neon. The whores were already out in numbers, their shiny cheongsams reflecting the colours of the Chinese characters which blazed from the shop fronts and hanging signs. Oblivious to them, he walked on, purging the disappointment from his system with every step.

In the South China Sea the typhoon seemed to have reached its apogee. Night had added its darkness to the storm's, the rain was doing a passable imitation of a waterfall, and the wind was lashing it into their faces with the power of a water cannon. If this storm had a still centre, the *Ocean Carousel* had managed to miss it.

The two men had looped the rope through handles on the containers, the straps of the bergens and the belts around their waists. Despite being soaked to the skin and colder than they had been since leaving England, both men were feeling thoroughly exhilarated. There was majesty and beauty in the frantic patterns of wind and water, as the storm crashed and danced around the lumbering behemoth of the ship. Only the dead man's body struck a sombre note, and not long after dark a particularly strong eddy of water washed it back over the edge of their loft among the stacked containers.

Around eight o'clock the rain suddenly slackened and stopped. As the sky began to break up, the clouds seemed to be racing each other along in huge arcs, like a celestial Catherine wheel. And then it seemed as if someone switched the wind off, reducing the sky to its normal speed.

The body was back where it had fallen the first time, the head badly disfigured by two hours of violent contact with the steel container sides. This time Cafell went down the rope. He edged an eye around the corner of the last container on each side of the ship, but there were no lights advancing towards him.

He went back for the body, grabbed the ankles and pulled it across to the edge of the deck. The dead eyes stared up at him from out of the ruined head.

Cafell took a deep breath. 'If by some remote chance there's a God up there wants to claim him,' he murmured, gently sliding the body over the side, 'here he is.'

He thought he heard a faint splash far below.

By the time he'd regained their hidey-hole the moon was out, the stars flickering brilliantly between the thinning clouds. The churning of the ship through the rolling sea was the only sound to break the silence.

'We'd better both stay awake tonight,' he told Finn. It was the first time in several hours he hadn't needed to shout.

'I suppose they'll come looking for sonny boy.'

Cafell nodded. 'They'll look, but probably not very hard. They'll assume he was washed overboard.'

'They're not likely to look up here,' Finn said.
'Let's hope.'

Rosalie got home a little after nine, still numb from her experiences that day. She supposed she ought to feel hungry, but nothing in the fridge looked like a gastronomic treat in waiting, so she settled for a packet of garlic breadsticks and a can of Guinness. On the TV a panel of Englishwomen in twin-sets and pearls were earnestly discussing the latest Charles and Di revelations. As if anyone in Hong Kong cared.

She picked up the phone and punched out the number of the Kwong Wah Hospital, which was where the Triad foot soldier had been taken. Eventually someone told her that he had been operated on, and was expected to survive.

She felt a surge of relief, and then anger for feeling it.

The phone rang in her hands, making her jump. Guessing it was Marker, she picked it up.

'If you don't find a way to terminate your investigation,' a man said in Cantonese, 'you will be next.'

She kept silent, hoping he would say something else, but there was only a click.

Dubery's head had felt better. A lot better. He tried taking deep breaths of the cold air coming in through the open taxi window, but it didn't seem to help.

After spending most of the daylight hours in Stanley and Aberdeen he had made his way back to Stonecutters' Island, thinking that he'd have a beer in the bar and then get an early night. He managed the beer, but had then been persuaded by some friendly Marines to accompany them back to the mainland for a few more. There were four of them: Mac, a pug-nosed fellow-Scot from Falkirk, the lanky Steve from South Shields, a curly-haired Welshman called Bev, and an overweight giant from God knew where whom everyone called Shaky.

They had started out in Harbour City's Canton Disco, but after four pints and a near-punch-up with some evil-looking locals, had decided to move on. Steve had suggested a place called Madame Chang's, but Bev had disagreed. 'They bore me,' he'd screamed, loud enough for most of Kowloon to hear. 'Little China dolls – they're more like cash registers than women. They take you in, give you a screw, spit you out and take your money, all with the same expression on their faces. It's not only fucking boring – it's boring fucking!'

'OK,' Mac had said equably. 'Since you've all been good, I'll take you somewhere different.'

And they were on their way there now, driving up Nathan Road in the general direction of China.

The cab eventually stopped, which was more than Dubery could say for his head. They all got out, and Mac paid the cabbie – 'Here y'a, slitty-eyes, and don't spend it all on opium' – before leading the group across the road and into what looked like a private house.

Inside, though, there was a bar.

They had just finished ordering when a middle-aged woman appeared. 'Mr Mac,' she said with apparent pleasure.

'Bring 'em in,' Mac ordered.

She disappeared through a curtain, and the five men sprawled on the available couches.

A few moments later she came back, a line of girls behind her. One had no arms, one was a hunchback, one was clearly blind. 'She no speak,' the woman said, indicating the fourth girl. The fifth, seated in a cart, was legless. All five were beautifully attired in silk.

Dubery could hardly believe his eyes.

'I think Shaky should take the blind one,' Bev said. 'Then no one'll have to look at him.'

'I suppose we should give the SBS first dibs,' Mac said. 'He may be a prat, but he is our guest.'

'No,' Dubery said, 'not for me, lads. I'm a happily married man.'

'She's ten thousand miles away, you silly fucker. Come on, take your pick.' There was an edge in Mac's voice now, as if he was determined to take refusal as a personal affront.

'Maybe he like straight girl,' the woman suggested, and as if by magic another girl materialized.

'OK,' Dubery heard himself say. He would go upstairs with her, and then once they were alone he would explain that he was married.

He looked at her for the first time and was almost struck dumb by how lovely she was.

She led him up two narrow flights of stairs, climbing slowly in the tight cheongsam, exposing her slender thighs with each step up. The room was furnished like a Victorian bedroom, or a whorehouse in a Western. The girl had a foot up on the bed, exposing more of her thighs as she undid the clasp on her sandals. Then she straightened up and began unbuttoning the front of the cheongsam.

Dubery felt paralysed, and not just by the beer and whisky swilling around in his brain. She was so beautiful, so different . . . He closed his eyes and tried to visualize Helen's body – the pale, translucent skin, the pink nipples, the dark-blonde tuft of hair – but he couldn't hold the picture in his mind.

The girl stepped out of the cheongsam and pulled down her knickers. Her breasts were small, the nipples dark and large. In the dim light her body seemed a deep golden colour. She let her hair cascade loose around her shoulders and walked across to stand a few inches in front of him, her nipples brushing against his shirt. He reached out a hand and cupped her right breast, and heard someone groan with pleasure.

It was him. You can't do this, a voice was saying somewhere in his brain. It's wrong, you'll regret it.

She unzipped his trousers and pushed two fingers in to find his penis. It wasn't a long search – he couldn't remember ever feeling this hard, this big.

She fondled him for a few moments, then took away her hand and walked over to the bed, where she lay back, one leg stretched out straight, the other bent at the knee, her fingers linked beneath her breasts.

He unbuttoned his boots and took them off, telling himself that it was nothing, everyone did it, that it had nothing to do with Helen. The rogue voice inside his head told him things would never be the same again, but the body on the bed pulled at him like a tide. He wanted to feel it, smell it, taste it, know it.

She's just a whore, the rogue voice said.

He didn't care. She was everything he had never had.

'Condom on table,' she said.

He picked up the packet like a sleepwalker and took it across to the bed.

She took it from him, slit one open with her fingernail, and deftly readied the purple sheath for him to don.

'Common sense, yes,' she said, and squeezed it over the head of his throbbing penis.

Somehow he didn't come.

She lay back again, this time with her legs spread wide, and as he gently lowered himself on top of her she took the sheathed penis, guided it expertly inside her, and squirmed to drive him deeper.

This time he did come.

On the *Ocean Carousel* the two men finally abandoned their joint watch. For four hours they had waited, Brownings in hand, for the expected search party, but none had come. Either the crew had yet to miss their comrade, or they simply didn't care.

Finn took the first sleep, leaving Cafell to stare at the stars and wonder what, if anything, it all meant.

7

The following morning Rosalie and Li held an impromptu conference as they waited for the coffee machine to deliver.

'One,' he said, holding a single finger aloft, 'as far as we know there's still a shipment waiting to be brought in. Two . . .'

'If they knew yesterday that Chen had spoken to us – which they did – then they also knew the godown wasn't safe. They could have arranged to bring the babies in somewhere else.'

'Maybe. But at a day's notice? My guess is they're still out there.'

'If any of them are still alive. Sorry,' she said, seeing the look of exasperation on Li's face. 'What was two?'

He smiled and raised another finger. 'We might not have a location to watch, but we do have suspects. I think we should put tails on the Blue Dragon enforcers – the Red Pole and his main helpers. We know who they are.'

She thought about it. 'Won't they be expecting it? We'd have to put on a five-star job – overlapping tails, the works. At least thirty officers for twenty-four-hour cover. I can't see Halliwell agreeing to it.'

'This time you are going to have to use your charms.'

'I don't think I have many today,' she muttered, fingering the sticking-plaster on her cheek.

'Oh yes you have,' Li said mischievously. 'Halliwell is what the English call a "tit man".'

She grimaced. 'What do English mothers do to their children?' she asked.

Marker was halfway through breakfast on Stonecutters' Island when an orderly came to tell him Chief Inspector Ormond was on the phone. He took the call in the base commander's office.

'Thought you'd like to know,' Ormond said, 'we've found a motive for suicide. Turns out Bellamy knew Lansing, the captain of the oil-tanker which was hijacked. More than knew him, in fact. His wife says they'd been drinking buddies for more than ten years. Lansing even stayed with them a couple of times when his ship was in port.'

'You think he passed on the information not knowing that his friend would take the fall?'

'Something like that.'

'And was then overcome by remorse . . .'

'More like self-disgust, from what I knew of him. I know it sounds a wee bit too much like Hollywood, but it's the best we've come up with so far.'

'Thanks for letting me know,' Marker said.

'All part of the service,' Ormond said drily, and hung up.

Marker was putting down the phone when the base commander walked in through the door. 'Everything OK?' he asked cheerily. 'We're looking after you all right?'

'Fine.'

'Oh, by the way,' the Marine colonel added when Marker was halfway out the door, 'there was a Signal 3 typhoon blowing around the Spratly Islands yesterday afternoon. Thought you might like to know.'

'Thanks,' Marker said soberly. There wasn't a damn thing he could do about it, but he supposed knowing was better than not. Cafell and Finn would be having a rough trip.

Down at the base dock he found Dubery waiting at the controls of the Rigid Raider which they had commandeered for the day. The lad looked terrible, Marker thought. He'd either had too much to drink, a sleepless night, or both.

'Where to, boss?' the Scot asked.

Marker looked at the map he'd borrowed. The idea of the expedition was to give the younger man a sense of the local geography, not to mention jogging his own memory. 'Let's head out this way,' he told Dubery, tracing a route with his finger, west towards the northern tip of Lantau, through the Kap Shui Mun channel and out towards the estuarine border between Chinese and British waters.

The Scot gunned the outboard and directed the powerboat out into the bay. Three miles to the south Marker could see two green and white ferries crossing in mid-harbour. Behind them the towers of Central and Wan Chai stood out sharp against the clear blue sky.

The Rigid Raider headed steadily west-north-west, its prow aimed at the gap between the hilly heights of northern Lantau and Tsing Yi, where smoke from a coastal power station rose straight as a beanstalk into the heavens. All around them the sea was full of small boats – the graceful junks with their latticed sails, sampans in all shapes and conditions, assorted powerboats and modern yachts, water taxis and ferries plying their trade between the colony's 230-odd islands. There was only one large ship in sight, an empty oil-tanker edging its way south into the West Lamma Channel, presumably bound for Singapore and the West.

Marker silently wished its captain luck.

It took them twenty minutes to reach the Kap Shui Mun channel and another twenty to pass the two islands known as The Brothers. Lantau was to their left now, and some twenty miles to the west they could make out the thin line of the Chinese coast.

'Let's just sit awhile,' Marker yelled, and with what looked suspiciously like reluctance Dubery cut the engine.

Motion suited the Rigid Raider – without it the boat bobbed in the swell like a large fibreglass bath. Marker waited until a Macau hydrofoil had thundered passed, and half jokingly asked the other man what he had got up to the night before.

The Scot actually blushed.

'Want to talk about it?' Marker asked.

Dubery exhaled noisily. He felt relieved to get the chance, but still didn't know what to say. 'I made a mistake,' he began, but even that didn't seem completely honest. Because when all was said and done he still wasn't sure it had been a mistake.

'What happened?'

'I went into the city with a bunch of lads. We had some drinks at a disco, a lot of drinks, and then one of the lads said he knew somewhere that was different. That was the word he used. And aye, it was different all right. They had all these girls who were, well, deformed, I guess . . . one had no legs and one was blind . . . it was disgusting . . .' He looked up at Marker. 'I don't mean the girls were disgusting – it was the whole thing . . .'

He stopped and looked out across the sea, and Marker resisted the temptation to fill the silence.

'Not all the girls were like that,' Dubery went on. 'There was one . . .' He stopped again, and turned to face Marker. 'Were you ever unfaithful?' he asked. 'When you were married, I mean.'

Not until I knew it was over, Marker thought, but he didn't think that was what Dubery needed to hear. 'Not in deed,' he said, 'but I thought about it more than once.'

'Isn't that what matters?' Dubery asked miserably. 'Having the strength to resist temptation?'

Marker shrugged. 'Maybe. I don't really know. I don't think there's any hard and fast rules. How would you feel if Helen was unfaithful to you?'

Dubery realized with a jolt that he had never even considered the possibility. 'I guess I would know she didn't love me any more,' he said after a moment's thought.

'Maybe that would be so, maybe not. People do things for the strangest of reasons, and most of the time they don't have a clue what those reasons are. Do you think you still love her?'

'Yes . . . And I want to feel sorry for what happened, but I know I'm not.'

Marker felt surprised for the first time. 'Are you planning to go back for more?' he asked, almost coldly.

'Oh no, I don't mean that. I . . .' Dubery had a

mental picture of the cheongsam sliding to the floor, and wondered if he did mean that. 'I don't know what I mean,' he said hopelessly.

'Well, that's probably a start,' Marker said. He felt sorry for Dubery, but there was no way for anyone else to work out what the lad's true feelings were. 'A friend of my dad's once said that everyone needs one story they can't tell to their grandchildren. Maybe this is yours.'

The Scot smiled back, and for the rest of the morning he seemed at least a couple of notches above suicidal.

Cafell and Finn had spent the first couple of hours of the day slowly drying out. The sea had seemed almost preternaturally calm, as if it was trying to make up for its tantrum of the day before, and the two men had kept their ears open for sounds of a search party, restricting their own vocal exchanges to whispers.

Once during the morning they had heard voices, but they had seemed some way away. This time they were closer, and growing more so.

Cafell pointed downwards with his finger, and Finn nodded. Whoever it was, they were in the channel below, where their ex-comrade had played pinball with his head. The language sounded Chinese, but neither SBS man was known for his linguistic abilities.

A laugh sounded not ten feet away. The two Englishmen held their breath, half expecting to see a head appear above the rim of the container, but instead a cloud of blue smoke suddenly came into view, dissolving on contact with the faint breeze. The smell of strong tobacco reached their nostrils.

A sudden shout erupted, and for a long moment

Cafell thought they must have left some tell-tale clue of their presence in the channel below, but a burst of laughter came hard on the shout's heels, and then the sound of receding footsteps.

They heard the voices once more, this time at a much greater distance, and then only the sounds of the ship and the sea.

The clock behind the bar of the Horse and Groom was showing only a couple of minutes past the hour when she walked in through the door, recognized Marker with a smile, and wove her way through the tables towards him. She was wearing a simple light-grey dress, flat shoes and hardly any make-up. Her blue-black hair was gathered at the nape in a burgundy-coloured scrunchy. There were more worry lines around her eyes than he remembered, but they didn't begin to make a dent in her beauty.

'What would you like?' he asked.

'What are you drinking?'

'Merlot. It's not bad.'

'I'll have some.'

He walked up to the bar and asked the young Australian for another glass of Merlot.

'Same one?' the Aussie asked, nodding in her direction. 'I'd say she was worth waiting twenty-four hours for.'

'Thanks,' Marker said. 'I really needed your approval.'

Back at the table they toasted their reunion.

'So what are you doing in Hong Kong this time?' she asked. 'Same as before, or can't you tell me?'

'It's no great secret. Not from the police, anyway,'

he added wryly. He told her about the international anti-piracy initiative, and the connection with Douglas Bellamy's death which they had discovered in Singapore.

'What do you think of Ormond?' she asked.

'He seems OK.' Marker suddenly felt anxious. 'Why, isn't he?'

'No, no, I think he probably is,' she said, wondering why he seemed so worried. 'But he doesn't like me very much, so if you need to keep in his good books . . .'

'I'd rather keep in yours. What's he got against you?'

'He was a friend of my father's, and I think he felt more betrayed than most. I guess I'm a constant reminder of it all.' She took a sip of wine. 'This is nice.'

He took a sip as well. 'You got promoted, I gather.'

'Twice. I'm Inspector Kai these days, with my own long-term investigation. Well, Li and I are jointly in charge.'

'What are you investigating?'

She explained about the baby-smuggling, and was pleased to see he made no flippant comparisons with the trades in drugs, dissidents and simple refugees. 'I was out with your Marines the other night,' she said, and told him about the appeal, Dr Chen's tip-off and the abortive sea chase. She decided not to tell him about Chen's murder the day before: for the first time in twenty-four hours those minutes in the corridor were consigned to the back of her mind, and she wanted them to stay that way. 'I'm hungry,' she said. 'Are you ready to eat?'

The restaurant was only a short walk away, up one of the steeply sloping streets on the other side of Hennessy Road. It was Vietnamese.

'This family came on one of the first boats to reach Hong Kong,' she explained. 'They own five restaurants now.'

Inside it was crowded, but a smiling old Vietnamese ushered them into a window seat for two and chatted to Rosalie in Cantonese. 'I booked,' she explained after he had left. 'At this table you can smell the jasmine in the garden,' she added.

He smiled at her, and grabbed a drinks list from an adjacent empty table. They both decided on a bottle of '33', a French beer long popular in Vietnam. 'Any recommendations?' he asked, switching to the food menu.

'The set meal is nice. Seven courses, all variations on beef.'

'And I don't suppose there's any Mad Cow Disease out here. Sounds good.'

She passed on the order in Cantonese.

'Are you going to stay in Hong Kong?' he asked, once the old man had shuffled away. 'Will it be safe?'

'I don't know. The Communists are bound to purge the RHKP, and I don't suppose being half-English will be a great asset.' She smiled wryly. 'But I can't pretend the idea of moving to England fills me with enthusiasm. This has always been my home.'

Marker could hear the bitterness beneath the surface. She had never seemed a contented person, but three years earlier there had been an optimistic energy to set against the legacy of her unhappy past. For the moment that energy seemed at a low ebb. Maybe it was just the

144

current investigation that was depressing her – it would be surprising if it wasn't.

'How is England these days?' she asked.

'Depressing,' he admitted. 'We've had fifteen years of government by people who don't give a toss for anyone but themselves and their friends, and it's taken its toll.'

'But has it changed the way people are with each other?' she asked. 'Can politics do that?'

He thought about that. 'I think it has,' he said eventually, and started to explain why he thought so.

She listened, noting that the intensity she remembered was still there, if perhaps a little tempered by age. But he would always be an outsider – that was why they had understood each other. She remembered their first meeting, at a restaurant table full of English officers. They had all been celebrating something, having a whale of a time, and although he had joined in, had done nothing to dampen anyone else's enjoyment, he had still seemed a man apart. There had been a certainty about him, an utter self-reliance, which at first she had found almost chilling.

It was, she had come to realize over the next few days, both his blessing and his curse. People with his kind of self-knowledge found it hard to understand others.

'Three years older,' he said, breaking the reverie.

'Three long years. Tell me what happened with Penny? Are you still together?'

'Nope. After I went back from here we lasted another year or so. It seemed to get a little worse each day . . . it was like being in a slow-motion car accident, just sliding towards disaster and nothing anyone could do about it.' He shrugged. 'And then one day she was gone. It was strange. It felt terrible, but it also felt like a huge relief. It was like reaching rock-bottom. Things could only get better.'

'And they did?'

'Yeah, I think so.'

'You haven't fallen in love with anyone else?'

'Nope. How about you?'

'I wasn't in love with anyone.'

'You know what I mean.'

'I've been too busy to fall in love,' she said, getting up to visit the ladies' room.

The conversation was going in the wrong direction, Marker thought, as he watched her disappear through the beaded curtain at the far end of the room. He didn't want to re-create the relationship they had had before, one of confidants who stared in at each other's lives from outside. But did he want anything else, and if so, what? He smiled to himself. He knew one thing he wanted.

It had been so simple in the old days, before Penny. If he fancied someone he had done his best to get them into bed, and only after that had been accomplished would he start wondering if there was anything else he wanted from the woman. Usually the answer had been nothing.

With Rosalie though, he knew there was something else he wanted. He liked her, liked just being in her company. What he didn't know was how it would work out. In the old days he would have just pushed ahead and seen which way the dice would fall, but now . . .

In the ladies' room Rosalie was leaning against the basin and staring at herself in the mirror. It would be so easy to take him home, to feel the warmth of another human being. It had been a long time since she had made love with a man – almost three years – and she knew that on that occasion she had been seeking some sort of compensation for the non-consummation of her friendship with the recently departed Marker.

They could consummate it now. What did she have to lose? A friendship? Two days ago she had never expected to see him again.

But . . .

She smiled wryly at herself. This would not be a casual thing, not for her at any rate. And not, she suspected and hoped, for him either. And if it wasn't a casual thing then there was something to lose.

A picture of Dr Chen's body flickered across her mind, both unbidden and unwelcome. It was too soon, or she was too tired, or something.

She walked back to the table, noted the look of uncertainty on his face. 'Do you know how long you are going to be here?' she asked.

'No. A few days at least.'

A few days, she thought. Enough time to turn each other upside down, but not enough to put each other right side up again. 'So will you come for a meal then?' she heard herself ask. When was the last time she had cooked anything?

'I'd love to,' he said. 'When?'

'That depends on work. I'll call you. I'm sorry,' she added, 'I'm really tired tonight.'

He nodded, feeling both relieved and disappointed. 'Car or tube?' he asked.

'The tube,' she echoed, and laughed.

'Whatever you call it. Can I walk you to the station?'

'Of course.'

Outside she slipped her arm inside his, and they walked back down the hill, turning right on Hennessy Road. At the entrance to the Wan Chai station she reached up and kissed him lightly on the lips, and then was gone, down the escalator, leaving him with the neon-drenched street, the roar of traffic and a hint of Shalimar.

'I want you,' he murmured to himself. It was a feeling that didn't fade as he walked back through the city centre to the Star Ferry.

By nine the following morning he was flying at five thousand feet over the South China Sea. They had long since left the small coastal islands behind, and only the faint line of Hainan's coast on the distant western horizon challenged the ubiquity of blue-green ocean and blue-white sky.

The density of boating had also dropped with every mile from Hong Kong, but there was still no shortage of shipping scattered across the waters below. At this particular moment Marker could see a couple of oil-tankers, a bulk carrier, two short-sea traders, a large junk and a Chinese warship. The latter, which looked like a Huangfen Fast-Attack Missile Boat, was heading south, probably bound for the disputed Spratly Islands and a spot of gunboat diplomacy.

The South China Sea had always meant trouble for someone, what with opium wars and Vietnamese boat people and seventeenth-century pirates attacking Spanish galleons from the Philippines. No doubt Rob Cafell could give a lecture on the subject, Marker reflected. In fact, with a week to spare on a container ship, he had probably already given it, with Finn the captive audience.

Still, the young Londoner was not short of retaliatory weapons. He had taken a pocket encyclopaedia to Florida the previous year, and bombarded the team with useless facts. Marker himself was still wasting brain cells holding on to the knowledge that the microwave had been invented in 1947.

He tried to refocus his concentration on the sea below. If the container ship was headed in this direction – and he didn't like thinking about the possibility that it wasn't – then it couldn't be that far away.

Another oil-tanker swam serenely into view. It was probably out of the Gulf, bound for Taiwan or Japan. Even from this height it was clear how low the ship sat in the water.

Had he done the right thing the previous evening? Marker asked himself for the tenth time that morning. Maybe she had wanted some clarity from him, some open declaration of something . . .

'Is that it?' the pilot's voice asked on the intercom.

The familiar green funnel was passing beneath them. The uneven arrangement of containers on the starboard side was as he remembered it from the Indonesian sea channel. Marker felt a leap of joy in his heart.

'Do you want to go in closer?' the pilot asked.

'No. Just get an accurate fix, and then keep on the same course until we're out of sight. I don't want to give them the idea they're being watched.'

'You're the boss.'

Marker squirmed round in his seat to keep the container ship in view, hoping to God that Cafell and Finn were still alive, free and on board.

Cafell heard the plane before it appeared in their rectangle of sky. It was a small plane, flying high enough for reconnaissance, with a familiar silhouette. But he was damned if he could remember the type. Neither could Finn. 'They all look alike to me,' he said. 'Like women in the dark.'

'No wonder you're single,' Cafell said, unfolding his map. 'I reckon we're only about twelve hours from the mouth of the Pearl,' he said, tapping the damp paper with his pen. 'I think it's time we did a little contingency planning.'

'OK. What are the contingencies?'

'There seem to be two. We're either headed for Hong Kong or somewhere else in the Pearl estuary, most likely Canton.'

'It's called Guangzhou these days,' Finn said.

Cafell resisted the temptation to hit him. 'If it's Hong Kong . . .'

'Then they'll have fallen into our trap,' Finn said triumphantly.

'If it's Hong Kong we can just wait for a good opportunity to go ashore,' Cafell said. 'If it's Canton – sorry, Guangzhou – we have to decide whether to go the whole distance. Do we want to end up in Red China?'

'Not particularly. Is there anywhere we can get off?'

'The gap between Hong Kong and Macau is about twenty miles,' Cafell said, pointing at the relevant spot, 'so we wouldn't have to swim more than ten.'

'You're kidding, right?'

'There's plenty of small islands we could break our journey on, but there's a slight problem there – they belong to the Chinese.'

'That's a *slight* problem?'

'The good news,' Cafell added, ploughing on relentlessly, 'is that I reckon the boss was in that plane, and that we'll be picked up before we've swum a mile.'

Finn sighed. 'Just supposing for one mad moment that I buy into this plan – how do you intend to get off without being seen?'

'At this speed we'll get there a couple of hours after sunset.'

'Oh I see, you want us to swim ten miles in the dark. That makes sense. And don't think for a minute that I'm against the idea, but aren't we supposed to follow the ship to its destination? I mean, look here' – Finn tapped the map – 'there are quite a few ports between Canton and the sea. Don't we need to know which one we're headed for?'

'Maybe you're right,' Cafell agreed. 'But it's only worth going in for the information if we think we can get back out again.'

'I like those odds better than your ten-mile swim through shark-infested seas.'

'They're not shark-infested.'

'Well, they sure as hell aren't full of kippers.'

As usual Rosalie had to fight her way off the train at Wan Chai, and as usual the invisible hands scrambled to get a feel of her breasts. It would almost be worth wearing a couple of mousetraps, she thought as the escalator carried her up to the street, and caught a glimpse of her own smiling face in a glass reflection. She felt good this morning. Alive.

A few minutes later she was walking through the doors of the RHKP building, and hoping that her mood would survive the day's work. The inquest on Dr Chen was scheduled for that afternoon, which didn't exactly bode well.

She would invite Marker for dinner the next day, she decided, stepping out of the lift on the OSCG floor.

There was a message from Li on their desk – his wife had come down with the flu, and he would be an hour or so late. He was probably taking his two daughters to school, Rosalie thought.

She angrily shook away the mental picture of her father, collected a cup of coffee from the machine, and started going through the reports of the surveillance team. Shu Zhi-fang, the Dragon Head, hardly ever seemed to go out, and when he did it was only to play golf with other old men at the Royal Hong Kong Golf Course a few miles up the winding coastal road from his home.

He was like a corporate boss, she thought – a long way above the fray. If anyone was to lead them anywhere useful it would have to be Lu Zhen.

The Blue Dragons' Red Pole at least moved around. He had spent most of the previous evening travelling to and from Macau, spending only half an hour in the colony, and most of that in the offices of the Casino Jai-Pek. The Blue Dragons probably had a controlling interest in the place.

There was one photograph of the Red Pole sitting on the hydrofoil, another of him emerging from the casino.

Returning to Kowloon around ten, he had not gone home to Mongkok – where, to Rosalie's surprise, he still lived – but to a woman's apartment in upmarket Kowloon Tong, where he had stayed the night.

There was a photograph of the apartment block.

So what had he done the previous afternoon? she asked herself, rummaging through the reports for the missing page.

He had come across to Hong Kong Island for a haircut. A place in Hollywood Road – photograph supplied – which looked fashionably expensive. Then he had taken the Star Ferry back to Kowloon.

She looked at the photograph, the two men sitting a foot or so apart on the seat, the newspaper between them. It was like a scene from a spy movie.

She smiled to herself and reached for the coffee. She was being ridiculous.

But why take the ferry? an inner voice asked. The man had a chauffeured limousine, or he could have taken a taxi. She studied the faces in the photograph, and made a mental note to talk to the officer who had taken it.

The other man's face was familiar, she realized.

Excited now, she racked her brain for an identity. Where had she seen this man before?

She got up from her seat and abruptly sat down again. For reasons of its own, her unconscious seemed reluctant to take the picture round the office. She scribbled a note to Li, cut the photo in two and put the unknown man's half in her bag, and took the lift down to the street. The offices of the *South China Morning Post* were only a short walk way.

Her old friend in the picture library had a desk covered with pictures of Deng Xiao-ping.

'He hasn't died, has he?' Rosalie asked.

Gu Yao-bang looked up with a smile. 'Just getting ready,' he said with an impish smile. 'How have you been?'

After they had swapped news for a few minutes, Rosalie brought out the photograph and showed it to Gu.

'What do you want to know?' he asked.

'Who is it?'

He clucked his disapproval. 'No wonder Hong Kong is going to the dogs,' he said. 'No one seems to have a clue what's going on. This man's had his picture in the *Post* nearly every week for the last six months.'

'So who is it?' she almost shouted in frustration.

'His name's Wang Xiao-bo, and officially he's a junior member of the team Beijing sent to scrutinize the run-up to '97. But everyone knows he's the PSB's man.'

Marker found Dubery waiting in the RHKP lobby for their noon meeting with Ormond. On the way up in the lift he passed on the news of the ship's sighting, and for the first time in several days saw a genuine smile break out across the young Scot's face.

Ormond was alone at his desk in shirtsleeves. A red tie hung loose around his neck. He seemed surprised to see them, but quickly made up for the lapse in memory, ushering the SBS men into two of a dozen seats left over from a recent team meeting. 'Some progress,' he announced, leaning back in his chair. 'We've pinpointed the Triad Bellamy did most of his dealings with. They're called the Blue Dragons.'

It was the same one Rosalie had mentioned in connection with her investigation, Marker remembered. He was wondering whether to say so when one of Ormond's team, a plump young Chinese, broke into the conversation.

'Boss, we've run into a snag. The Blue Dragon principals are already under surveillance.'

Ormond's eyes narrowed. 'Who the fuck by? Anyone dealing with the Triads knows they have to clear it with this office.'

'It's the baby-smuggling team,' the subordinate said, almost apologetically.

'Shit!' Ormond said vehemently, his head swinging round in the direction of Rosalie's desk, just in time to catch her framed in the opening lift doors. She looked happy, Marker noticed, and he found himself hoping that her raised spirits had something to do with him.

'Go and get her over here,' Ormond said brusquely.

Rosalie came back with the subordinate, her lithe walk making his seem like an awkward waddle. The smile didn't disappear when she saw Marker, which he supposed was something.

Ormond didn't offer her a seat, but she sat down anyway. He started a sentence, then stopped, as if the memory of seeing Marker at her desk forty-eight hours earlier had suddenly surfaced. 'Am I missing something here?' he asked.

She looked at him blankly, but Marker realized what was happening. 'We're old friends,' he explained. 'If these two cases are connected neither of us was aware of it until now.'

'I'm still not aware of it,' she said. 'What's going on here?'

'I've just been told you have the Blue Dragon principals under surveillance,' Ormond said. 'Why?'

She shook her head. 'Our investigation is on a need-to-know basis – you know that.'

'If I didn't need to know I wouldn't be asking,' Ormond said.

'Why? What's your interest?' she asked, not giving an inch.

Ormond opened his mouth to say something, but then appeared to think better of it.

'Look,' Marker said. 'It seems obvious that these two investigations are linked, if only by the Blue Dragon Triad. They seem to be heavily involved in the organized piracy, and' – he turned to Rosalie – 'I gather that they could be behind the baby-smuggling?'

'No doubt about it,' Rosalie said.

'But the Blue Dragons' reach doesn't seem to stretch beyond Hong Kong,' Marker persisted. 'They must have other partners as far as the piracy is concerned, and they can't be organizing the buying of babies on the mainland, can they?'

He looked at Rosalie, who turned to Ormond. 'Can we spread the need-to-know net across both teams?' she asked.

Ormond looked hard at each of them in turn. 'OK,' he simply said.

Rosalie took the photo from her bag. 'I think this is the other partner,' she said.

Ormond took one look and closed his eyes.

'Who is he?' Marker asked.

The Chinese Public Security Bureau's man in Hong Kong,' Ormond said slowly. 'Which means three things. One, someone on the other side of the border – a Party chief, police chief, economic chief, you name it – is up to his ears in both babies and piracy. Two, at least one Triad has found a way of dealing with the Communists, which means Hong Kong will have to deal with both sets of bastards after '97.' He grunted in disgust.

'And three?' Marker prompted.

'It means we haven't got a hope in hell of stopping whoever it is, because Whitehall would rather sell the Governor's daughters into white slavery than risk offending Beijing.'

'He's probably right,' Rosalie told Marker and Dubery over lunch in the RHKP canteen. 'But it's not just Government House – there are about five million people out there who either want to stay or have no way of getting out, and none of them want to tangle with their future masters. And that includes most of the police. By going into business with the Communists the Blue Dragons have bought themselves the best protection they could hope for.'

'But only if their Communist friends are influential ones,' Marker said hopefully.

'They will be. And if those piracy figures of yours are accurate they'll soon have enough money to buy off any potential threats. These days, money is about the only thing that counts in China.'

'What's the situation like now?' Dubery asked, partly because he was interested, partly because he felt more like a gooseberry if he kept silent. The boss certainly seemed interested in this woman, and he could see why.

'It's chaos,' Rosalie replied. 'There's this frenzy to get rich. Some people say it's like the Cultural Revolution, and it is . . . It's the same collective obsession with a single goal, and the same indifference to the damage that's being done to people in the process. I used to listen to escaped dissidents telling me how wonderful it was to be free. Nowadays the dissidents I meet are mostly Communists who've been locked up for opposing corruption in the Party.'

'A political dictatorship and a rampant free market – it's hard to think of a more toxic blend,' Marker observed.

'Well,' she agreed, 'it's certainly not a recipe for peace and tranquillity, but what you've just described also sums up a century of British rule in Hong Kong.'

He grinned. 'No argument from me,' he said. 'You convinced me last time I was here.'

'What about crime?' Dubery asked.

'In China? It's mushrooming, especially in the Special Economic Zones . . .'

'Which reminds me,' Marker interrupted. 'I was thinking – say these pirated ships were taken back to China, up the Pearl River to somewhere. The cargoes could simply be re-exported. Sold twice, in effect. But they would need the use of a decent-sized port, and a lot of authorities willing to turn a blind eye.'

'I don't think that would be a problem,' Rosalie said. 'You could probably buy Canton with the profit from one ship.'

Marker looked at his watch. 'Five in the morning in England,' he said. 'I'll give the old man another couple of hours' sleep.'

'I hope he's persuasive,' Rosalie said, 'because I wouldn't hold out any hope of Ormond getting anywhere with our bosses here.'

'You still don't trust him?'

'No, I think I do. There's just too many powerful people in Hong Kong who won't want the boat rocked.'

'In London as well,' Marker added pessimistically.

'I've just had an idea,' Dubery said suddenly. 'If the Blue Dragons are selling information to the Communists, then how are they being paid?'

The other two looked at him blankly.

'In bairns,' the Scot said. 'Babies.'

8

It had been dark for over an hour and a huge red-orange moon had just risen from the black ocean. In their niche among the stacked containers the two SBS men could feel the adrenalin beginning to pump through their veins as the ship approached the end of its six-day journey. By Cafell's reckoning the distant islands passing by off either side belonged to Beijing, and the *Ocean Carousel* was now deep inside the waters of the People's Republic.

'Do you think it's time we took a look forward?' Finn asked softly.

'Maybe,' Cafell said. Their narrow field of vision was certainly not good for the nerves, but getting spotted and caught trying to improve it was likely to be considerably more injurious to the health. And if the ship was nearing its destination the chances of there being crewmen this far forward would have greatly increased.

He looked at the map again, but it simply wasn't detailed enough to offer him any answers.

'Look,' Finn whispered.

Off the starboard bow land had suddenly loomed into view. No more than a mile to the east a rocky headland was rising into a bare hill, momentarily eclipsing the moon, and with every passing second the shoreline seemed to be growing closer.

'OK, I'll go,' Cafell said.

A minute later he was down in the corridor between containers and working his way slowly towards the starboard side. A few feet from the edge of the deck he stopped, listening for the sound of feet or voices on the walkway below. Hearing nothing, he climbed a couple of rungs down the ladder and leaned out into space, hanging on with one hand.

The boat was slowing, he realized, and up ahead he could see the reason – a port of some sort. The dark line of a long jetty divided the water from the heights of the island behind, and silhouetted against the latter Cafell could see the tell-tale pattern of gantry cranes. Onshore a cluster of lights twinkled in the shadow of a small, sugar-loaf-shaped promontory.

He climbed back on to the deck, and made his way across to the port side, again stopping and listening before leaning out to scan the way forward. This time he found ships, seven of them, all apparently at anchor within half a mile or so of the shore. One looked like a patrol boat of some sort, but the other six were short-sea traders. Though of various types, each had the usual squat superstructure set aft and prominent lifting gear amidships. They were about a quarter of the size of the *Ocean Carousel*.

This was the transhipment point, Cafell realized.

He made his way back to Finn, pulling the rope up after him, and told the younger man what he had seen.

'Plan B?' Finn asked.

'Since we don't have a Plan A, I guess so.'

The previous night they had scouted their immediate neighbourhood, looking for a short-term hiding place which would give them both a better view of what was happening and more flexibility of manoeuvre. The niche among the containers had served them well at sea, but in port it could swiftly turn into a death-trap.

'Home sweet home,' Finn murmured, taking one last look at the square of shadow before starting down the rope. Once both men were down in the trench between containers, he worked the improvised grab-hook loose and deftly caught it as it fell.

The ship was now moving at only a couple of knots, and off the port side the first of the anchored boats was visible between the walls of stacked containers. Cafell gestured to Finn to stay where he was and advanced stealthily to the other side, where the lights of the port installation buildings were now reflected across a quarter of a mile of sea. On the long concrete jetty the container lifting gear was bathed in yellow light. A few figures were visible, and on the far side of the jetty's longer arm two more short-sea traders were berthed.

A host of smaller boats were drawn up beside a smaller, L-shaped jetty in front of the installation buildings. More men were emerging from one of these, and for a second Cafell assumed the voices were carrying across the water. Then he realized they were coming up behind him.

He decided not to move, and hung there above the deckwalk like an angel about to take flight from the buttress of a church, working out the sequence of movements he would need to make if he was seen. Swing back on the left arm, he told himself, moving the body into a crouch as the right hand pulls out the Browning . . .

That would be the easy part. It would start getting difficult when fifty Chinese overheard the shot.

The men were only about ten yards away, then five,

then passing beneath him, still talking, two men in T-shirts and loose trousers, one of them with a pigtail. As they walked away their shiny black hair turned gold in the reflection of the jetty lighting. Cafell let go of the breath he had been holding, and pulled himself back up on to the main deck.

The ship was inching in towards the jetty, the men on both ship and shore exchanging shouted greetings. This crew of pirates had obviously been here before.

Cafell worked his way back to Finn.

'Time to say goodbye?' Finn asked in a whisper.

'I think so.'

'If we're caught don't forget to tell them you're Maurice Chevalier,' Finn added.

Cafell looked at him blankly.

Finn shook his head. 'I'll explain later. Let's go.'

They hoisted the bergens on their backs and started towards the port side, with Cafell scanning ahead, Finn watching their backs. There was no visible movement on the port walkway, and the nearest of the anchored traders, some three hundred yards in front of them, seemed devoid of human life.

'As good a time as any,' Cafell said, starting down the iron ladder to the walkway. If they were seen now it was just bad luck, for on a docking ship the crew's attention was normally focused on the dock.

He let the rope out across the side, hearing a faint thump as it struck the metal hull. 'You first,' he told Finn, holding their wooden grab-hook against the rail until the Londoner's weight had pulled the rope tight.

As Finn's head disappeared into the darkness it occurred to Cafell that the circumstances had been kind – both the moon and the jetty lights were bathing the other side of the ship, creating a deep cloak of shadow for their disembarkation.

A tug on the rope told him Finn was in the water. He clambered across the rail and started down, using the soles of his feet to run backwards down the ship's side. The last time he had done this was in a Poole Harbour training exercise earlier that year.

This time the water was about forty degrees warmer – sliding into the South China Sea was like entering a lukewarm bath. Finn was waiting for him in the prearranged spot twenty yards from the ship's side, a big schoolboy grin on his face, leaning on his watertight bergen as if it were a beach ball.

They started swimming, dragging the bergens with one hand and using the other three limbs to pull them through the water. Taking care to keep beyond the range of the lighting, Cafell led them round the bow of the halted ship in a wide circle, past the end of the concrete jetty, and in towards the shoreline of the wide bay which lay behind. The moonlight was brighter now, but there was enough surf to hide them from anything but the most rigorous watcher, and soon they were back inside the moon-shadow cast by the island itself. Behind them on the jetty they could hear the whine of the gantry crane in motion – the unloading had begun.

In front of them, a small and apparently empty beach sat beneath low cliffs. At either end of the bay these merged into rocky headlands: the sugar loaf on the right masking the installations in the small bay next door and a much larger, less elegant hump on the left rising almost sheer from the sea.

The two men swam until the water grew too shallow, then lay with only the tops of their heads above water for several minutes, searching the beach for any sign of movement. At Cafell's signal they crawled ashore and slowly up the beach, stopping only when they reached the shelter of some bushes at the foot of the cliff.

'If this is China I want my money back,' Finn murmured.

Marker sat with one elbow on the side of the unmarked Fast Patrol Craft, gazing out across the night sea. He was beginning to feel anxious. It was almost nine o'clock, and by his reckoning the container ship should have hove into view more than half an hour ago. So where was it?

If it wasn't headed up into the Pearl River estuary then where the fuck was it headed? Up until now his main concern had been trying to gauge the stowaways' intentions. Were they committed to seeing the voyage through, even if it meant sailing into the maw of the Chinese dragon? Or would they try and jump ship? He had wondered what he would do in their place, and decided that, on balance, he would jump.

That afternoon he had phoned Colhoun in Poole and explained the situation. After a round of phone calls between the various military and political parties involved, it had been agreed that, while there were no circumstances in which the Marines' 3rd Raiding Squadron could trespass in Chinese waters, two non-uniformed SBS men might be allowed a slightly wider latitude. So he and Dubery, wearing the plain clothes of innocent boating enthusiasts, were sitting plum in the middle of the estuary mouth, some eight miles west of the diplomatically correct cordon of FPCs.

'Just use your discretion,' Colhoun had said drily. 'If

you see someone in trouble at sea, then it's your duty to pick them up.'

'And to use reasonable force in helping them evade capture by known pirates,' Marker had added hopefully.

'Aye, that sounds reasonable enough,' Colhoun had agreed.

But it was hard to meet people off a boat which refused to arrive.

Having found a relatively easy place to scale the low cliffs, Finn and Cafell started south across the uneven slopes in the general direction of the port's onshore installations. On their left more rocky hills stretched into the darkness. If this was the island Cafell thought it was, then it was about two miles wide and three miles long. It didn't seem overcrowded.

After about five minutes they came upon what they were looking for. A stream had cut a small valley in the hillside, and among the trees they could find a place to rest up and take stock. The noise of the stream would even mask their conversation.

A few yards downstream they found a bamboo grove which offered both invisibility from the landward side and a fine view of the distant jetty, where the loading of the two short-sea traders was now in full swing. Cafell studied them through the nightscope.

'We should be on one of them,' Finn said quietly.

Cafell disagreed. 'Their names are in Chinese, not English. They must be headed up the coast or the estuary. If this was Europe or South America I'd say risk it, but white faces in China? We'd stick out like a dog's bollocks.'

'So how far are we from Hong Kong?'

'About fifteen miles from the nearest island.'

'OK,' Finn said, 'so unless you're planning to open a business here we're going to need some kind of transport.'

'Yeah. I thought . . .'

'Of course we could always build a raft from driftwood.'

'I was thinking more in terms of simple theft.'

'The boss'll be proud of you. So what are we waiting for?'

'Patience,' Cafell told him, rummaging in his bergen for paper and pencil. 'First off, I want to copy down the names of these ships,' he said, putting the nightscope to his eye and starting on the first Chinese character.

Finn watched, feeling disappointed in himself for missing it.

'We need as much evidence as we can get,' Cafell said as he drew. 'By this time tomorrow the containers will be gone – in half a dozen different directions, for all we know. And without them we might even have a hard job proving that ship out there was ever the *Ocean Carousel*.'

'Ships should have serial numbers stamped on their hulls,' Finn muttered.

'How about some pictures?' Cafell asked.

Finn shook his head. 'There's not enough light. You'd need a special job for this. Even that camcorder we used in Florida wouldn't do it – not at this sort of distance.' He thought for a moment. 'But we could stay the night and take some pictures in the morning.'

Cafell considered the suggestion. 'No,' he decided, without being sure why. Certainly there was a noticeable shortage of cover on the island, but they could always dig in somewhere . . . No, it was more a feeling that they would be pushing their luck. And during his years in the SBS Cafell had learnt to take such feelings seriously. 'The boss would be worried about us,' he told Finn.

'Oh yeah? He's probably sitting in some ill-lit room with a Suzy Wong on each knee and opium pipes sticking out of every orifice.'

Cafell laughed in spite of himself. 'Has anyone ever told you how disgusting you are?'

'No. But thanks.'

Cafell admired his own calligraphy, and started on a rough sketch of the scene in front of them. Five minutes later he was stowing the folded drawing in the bergen. 'OK, let's go. And the more info we pick up *en route* the better.'

'Land or sea?' Finn asked.

'Land. We should be able to circle round above the buildings and get down to the water within reach of the smaller boats.' He stopped and turned to Finn. 'Why Maurice Chevalier?' he asked.

Finn grinned. 'The boss and I got the stowaway idea from the Marx Brothers . . .'

'No wonder I spend half my time feeling like I'm trapped in a farce,' Cafell murmured.

'They stow away on this transatlantic liner,' Finn went on, 'and when they reach America, and they have to go through immigration, all four of them claim to be Maurice Chevalier.'

Cafell just looked at him.

'It's one of the funniest scenes ever shot.'

'I'll take your word for it.'

It took them the best part of an hour to reach a point

overlooking the onshore port installations. A line of three modern warehouses had been built on levelled ground between the sugar loaf and the roadway which continued out on to the main jetty. On their left, facing the smaller jetty, there was a cluster of smaller, much older-looking buildings – the remnants, Cafell guessed, of a bygone fishing port. Even further to the left, beyond a grove of palm trees, a line of connected cabins climbed the hill like a giant's stairway.

'Aim for the palms?' Finn suggested.

'Yeah. But I'm going to do another drawing first.'

Finn watched as the scene below was transferred on to a clean sheet of paper. There was no doubting the man could draw. 'I can smell food,' he said.

'So can I,' Cafell agreed. It was six hours since they had eaten the last of their rations. 'I expect there'll be a McDonald's for you in Hong Kong,' he added unkindly.

'The rate you're going it'll be closed by the time we get there.'

Cafell put away the drawing, made sure the bergen was sealed against the water, and led the way down the hill. There was no sign of life around the buildings below – it looked as though everyone was out on the jetty getting on with the job in hand. A previously anchored ship was now moving in, presumably to take its turn beside the loading berth.

The two men crossed a narrow road, and carefully picked their way down a grassy slope towards the palm grove. As they entered the shelter of the trees a baby suddenly started wailing in the cabins above, the sound merging with the distant whine of the gantry crane.

They clambered across the rocks on the edge of the

water, slid into the lapping waves and swam towards the end of the L-shaped wooden jetty. Cafell left Finn to keep watch while he checked along the line of tethered boats for a suitable candidate. The selection was impressive – there were eight sleek-looking speedboats, each equipped with radios and loaded with extra fuel cans. All but one had their keys in the ignition.

There were also a few decrepit wooden boats, and in one of these Cafell found the oars he was looking for. He placed them in his chosen speedboat, slit through the securing ropes with his knife and started gently pushing the boat towards the mouth of the harbour. Finn joined him, and the two men eased the vessel down the shoreline for fifty yards or so. Once confident that the dark line of coast would hide them from watchers on either jetty, they clambered aboard and began to row.

Twenty minutes later they rounded the southern tip of the island and the last of the anchored ships was lost from sight. Cafell engaged the outboard and Finn let out an exultant whoop as the craft gathered speed.

Marker and Dubery got the news over the radio about fifteen minutes later: the two FPCs at the southern end of 3rd Raiding Squadron's cordon were running an intercept course on a speedboat coming out of Chinese waters. After a tense few minutes a laconic voice announced: 'We've picked up a couple of Poole's finest.'

By the time Marker and Dubery got back to Hong Kong waters, Cafell and Finn had consumed all the sandwiches they could lay their hands on and swallowed about a gallon of tea. The ex-stowaways switched boats, leaving an eager Marine to take the captured speedboat back to Stonecutters' Island. The four SBS men shook hands, high-fived, hugged and grinned at each other.

'Nice trip?' Marker asked once they were underway.

'Apart from the accommodation, facilities, food and entertainment,' Finn told him.

'So where's the *Ocean Carousel*?'

'About fifteen miles back,' Cafell said, gesturing over his shoulder. 'Unloading.'

He seemed more sombre than usual, Marker thought. 'Why don't you start at the beginning?' he suggested.

Cafell went through the main events of the voyage: the murder of the crew, his and Finn's killing of the pirate who had somehow stumbled across their hiding place in the hour before the storm. He talked dispassionately, but Marker had spent enough time with him to know that both events had left their mark.

Cafell described the island base, their brief recce and escape. 'I did some drawings,' he added. 'It's a professional set-up, all right. They've got a modern container gantry and the usual derricks, and I'd guess some heavy dredging has been done to let them take large ships. There's no way someone could put together a facility like that on the quiet.'

'The patrol boat was a bit of a give-away,' Finn added.

'One patrol boat's not the Chinese Navy,' Marker argued. 'And the local authorities might have sanctioned the set-up without knowing who was going to use it.'

'Maybe,' Cafell agreed, 'but I wouldn't bet Finn's shirt on it. And it's a good job we got a look at the place, because otherwise we'd have been wasting our time for six days. How did you find out we were headed this way?'

Marker went through his and Dubery's story: the discovery of the fax in the office on Rempang; the raid on the Wu brothers' warehouse in Singapore; the tapped phone call from Hong Kong and the light it threw on Douglas Bellamy's suspicious death; the emerging role of the Blue Dragons Triad, and the discovery that day of their link with powerful interests across the border in China. 'And there's also a tie-in with a baby-smuggling operation,' Marker concluded, 'but I'll save that for later.'

'Christ,' Finn muttered. 'We only need a few international drug smugglers and we'll have the full set.'

'So what's next?' Cafell asked.

'A good night's sleep,' Marker said. 'We'll worry about the rest tomorrow.'

'Things always look better in the morning,' Finn muttered facetiously.

Marker doubted it. With the moon shining on the sea, and his men back safe, he felt pretty damn good right then.

They got back to Stonecutters' Island shortly before two, and after making sure Cafell and Finn had beds Marker borrowed the CO's office to call Colhoun in Poole.

'Thought you'd like to know, the wanderers have returned,' he told the SBS boss.

'Good,' Colhoun said, his relief apparent even in the one syllable.

Marker gave him a brief summary of what had happened on board the ship, and Colhoun said he'd get in touch with those authorities in Singapore who were officially handling the ship's hijacking. 'I've sent the lads to bed,' Marker went on. 'I'd like to talk the whole operation through with them sometime later today, and come up with some recommendations.' He did a quick mental calculation. 'Four in the afternoon here will be eight hundred hours GMT. Can I ring you then?'

'Fine.'

Marker hung up to find Cafell leaning against the door jamb.

'I thought I'd ring Ellen,' he said.

Marker smiled and left him to it. Cafell punched out the number and hoped she was home from school.

She was, and she sounded happy to hear his voice. 'How are things?' she asked.

'Pretty good. We've been incommunicado for a few days, so I haven't been able to phone.'

'You told me that might happen.'

'I know, but . . .'

'Have you been chasing pirates?' He had told her of their secondment to the Anti-Piracy Centre.

'Something like that.' It was so good to hear her voice. He felt almost like singing. Or crying. Something to express the relief he was suddenly feeling that they had survived the last six days. The crew of the *Ocean Carousel* had not been so lucky. Their girlfriends wouldn't be getting calls.

'Are you OK?' she asked, anxiety in her voice.

'I am now. I miss you.'

'I miss you too. Have you any idea when you'll be back?'

'Not yet.' One part of him wished it could be tomorrow, the other part reminded him how much he loved his work. 'How are you doing?' he asked.

'Oh, fine.' She talked about a friend at work, what she

was going to eat that evening, how the cat was staring at her as if he knew who was on the other end of the telephone line. He saw the pictures in his head, and felt ordinary life bathing him with its wonderful simplicity.

They told each other they loved each other, and how much they missed making love.

Cafell went back to his bunk feeling both full and empty. This was what it was going to be like from now on, he thought. This was what it was like, trying to share your life in a single man's job.

The following morning Rosalie had no sooner stepped into the OSCG office than she received an invitation to visit Ormond's desk. He wasted no time on preliminaries. 'The hatches are being battened shut,' he told her in an uncharacteristically low voice. 'I don't know how your friend Marker is doing, but I'm getting nothing but the bloody run-around. Very apologetically, of course, but the run-around just the same. I imagine Chatfield upstairs is getting it too. Someone in Government House has probably grabbed the ball and sat on it.'

'I haven't seen Marker since yesterday,' she said.

Ormond sighed. 'Well, I guess I've got other work to get on with,' he said. 'What are you working on?'

'The same old stuff,' she said. 'Li and I are checking out the adoption agency which one of the buyers went to.'

He nodded. 'Good luck.'

She went back to her desk, feeling a little guilty for not trusting him more. Li was indeed working on the line she had suggested, going down the list of clients in search of women who had not been offered legal babies, in the hope that eventually they could narrow the field of suspicion to a particular office and adviser. She, however, had decided to devote at least half the day to running down information on Wang Xiao-bo.

The police computer entry on the Beijing envoy told her only his date of birth – 4 October 1949 – and his current position as a member of the delegation from the People's Republic charged with facilitating the transition from colonial rule.

'Facilitating,' she murmured to herself. It was one of those Americanisms which the English really should have invented themselves. The very word reeked of hypocrisy, of fists curled up in velvet gloves.

She reached for the phone and punched out the number Marker had given her on Stonecutters' Island. Someone with a pronounced Welsh accent answered and good-naturedly offered to go and look for the man in question. There was no doubt the British were leaving, she thought.

'Rosalie?' Marker asked.

'How many other women are you expecting a call from?'

'None.'

'Good. Can you come for dinner tonight?'

'As far as I know. What time?'

'Seven, seven-thirty?'

'Great. I'll see you then . . .'

'I've also got some news,' she told him, looking across the office. The ginger head was nowhere in sight. 'Ormond tells me he's getting the run-around. No direction, no response at all, as if the politicos are hoping the whole business will just go away.'

'Sounds par for the course.'

'Have you heard anything?'

'I'm talking to my boss at four. I'll give you an update tonight.'

'OK, I'll see you then.' She put the phone down, her mind made up.

Later that day the four members of the SBS team were sitting round a table in the empty canteen on Stonecutters' Island. Through the window beside them the towers of Kowloon glittered in the afternoon sun.

'So what do we have?' Marker asked, and proceeded to answer his own question. 'We have photographs of the ship before, during and after its face-lift at the Indonesian base. We have two eyewitnesses to the murder of the original crew at sea and the unloading of the ship on the Chinese island of Chuntao. We have the names of two of the boats which took the cargo on to God knows where.' He paused. 'The people in Singapore think they have enough evidence to shame the Indonesians into some sort of action against their own people on Rempang, and now that you two' – he nodded in the direction of Cafell and Finn – 'are safe, I expect they'll get moving on that.'

'That's something,' Finn said.

'But not a lot,' Marker said remorselessly. 'We have no evidence connecting any Chinese authority with the piracy . . .'

'The patrol boat?' Cafell asked.

'A case of mistaken identity. A fantasy dreamt up by imperialist trespassers on Chinese soil. They'll probably demand an apology.'

Cafell looked suitably rueful. 'So where do we go from here?'

'That's what we're here to decide. Or at least, to come up with some ideas.'

There was silence for a few moments.

'If we could get Singapore to hold their horses,' Finn said, 'we might be able to set a trap, and get the Navy to intercept the bastards in international waters.'

'Even if Singapore was willing, which I doubt, it would be a hell of a tall order to set up a ship, monitor it across two thousand miles in both directions . . . No, sorry, I don't think so. This bunch are too well organized, and they'll be even more careful over the next few weeks. Think about it – the Wu brothers in jail, Bellamy's death, the operation against the Blue Dragon smuggling boat the other night – if you were in Fu Manchu's position wouldn't you start getting a little paranoid? And they've probably realized by now that one of their boats is missing from Chuntao. Once the Indonesian shit hits the fan they'll *know* something's up. They'll be waiting for us.'

'So what's the good news?' Finn wanted to know.

'There isn't much,' Marker said brutally. 'Their operation may be fraying at the edges, but the centre hasn't been touched. They've lost their go-betweens in Singapore, the Indonesian base and an inform-ant in Hong Kong – all of which are replaceable. The only really good news is that we now have a damn good idea how the whole thing works. When we have some hard evidence, then we'll be in business.'

'Chuntao,' Cafell murmured.

'Yeah. We need the same sort of pictures that Finn took on Rempang.'

'A Chinese Navy patrol boat sitting in front of

a hijacked freighter,' Finn remarked. 'Framed by a gorgeous sunset,' he added unnecessarily.

'I didn't get the feeling that Chuntao was much more than a transhipment point,' Cafell said. 'And if it isn't, won't we still be fraying the edges?'

'That gantry crane was an expensive investment,' Finn argued.

'And the monster's lair is probably somewhere on the mainland,' Marker told Cafell. 'I think we're going to have trouble getting the go-ahead for another visit to Chuntao. Our chances of getting anyone to let us loose on the mainland are a lot less than zero.'

Cafell grinned at him. 'We can only ask.'

Marker pushed back his chair and got up. 'I'll go and do that now.'

As Marker spoke to Colhoun, Rosalie was sitting in a Wan Chai coffee shop, scrutinizing the several pages of notes she had amassed in visits to three newspapers and the reference sections of the city and British Council libraries. Wang Xiao-bo might represent the Public Security Bureau on the Beijing delegation, but he had made his career as an economic fixer, not as a policeman in the shadows.

He had made no mark at all until after the Cultural Revolution, emerging into public view in the late seventies as the successful director of several semi-privatized industrial concerns in Guangzhou. He had then disappeared again for several years, but his re-emergence in the prestigious post of PSB chief for the Shenzhen Special Economic Zone seemed to rule out the possibility of disfavour.

Rosalie thought it most likely he'd spent the missing

years involved in either a military project or the enormous prison labour sector. Either of these would have made it easier for him to set up the sort of organization they now seemed to be facing, and later, as PSB chief in Shenzhen, he would have had access to every economic and military facility. He could have introduced his own men wherever he wanted. Given the experimental nature of the Zones, given their proximity to the outside world, he could have used national security as an excuse to set up, or help set up, any number of no-go areas.

And one of them would have to be a port, she thought.

She needed more information about his years in Shenzhen. She needed to know who his cronies had been, and where they were now.

In his Poole office Lieutenant-Colonel Neil Colhoun replaced the phone and stared thoughtfully out across the rain-swept harbour. It looked miserable out, but he wouldn't have swapped it for the weather he knew Marker and his team would be enduring. It was always the same in Hong Kong, like walking around with a hot flannel a couple of inches from your face.

He looked over the notes he'd made during the conversation, and didn't feel hopeful. In fact, in a situation like this, he had no real idea where to begin. There were too many important interests involved, most of them with no higher objective in mind than the preservation of a barely defensible status quo.

The Foreign Office had set up the liaison with the Kuala Lumpur people, he thought – someone there should have some interest in following through against the pirates. And the insurance companies were certainly more interested in stanching their financial haemorrhage than in preserving Beijing's sensitivities. They would have some clout in the Cabinet Room.

Colhoun wondered if Marker was right in thinking the men in Beijing could be shamed into acting against the pirates. In his years in Hong Kong he had been baffled by the Chinese, and had almost come to believe the nostrum proposed by his CO at HMS *Tamar*, that the only two motivating forces in the Chinese psyche were greed and the need to save face.

He supposed the latter was what Marker was counting on. He was the man on the spot, a man whose judgement in such situations had always been good. If Marker wanted his team to do a photo shoot behind Chinese lines then Colhoun would do his best to get the man a diplomatic green light.

The problem remained – where to begin? Colhoun decided he needed advice from a disinterested quarter, and flicked through his tattered leather telephone book for Oliver Bradburn's number. They had both been in Hong Kong for the same two-year period in the mid-eighties, Colhoun with the Marines, Bradburn completing the last phase of a long diplomatic career, and a friendship between their wives had widened to include them. Jenny still wrote to Alice Bradburn, but he had not talked to Oliver since a chance meeting at Twickenham a couple of years ago.

'He's sitting in the garden,' Alice told him, and there was a long wait.

Her husband would be in his early seventies by now, Colhoun thought. He hoped that Bradburn had not lost touch with, or given up on, that world he had lived in for so long.

'Long time no hear,' the familiar voice exclaimed. 'To what do we owe the pleasure?'

'I need some advice,' Colhoun said honestly. 'I want to ask you about the situation in Hong Kong.'

'Fire away. I haven't been back for three years, but I think I have a pretty good idea of what's going on.'

Colhoun felt relieved. 'Say I wanted to do something which would irritate the Communists, make them lose a lot of face, make them angry – where would I find support for doing something like that in Hong Kong?'

'What are you planning to do? No, I know you can't tell me. Well, the answer's pretty easy – hardly anywhere. Nowhere that counts.'

'Why?'

'They've made this deal with Beijing and they're hoping it will stick. They may not like it very much, and they may not trust Beijing, but they're still hoping. And they're terrified of giving the Communists an excuse to tear it up. It's like the thirties, but you wouldn't remember that. It's appeasement.'

'Who are the "they" you're taking about?'

'The business people in Hong Kong are the most influential people involved. They can put pressure on both the Governor there and the Government here. And they'll have friends and partners in the business world here who'll do the same. There's probably a few local politicians who'd like to stand up to the Chinese, but you'll always find a few Don Quixotes. When all's said and done, in two years from now Beijing will be in charge. It's not in anyone's interest to stir things up.'

'What about here in the UK?'

'Hmmm. There's a lot of people who find the whole

deal shabby, and are happy to say so. Of course they won't have to live with the consequences. I know the MoD's pretty fed up with drug smugglers using Chinese waters as a sanctuary, but you'd know more about that than I do.'

'Aye,' Colhoun agreed noncommittally. 'So how are you coping with retirement?'

The two men talked for another ten minutes, concluding with vague promises of a visit. Colhoun put the phone down, hoping his mind would still be as sharp when he was Bradburn's age, and feeling profoundly pessimistic about the chances of getting his team the green light they wanted.

Marker arrived at the Quarry Bay flat with a bottle of wine in one hand, a bouquet of lilies in the other and a packet of condoms in his pocket. The latter two made him feel about seventeen years old, which was not an age he looked back on with any great fondness.

Rosalie's eyes lit up when she saw the flowers, and as she stretched up on tiptoe to kiss him on the cheek he smelt the familiar perfume. 'Come through,' she said, leading the way. She was wearing a sleeveless dress in deep indigo, and her long black hair danced on her back as she walked. It was the first time he had seen it down for three years.

The savoury-sweet smell of oriental food was coming from the kitchen. The living room seemed unchanged, though perhaps the TV was new. The pale-grey futons, the carved wooden table and the neat bookcase all looked the same; the large Chinese watercolour and the Turner print still faced each other across the room. On the one side tranquil trees and pool, on the other a raging sea squall. He remembered thinking that they represented the two sides of her heritage, staring at each other in bemusement.

'Go out on the balcony,' she called from the kitchen. 'I'll bring the wine.'

He went out through the sliding glass doors and leaned against the balustrade. A mile to the north the airport runway ended in mid-bay; two miles to the west the building blocks of Kowloon started rising towards the New Territories. The sky was overcast, but who needed stars when humankind had supplied its own thousand points of light? All those lives, he thought. All those worries and moments of pain. All that contentment, all the moments of joy.

He sounded like his father on Shakespeare.

He heard her footfall and turned to find her smiling at him, a glass of wine in either hand. He took one, then the other, placed both on the balcony table and turned back towards her. With what seemed perfect timing their arms moved to encircle each other, and their lips met in a gentle, unhurried kiss.

'I wanted to do that three years ago,' he said.

She looked in his eyes, as if she was searching them for truth.

He smiled and they kissed again, harder this time, and longer, leaving each other breathless. Her nipples were pressing against the dress, and he lightly brushed one with the palm of his hand.

She ran the palm of hers against the swelling in his trousers.

'Dinner will keep,' she said softly, before taking his hand and leading him back into the flat.

9

Marker shared the early-morning ride back to Stone-cutters' Island with about a dozen Marines in varying states of dissipation. Friday night furloughs in Hong Kong obviously hadn't changed that much – if the drink didn't get you then something else would.

It was a beautiful morning. The day's blanket of wet heat had not yet fallen across the city, and the air was clear and almost cool. He could still see her face at the door as he left, feel the last kiss on his lips. I'm in love, he thought.

An adjutant let him into the CO's office with ten minutes to spare before the expected call from Colhoun. He sat in the swivel chair, gently turning to and fro, mulling over the previous night. He couldn't remember ever feeling so good about making love with someone. It had seemed so easy, so natural.

As if they were made for each other, he thought, wincing at the cliché. But it really had felt like that. Like he had finally come home . . .

The phone rang, startling him out of his reverie.

Marker knew the news was bad from Colhoun's tone.

'I've been getting nothing but red lights all day,' the CO confirmed. 'The MoD's sympathetic in theory, but no one's willing to put a head above the parapet. The

FO's South-East Asia people are keen to see progress with the anti-piracy campaign, but they don't have much of a say any more. The Hong Kong people almost had a fit when I just hinted at the possibility of action in Chinese waters. It looks like our only hope is the Intelligence network, so I'm seeing a couple of people in London this evening. If we can' get an OK from the Joint Intelligence Committee, then no one else need know. But I'm not optimistic.'

Marker sighed. 'So you'll call again tonight?'

'As soon as I know anything. You and the lads can have a day off. Enjoy the sights.'

'OK, boss.' Marker hung up. He didn't want to think about an immediate recall – not now.

Given the news of their free day by Marker over breakfast, the three other members of the team took the launch across to Kowloon, walked through to the bottom of Nathan Road together, and then went their separate ways. Cafell walked south and turned left on to Salisbury Road, looking for the New World Shopping Centre Mall, which, according to Marker, housed the Chinese Arts and Crafts Bazaar. He found it without difficulty, and spent half an hour browsing through the paintings, seal carvings, calligraphy and dolls, wondering what Ellen would like best.

She would prefer materials to the finished goods, he decided. Some different papers, a set of watercolours, calligraphy pens and inks. Another half hour and he had gathered together a traditional Chinese arts DIY kit of awesome proportions. It cost him most of a week's wages, but then there hadn't been many places to spend money on the *Ocean Carousel*. And he was pretty certain she would love it.

Leaving the air-conditioned bazaar for the steam bath outside was a traumatic experience, but the view from the Waterfront Promenade was almost worth it. Cafell walked slowly east, dodging joggers with sweat-banded foreheads and the occasional roller-blade enthusiast. To his right the waters of the harbour played host to moving boats of every known type and size, and the non-stop wailing of horns, bells and what sounded suspiciously like gongs floated across the water like a maritime symphony. On the other side of the harbour the skyscrapers of Hong Kong Central and Wan Chai clustered beneath the grey-green haze of Victoria Peak.

He found a seat and let his eyes feast on the scene. Almost out of sight behind the tip of the Kowloon Peninsula, he could just make out the abandoned buildings of HMS *Tamar*, where his father had been stationed in the fifties. His father, who had served in the Navy for over thirty years and never seen action.

The SBS was not like anything else, Cafell thought. Except perhaps the SAS. Barring another Falklands, the members of these two units were the only British military personnel who were likely to see action in the old sense of the word. He supposed the poor bastards on secondment to the UN in Bosnia were seeing action of a sort, but then so were the rows of ducks in a fairground shooting gallery. And all of the UN jobs which came the Navy's way were pretty low-risk affairs.

No, he had to face it – the SBS was about the only way for a sailor or Marine to get killed these days. Looking back on it, he still thought it some kind of a miracle that none of them had died in Haiti the previous summer.

He had nothing to prove at any rate, not to himself or anyone else. He had been brave or stupid enough – and he didn't think he would ever know which – to take the sort of risks which a married man and a father ought not to take voluntarily. He wasn't hooked on danger, wasn't interested in it for its own sake. And there were other places to indulge a love of the sea than in the SBS.

It would soon be time to move on, he thought.

Since this was his first trip to Hong Kong, Finn did what most tourists do, and took a trip on the Star Ferry. From the island terminal he wandered up Harbour View Street, watching the activity around the piers, and then turned left up the hill with the vague notion of finding the Peak railway. Hollywood Road looked interesting, so he turned left again, and strolled slowly along, looking in the shop windows and watching the women walk by. There were some real beauties, he decided.

The one he had paid for on the previous evening had been a disappointment. He wasn't at all sure why, but he had expected more from a Chinese woman. Maybe it was a combination of the slit dresses and coy faces, but he had been looking forward to something really exotic. The woman had been good-looking enough, even when the booze wore off, but there had been nothing special about the way she fucked. The most exotic thing about her had been the abacus she used to tot up her services.

He wondered if the phrase 'missionary position' had

been invented by disappointed missionaries in China, and then remembered Ingrid Bergman in *Inn of the Sixth Happiness*. Finn sighed out loud. One of these days he had to visit Sweden.

On leaving the others Dubery had walked north up Nathan Road. Reaching Temple Street, he thought he recognized the brothel, but a busy market filled the roadway and it was hard to tell one building from another. Not that it really mattered – he didn't want to go in, he just wanted to see her again, fully clothed, looking normal. If he could see her as a human being, and not as the sad eyes and glistening naked body which haunted his daydreams, then perhaps he could start to pull himself together.

He had finally phoned Helen that morning, and she had picked up the difference in his voice, as he had known she would. She had kept asking if he was OK – she knew something had happened.

He had dropped hints of a close escape at work, and felt even more guilty when she flooded him with sympathy.

A car horn suddenly blazed in his ear, and he realized he had stopped in the middle of the street. A Chinese man leaned out of the window, showing gold teeth as he shouted, and Dubery was engulfed in thick black exhaust smoke.

This is ridiculous, he thought. One more walk down the street and he would head back down Nathan Road. At least the girl had made him wear a condom, or God only knew what he might have taken home. And then he would have had to own up . . .

He knew he could never tell her, and his heart sank

at the thought of this secret which would always be between them.

Soon after breakfast on Saturday morning Colhoun finally reached the end of the road. He had a less than perfect idea of how far up the chain of government his request had gone, but a Foreign Office Junior Minister named Manning had somehow ended up with the task of making the refusal official.

'We've considered your proposal very carefully,' Manning told him, with about as much sincerity as a spokesman for the Bosnian Serbs. 'But, as I'm sure you can understand, this is a particularly sensitive moment in Sino-British relations, and we simply can't afford to put at risk all the diplomatic efforts of the last few years. It wouldn't be fair to the people of Hong Kong.'

You bastard, Colhoun thought.

The unctuous voice rolled on. 'And your boys seem to have already done a great job. Now that we are aware of the people who are responsible, I'm sure all the interested parties can do more on the preventive side. Re-routing of ships, more armed guards and deck lighting, a tighter watch on cargo information – you know the sort of thing.'

The bastard had done his homework. Colhoun wanted to argue that ships using Hong Kong had no choice but to pass through Chinese waters, that reams of official advice on how to deter and deal with piracy had already been issued, but he knew there was no point.

He could recognize a bottom line as well as the next man. There was obviously more money invested in Hong Kong's stability than there was in the maritime insurance companies.

* * *

It was ten to six in Hong Kong when Marker took the call from London. He stared out across the harbour at the darkening sky as Colhoun gave him the bad news. 'You're all due a week's leave,' the CO concluded. 'If you want to take it there I'm sure we can arrange something.'

Marker went for a stroll around the base, feeling both angry and depressed. It seemed as if Cafell and Finn had risked their lives on the *Ocean Carousel* for nothing. The pirates would make good their losses, regroup, and soon be back in business. He could understand Whitehall's reasons for not wanting to upset Beijing, but that didn't mean he agreed with them. The future of Hong Kong's people was worth considering, but he refused to accept that there should be a safe haven anywhere on earth for people who murdered an entire ship's crew.

He stopped at the edge of the dock and sat down with his back against a bollard, knowing that the end of the operation was not the real reason for his sense of frustration. One week's leave and he would be on his way back to England. In the meantime he and Rosalie would be forced into decisions that he didn't think either of them were ready for.

He knew she was fond of him, and the previous night there had been a passion in her eyes and her physical responses which seemed to indicate a great deal more. But loneliness could confuse anyone's feelings, and he knew she had been lonely.

He thought he was certain of how he felt about her, but he had been just as sure about someone else. Sitting on the edge of the dock, watching the lights across the harbour sharpen against the gathering darkness, he could still remember feeling that Penny was the only woman he could ever really love. And after the first time it was never quite the same. He was too old to pretend that one love was more real than another; he couldn't do what some of his friends had done, and rewrite his own history to keep the myth of a 'one and only' alive.

Still, one thing at least seemed clear. With the Communist take-over on the horizon there was no chance of him living in Hong Kong. So would she come to England? He realized with surprise that they had hardly talked about what she intended to do in 1997. And he had to admit, he found it hard to imagine her anywhere else.

It was fully dark now, the waters of the harbour awash with their nightly carpet of neon reflections. In an hour he was supposed to be meeting her.

He strode back to the barracks, showered, changed, and left a message for Cafell and the others containing the gist of his conversation with the CO. He told them he would be staying another week, and that the three of them should each decide when they wanted to return to England, and get Fergie to book them flights accordingly. Cafell and Dubery would be on the first plane, he guessed, eager to see their better halves. Finn would probably stay around for a week of tourism and debauchery, though not necessarily in that order.

Marker took the launch across to Kowloon, and as the wall of lights loomed above the approaching quays he found himself wondering how anyone would willingly exchange this for the suburban delights of downtown Poole.

She was waiting for him in the Horse and Groom, sitting at the same table, one glass into a bottle of Merlot. There seemed no trace of reserve or inner retreat in the warmth of her greeting, but it soon became apparent that there was a remarkable shortage of conversation topics which didn't touch on the future, and she seemed every bit as anxious to avoid talking about that as he did.

She suggested a film, and he readily agreed. Zhang Yimou's most recent was showing at the Cine Art House in Wan Chai, and for almost three hours they watched a brilliant but profoundly depressing story of urban punks in the new get-rich-quick China. Marker found it hard to imagine why anyone would want to stay and share in such a future, but then he remembered all the friends of his parents who had sworn to leave England if the Tories won again in 1983. And again in 1987. And yet again in 1992. They were all still there. Home was home, even with the enemy in power.

On the subway train home their conversation about the film inevitably edged towards a discussion of the future – China's, Hong Kong's, hers and theirs. 'Let's not talk about it, not tonight,' she said, as they ascended the escalator at Quarry Bay.

'Suits me,' he said, pulling her towards him.

They kissed their way up in the high-rise lift, and once inside her apartment left a trail of clothes from the front door. He pulled her towards the bedroom; she pulled him harder towards the shower cubicle. They lathered each other with soap, and kissed some more as the streaming water rinsed it away. She put her arms round his neck, let him lift her up by the buttocks, braced her feet against the wall behind him, and felt him slide inside her.

About ten miles to the south-west, on the bridge of the twelve-thousand-ton dry-cargo liner *Indian Sun*, Captain Giuseppe Berti drained the last drop of brandy from his glass, stretched his shoulders and yawned. Through the window he could see the three giant derricks amidships, and beyond them the white forestay light of a ship lying at anchor. Off the port bow, some two miles away across the black water, the hilly outline of Lamma Island was just about visible against a starless sky.

With a dawn start in prospect it was time for bed. About half the twenty-seven-man crew was already on board, and the rest would be arriving over the next couple of hours. In years gone by Berti had worried about last-minute no-shows, dreading the prospect of having to sail without a full complement, but all of his current crew had proved their trustworthiness through more than a year of round trips, and if half of them were willing to shell out the cost of a water taxi so that they could enjoy one last evening on the town then he had no objections. After all, for the next four weeks their only excitement would come courtesy of the ship's VCR.

He yawned again, but didn't move away from the bridge window. The sense of excitement which accompanied a new voyage had grown dimmer over the years, but it was still there, lurking in the corners of his mind like a reluctant smile. Four weeks of a routine that he knew off by heart, four Sampdoria results which he would hear through the crackle and hiss of the BBC World Service.

He was not looking forward to their passage through the Singapore Straits and Phillip Channel, even in daylight. Tomorrow, once they were underway and clear of the coastal islands, he would discuss the drill with his officers and then talk to the rest of the crew.

And, speaking of the devil – as the English would say – he could hear the drone of an approaching water taxi. Or even two.

Berti strode across to a side window and looked down. There were three speedboats bobbing in the water off the port bow, and several uniformed men were already ascending the lowered stairway. The flag of the People's Republic was fluttering in the stern of each boat.

For a moment he considered the absurd idea that his ship was in the wrong place, but the familiar silhouette of Lamma Island offered the necessary reassurance. The *Indian Sun* was riding at anchor in her usual pre-voyage spot, some five miles inside British waters. It was the Chinese who had got their navigation wrong, or at least he hoped they had.

Berti left the bridge and walked swiftly through the officer quarters to his radio officer's cabin. He opened the door to find the man studying a porn magazine centrefold in his bunk. 'Paolo, emergency,' he said. 'Get hold of the Marine Police and tell them we're having a visit from the Red Chinese.'

In the flat in Quarry Bay Rosalie awoke with a start to feel the end of the gun against the side of her head, and to see the dark shadow looming over her. 'Don't make a sound,' a male voice said in Cantonese. It was the second time he had said it, she realized – the first time was what had woken her up.

She suddenly realized she was alone in the bed.

'Come on,' a nervous voice said from a few feet away. Another figure was standing in the open doorway.

'Get up,' the first man said. 'Slowly,' he added, keeping the barrel of the gun no more than a few inches from her head.

She got slowly to her feet beside him, and he wrapped an arm almost lovingly around her neck.

The other whistled softly. 'Pity we haven't got more time,' he murmured.

She could almost feel his eyes wandering over her naked body. Where was Marker? Her heart sank at the thought that he had gone, that there was a note on the kitchen table telling her he had an early meeting.

'Walk,' the man was saying. She could feel his breath in her ear, which meant he wasn't much taller than she was.

They moved out into the passage which ran through from the front door to the living room. Out of the corner of her eye she could see no sign of a light under the bathroom door, but then she supposed he would have turned it off.

And then, with a surge of relief which caused her heart to skip a beat, she saw that both their clothes were still scattered across the floor. He hadn't gone. And they hadn't noticed his clothes. There was still hope.

Only about ten minutes had passed since Marker had left her sleeping peacefully and walked out on to the balcony, wanting to feel some breeze on his body and share his sense of joy with the night. He had heard the click as the flat's front door sprang open, and had seen the silhouetted men and guns against the bright light of the corridor beyond as they let themselves in.

For a moment all he could do was curse his own incompetence. Their passion had overridden every basic security precaution, from the double bolting of the door to keeping his gun within reach. As far as he knew, the holstered Browning was still attached to the trouser belt she had undone for him in the hallway.

The options flashed through his head. If they were going to kill her immediately – the thought dropped his stomach about a mile – then the best he could do was to die with her. But if they planned to take their time he had a chance.

He offered a prayer to whatever god might be listening, and in the silence heard one of the men say something in the bedroom. He didn't understand the Cantonese, but words in any language had to be better than the apologetic cough of a silenced gun.

He paused on the balcony's threshold, torn between the knowledge that any hesitation might be fatal and the fear of blowing his one chance by moving too soon. Give them a few minutes, his rational self insisted, give them time to feel secure, to let their guards down. But he found himself leaning into the living room regardless, as if a more primeval voice was pulling him forward.

He was saved by the enemy. One of the men backed out of the bedroom, his eyes on what was happening inside, and Marker had time to slip back out on to the balcony. Through the door curtains swaying in the breeze he saw the other man follow, pushing Rosalie in front of him. His left arm was wrapped around her throat, the right held a gun against her right temple.

They were walking straight towards him. Two guns against his none, and one of them poised to blow away the person who meant most to him in the world.

Go with the motion, his kung fu teacher in Kowloon had always told him. He should have continued the classes in England, but at the time it had seemed better, as far as he and Penny were concerned, if a line could be drawn under his months in Hong Kong.

And now it might cost both him and Rosalie their lives.

He took a deep breath, calculated distances, and as the first man came out he grabbed the arm with the gun, pivoted on both feet like a discus thrower and pulled in the direction the body was already travelling. There was a crack of bones breaking, and a scream of pain rising to a wail as the man crashed across the parapet, teetered on its edge like an acrobat, and tumbled from sight.

As she and her captor had advanced across the living room Rosalie had listened in vain for the slightest sound behind them. So Marker had to be on the balcony, and he would have to tackle the first man through the door. The man holding her would get a shock, and she would have a split second to make her move.

The man in front was only a couple of feet from the doorway. She let her knees buckle and went limp in her captor's arms, as if she had suddenly fainted. He cursed, let her sag for a moment, and then encircled her beneath the breasts with his other arm.

He had put the gun away.

As the first man stepped out on to the balcony, and she saw Marker's two hands reach out for his gun arm, Rosalie dug both her elbows backwards into the second man's ribs with as much force as she could muster. He grunted, but the arm around her throat only loosened for a second, and she could feel the other hand desperately reaching for his gun.

She pushed her foot against the door jamb and shoved with all her might, forcing them both backwards, and as they tottered in unison across the floor she managed to entangle one leg through his.

They both went down, she on top of him, he on to the TV, his head striking the corner of the set with sickening force.

She whirled away, but there was no need. He was out cold, and Marker was holding his dead partner's gun in the balcony doorway.

Some six miles to the north-west, one FPC and two Sea Rider inflatables belonging to 3rd Raiding Squadron were lurking close to the island of Peng Chau on the western side of the West Lamma Channel. They were sitting in silence, with lights out, on the lookout for smugglers. There were two Marines in each boat, and the FPC also carried a Chinese interpreter from the Marine Police. Corporal Taff Saunders was in overall command.

It was about half an hour after the Chinese first set foot on Captain Berti's ship that the order to investigate reached the patrol. Reckoning that an early appearance by the British authorities would count for more than numbers or fire-power, Saunders took the decision to make best speed in the FPC, and leave the Sea Riders to catch him up as quickly as they could.

'Go and take a look, but be bloody careful,' the voice on the radio had advised, and the latter half of the instruction had not been lost on Saunders. He had been in Hong Kong long enough to remember several such incidents turning sour. In one, not more than a year earlier, an inexperienced young Marine had stepped on to a Chinese boat thinking that his comrades were right behind him. They hadn't been, and the Marine had been forced to leap from a speeding boat into the dark waters.

'Whatever you do,' Saunders yelled at the young Marine who was with him, 'don't leave the boat. I'm not spending half the night looking for your body.'

'No, Corp,' the young man said with a grin. His name was Branston, and everyone called him Picklehead.

In the bow of the FPC the Chinese interpreter seemed more concerned with the immediate perils of a sixty-five-mph journey across the choppy centre of the Channel than any upcoming confrontation with the People's Republic. As he bounced around in his own seat Saunders could appreciate why.

'Why would they board a ship in our waters?' Picklehead was shouting. 'Why not wait until it's in theirs?'

'Because it's a bloody sight harder to board a moving ship in daylight than an anchored one at night. A lot of the freighters don't want to pass through the offshore islands in the dark, but they don't want to pay an extra night's harbour dues either. So they move out here in the evening, spend the night at anchor, and head on out after a hearty breakfast.'

Picklehead nodded his understanding.

They could see the ship now, a couple of miles ahead of them, a long, black wedge against the shadowy background of Lamma Island.

'It's moving,' Picklehead yelled.

It was. Saunders altered course slightly, wondering where the Chinks got their nerve from.

Picklehead's hands emerged from the watertight bag with the low-light camcorder which had been specially designed for 3rd Raiding Squadron's smuggling patrols.

'Don't go flashing that around,' Saunders yelled at him. 'The bastards may be camera-shy.'

They were about a quarter of a mile from the slow-moving cargo liner when it became apparent that the Chinese had spotted them. Two of the speedboats were arcing away from the freighter on an intercept course, like dogs leaping to the defence of their prey.

'What now, Corp?'

Saunders throttled down. 'Jesus, I don't know. I guess we see what they have to say.'

The three boats decelerated towards each other, the Chinese moving in on either side of the FPC. In the latter's bow the interpreter looked distinctly apprehensive.

A uniformed officer shouted out something in Cantonese across the few feet of water which separated the craft.

'He says you will not be permitted to interfere in the internal affairs of the People's Republic. This ship has been engaged in smuggling and is being taken into port for investigation. The captain is under arrest.'

Saunders looked the Chinese officer in the eye. 'Tell the little fucker that he's in British waters. Tactfully, of course.'

The officer listened, smiled, and said in perfect

English: 'This is the South China Sea, not the English Channel.'

'Tell him 1997 is still two years . . .'

One of the Chinese in the other boat suddenly shouted, turning Saunders round. He was pointing at the camcorder which Picklehead was holding loosely in his hand.

'Put it down,' Saunders said, and turned with upraised hands and an innocent expression to find two Chinese officers in the process of jumping aboard the FPC, both of them brandishing automatic pistols.

'Hey!' he shouted impotently.

Suddenly everyone seemed to be shouting at once.

'Give him the camera,' Saunders told Picklehead, who went to pull the strap off his shoulder, and ended up jerking the sub-machine-gun into his hand.

One of the Chinese officers fired point blank at the young Marine's chest, and he sank to the floor of the FPC with a look of astonishment on his face.

There was a moment's stunned silence. As Saunders bent to see how badly Picklehead was injured, the Chinese officer rapped out an order, and his men returned to their boat, taking the camcorder with them.

The freighter was already a mile away, and the two Chinese speedboats raced off to catch it. This was one for the politicians to sort out, Saunders thought. He was sorry he had ever heard the fucking distress call.

He was sorrier still when Marine Branston died on his way to hospital.

In London it was shortly after seven-thirty, and Sir Willoughby Winterton was just about to leave for his club and an evening of bridge when the telephone rang. He would not have answered it, but his elder son, recently sent down from Cambridge, had probably been expecting a call from one of his druggie friends. 'It's for you, Pops,' the young man called out in his usual mocking tone. 'Someone named Beeston. I told him you were home.'

Winterton sighed. 'I'll take it in the study,' he called out. As the chief executive of a huge insurance conglomerate which had long been a major contributor to Party funds, Brian Beeston was not someone a Party Chairman could afford to antagonize.

'Hello, Brian,' he said cheerfully. 'What can I do for you?'

Beeston wasted no time on niceties. 'I heard it on the grapevine that the Government has just put new handcuffs on our lads out in Hong Kong,' he said. 'Can you confirm that?'

'More or less,' Winterton agreed. He knew there was no point in denying it. 'It's a matter of . . .' he started to say, but Beeston was having none of it.

'Well, I've just had news that another one of our ships has been hijacked,' he ploughed on remorselessly. 'In Hong Kong waters, no less. And it seems as though a Royal Marine was killed trying to stop the bastards.'

Hell's bells, Winterton thought. A dead serviceman meant Questions in the House.

'Do you know how many millions this is going to cost us?' Beeston asked. 'And can you guess what our shareholders will want us to cut back on?'

Winterton could.

'From what I've heard,' Beeston went on, 'your contributors in the Hong Kong business community are deserting you in droves. Perhaps it's time you took a hard look at who your real friends are.'

In Hong Kong it was almost dawn when her police colleagues finally left Rosalie's flat. The locals had arrived first, followed by CID officers from Central and a couple of Ormond's OSCG team. Finally an anxious Li had put in an appearance. He had received a garbled message on the phone saying only that she'd been attacked at home, and was relieved to find that she hadn't been injured. He confirmed her recognition of the injured man as a Blue Dragon foot soldier, and agreed that the dead man was likely to be the same. Since the latter had fallen seven storeys on to his face a definite identification was going to take time.

After everyone had gone Rosalie and Marker went back to bed, and fell swiftly asleep in each other's arms. Two hours later by the clock – it felt more like two minutes – they were woken by the phone.

'Kai,' she said sleepily, listened, and handed it to Marker.

It was Cafell. 'I thought you'd like to know – leave's been cancelled. Colhoun just phoned. He thinks we'll get the green light in a few hours.'

'What changed their minds?' Marker asked. He felt suddenly awake.

'Our pirate friends. They took another ship last night, off Lamma Island. Right from under our noses,' he added disgustedly.

'Christ . . .'

'And a Marine was killed,' Cafell added.

'Oh shit,' Marker murmured.

'Name of Billy Branston.'

Marker had never heard of him.

'If the ship was taken last night,' Cafell went on, 'there's a good chance it'll still be at Chuntao.'

'Right,' Marker agreed. 'It'll have to be tonight.'

'Well, I hope you've had a good night's sleep,' Cafell said mischievously.

Marker grunted. 'Not so as you'd notice. I'll be there as soon as I can. Get started on the usual, OK?'

'Gotcha.'

Marker hung up, and turned to Rosalie. 'I have to go,' he said, and wished he didn't.

'Chuntao?' she asked, worry in her eyes.

'Looks like it.'

She nodded, as if in acceptance. 'I'll take the train in with you,' she said. 'I want to be there when they bring Lu Zhen in for questioning.'

They showered, dressed, drank a cup of instant coffee, and walked down to the MRT station. With a gentle breeze blowing in off the harbour and the sky still blue, it was hard to believe that less than six hours earlier they had both been fighting for their lives.

At Wan Chai he watched her walk away down the platform, and then turn at the last minute with a wave and a smile.

Back on Stonecutters' Island Marker eventually found Cafell in one of the instruction rooms, hard at work on a model of the Chuntao port and its surroundings.

'It's Play-do,' the younger man explained as he added more height to a headland. 'I found it in the crèche.'

'Where are the others?'

'Ian's checking out the available boats, and Finn's looking for photographic equipment.'

Marker went in search of Dubery. He already knew what sort of boats he wanted to use.

Rosalie stood behind the one-way glass, studying the seated figure of Lu Zhen. They were in the Kowloon Regional HQ on Argyle Street, the station where she had started her career, and even now, a decade later, the place still felt oppressive. This was where she had begun the process of exorcizing her father's ghost.

And now she was looking at the man who had acted as the executive officer in the small matter of her attempted murder. Not that there was any hope of proving it.

The Blue Dragon Red Pole knew he was bright, but there was no bombastic arrogance – he wouldn't trip himself up with his own cleverness. There was something so smooth and self-assured about the bastard – 'urbane' was the word her father's circle would have used. He probably liked Zhang Yimou's films.

Ormond's two men were trying to convince Lu Zhen that the survivor of the previous night's attack had implicated the Blue Dragons in general and him in particular. Of course he had done no such thing, and the Red Pole knew it as well as the two detectives. His mouth was still creased in amusement at the thought.

If they ever got this one, she thought, then it would only be for something like tax evasion. He might run a gang of vicious thugs, but he had risen above personal participation in the sort of crime which left DNA traces or fingerprints. The only sure method of stopping Lu – and his equally immune boss Shu Zhi-fang – lay in the destruction of that cross-border alliance which had facilitated the Blue Dragons' spectacular rise.

*   *   *

By three in the afternoon the SBS team had finished sorting out their transport, weapons and equipment, and had gathered together every scrap of available information on Chuntao Island and the surrounding waters. The four men had sat around Cafell's model making plans for all the contingencies they could think of. The usual litany of hysterical jokes had reached a peak around noon and declined thereafter, leaving each of the four men as ready as he would ever be to risk life and limb in the service of Queen, Country and SBS.

At four Colhoun rang with the expected news. 'So plain clothes,' he concluded, 'and no traceable equipment. Needless to say, if anything goes wrong you'll be on your own as far as the politicians are concerned. I'll do what I can from this end, but it may not be much.'

'We know,' Marker said.

'Oh, by the way, the Chinese Ambassador has been called in to the FO this morning. He's going to be given a stern rap on the knuckles, and with any luck they'll assume that that's it as far as any British response is concerned.'

'That's good,' Marker agreed. Maybe they wouldn't be expected, after all. It was just difficult to believe that no one had missed the boat which Cafell and Finn had stolen, and put two and two together.

He supposed they would soon find out.

Colhoun was wishing them luck, saying goodbye.

Marker pressed the disconnection bar and punched out Rosalie's number at the OSCG office, half expecting she wouldn't be there.

She was.

'We'll be off soon,' he told her. 'And we're planning to be back in about thirty-six hours.'

'Good luck,' she said, and he could hear the tightness in her voice.

'I love you,' he said, the words sounding both strange and true.

'I love you,' she echoed, after only the slightest hesitation. And for better or worse, she knew she did. 'You be careful,' she added almost angrily.

'And you,' he said. 'There's plenty of Blue Dragons still out there.'

'I'll be OK.'

For a moment he doubted it, and an almost overwhelming urge to stay and protect her welled up in his heart. But a man had to do what a man had to do, he thought sourly. How fucking ridiculous that sounded.

'Come back to me,' she said, and put the phone down.

He did likewise, and stood there for more than a minute, wondering if he was making the biggest mistake of his life.

10

About a quarter of a mile south of Tai A Chau Island, at the extreme south-western corner of Hong Kong waters, the Rigid Raider bobbed in the gentle swell as the four black-faced SBS men manoeuvred the two Klepper canoes over the side. Finn and Cafell lowered themselves into the back seats, took the MP5s and bergens that were passed down, and held the canoes steady for Marker and Dubery to follow. The spray deck was positioned, clamped and tied. The four men started paddling, oblivious to the hands raised in farewell by the Raider's two-man crew.

Marker and Finn took the lead, the former steering a course west by south-west on the rudder bar with his feet. By Cafell's reckoning Chuntao was eighteen and a quarter nautical miles ahead of them, and provided the sea remained calm they should be there in under an hour and a half. 'Just like a row across Poole Harbour,' Finn had joked, but there were few men on earth who could have taken on a journey like this with such equanimity. This was what they had been trained for – to perform tasks as ordinary as paddling a canoe better than anyone else.

They could hardly have hoped for better conditions, Marker realized. The sky was overcast, reducing visibility; the sea was calm enough to make progress easy, yet choppy enough to hide the Kleppers from either human eye or radar scanner. A cool breeze would have been nice, but then nothing was ever perfect.

The four men paddled on, not speaking, each feeling the tension. If a Chinese patrol boat found them it would all be over – the weapons and equipment would have to go over the side, and they would have to trot out their ludicrous cover story of British athletes in training for the Olympics. If they ever got back to Hong Kong the RM Quartermaster would probably kill them for losing his second and last low-light camcorder.

Islands loomed out of the darkness to both left and right, but the sea dead ahead remained empty. Marker paddled on automatically, letting his shoulders glide through the rhythmic motion as the blades sliced through the water. He was thinking about Rosalie, and about feeling hungry for life again, and hoping that his sense of obligation to her would not make him overcautious. In the seat behind him, synchronizing the strokes of his paddle, Finn was thinking about the life his schoolfriends still lived in Hackney. Bored and angry, they hated themselves and everybody else. And here he was – it was like being in a fucking movie!

In the following canoe Dubery was thinking about the past, his and his family's, and nights like this which were not like this – another sea full of islands, with cold winds scouring his cheeks and his father's boat tossing in the swell. Behind him, Cafell had his mind on the future. Perhaps he could make a living as a model-maker – mostly ships, of course, but he could model anything, and there was nothing quite as satisfying as working with his hands. He and Ellen could have a studio together, somewhere by the sea. Somewhere near Lyme Regis.

They paddled on, reaching what marathon runners call the 'wall' and pushing right through it. About an hour into the journey a short, dark line appeared in the distance, and slowly but surely it grew into the shape they expected. Chuntao had a pair of six-hundred-foot peaks in its six square miles, and from either east or west its silhouette was shaped like a saddle.

According to the information Cafell had gathered from several sources that afternoon, the island had been uninhabited until recently, and as the Kleppers drew nearer the lack of any welcoming lights suggested this was still true of the eastern side. There was supposed to be an abandoned monastery in the centre of the island, but there had never been any agriculture of note, nor any local fishing community. The older buildings by the small bay which Cafell and Finn had seen on their previous visit were all that remained of a settlement set up by fleeing Japanese soldiers in the last days of the Second World War but disbanded a few years later when the victorious Communists asserted their control throughout the southern littoral.

The Navy had received satellite photographs of the whole region from the Americans in the late seventies, and a study of these had shown Cafell that his impression of the island as rocky and sparsely vegetated had been a misleading one – most of Chuntao was thickly vegetated. For this reason it had been agreed that they would make landfall in one of several bays on the nearer, eastern side of the island, and then make their way across country to establish an OP overlooking the port facilities.

It had sounded dead simple in theory. But looking across the Klepper's bow at the island's rugged contours, Marker wondered how easy it would be in practice.

'Ship ahoy,' Finn whispered behind him. 'Off the stern.'

Marker turned to look, and saw the ship's lights, a mile or so behind them.

Cafell was examining it through the nightscope. 'Warship,' he said, his voice barely audible. 'An EF5 Guided Missile Destroyer.'

It was heading north into the Pearl River estuary. Ten minutes earlier and it would have come close to running them down. There was no doubt at all that they would have been seen.

'Let's give it a little while,' Marker whispered, and the four of them sat there in the bobbing Kleppers, watching the dark wedge of the Chinese destroyer steadily shrink into the distance.

He gave the order to resume paddling, and soon they were inching towards the inviting beach, not expecting any defences, sophisticated or otherwise, but preferring to be safe than sorry. Once ashore they found the sands surrounded on all sides by dense vegetation, and had no trouble finding a reasonable hiding place for the Kleppers. The intention had been to disassemble and bury the canoes, but Marker decided the chances of their being found in such a place were remote, and there was always the possibility they would need a quick getaway. Having to build your own boat tended to slow down an escape, so they left them intact.

The Kleppers hidden, their make-up retouched, the four men started up what once might have been a track.

Marker supposed that its near-impassability was a good sign, but with knife-edged leaves whipping him across the face and God only knew what varieties of local fauna lurking in the trees above and on the ground below, he found it hard not to wish for a broad and well-lit path. Concrete if possible.

Finn took the lead scout position, eyes and ears alert for possible trouble up ahead. Cafell came close behind him with their map, Marker in third place, Dubery the Tail-end Charlie responsible for their rear. Each man cradled the silenced MP5SD in his arms.

The quickest route probably lay across the saddle, but they had decided on the longer route around the southern peak, partly because it seemed from the satellite photos to offer slightly less chance of either an unforeseen meeting or a long-distance sighting, and partly because it would bring them straight to their chosen destination on the wooded headland south of the port facility.

It took them about an hour and a half to cover the two miles, and it was shortly after three in the morning when Marker and Dubery had their first view of the two jetties, gantry crane and buildings. It was not the same spot Cafell and Finn had used: this time one line of sight lay straight down across the cabins which climbed up the hill from the small bay, and another, some thirty degrees around to the north, looked down the length of the broad main jetty.

It was a perfect place for taking pictures. The only trouble was, most of what they had hoped to immortalize on video was gone. Scouring the jetties and adjacent ocean with the nightscope, Cafell could find no patrol boat, no *Ocean Carousel* and no *Indian*

Sun. There was not a single freighter at anchor, and even the speedboat population had shrunk to five.

The four men dug out a good-sized rectangular scrape among the trees, covered it with the light tarpaulin, and then added various pieces of vegetation for camouflage. A breeze was now beginning to blow, and the sky seemed even darker than before. Cafell and Dubery lost the toss for first watch, and the other two snuggled as cosily into their damp earth beds as they could. It was a far cry from the silk sheets of the previous night, Marker thought, as the first drops of rain started beating a tattoo on the tarpaulin.

There was nothing in the papers and nothing on the radio, but Rosalie still arrived at the OSCG offices half expecting to hear that a major diplomatic incident had taken place in the South China Sea that morning. The normal buzz of activity told her it hadn't, for which she felt only half grateful. It might well mean that the SBS team had been neither intercepted nor observed, but there was always the possibility that the Chinese had simply arrested them and decided not to make the matter public.

She told herself there was no point in worrying about him, that she had her own work to do. Unfortunately there weren't many grounds for optimism in that regard either. The Blue Dragon Red Pole had been released the previous evening, and unless he made an uncharacteristically stupid mistake, was likely to remain so – a free and prosperous executive in a rising corporation.

Rosalie remembered her father once saying that the less regulated free enterprise became the harder it was to distinguish from organized crime. He had been in a good position to know.

She yawned, stretched and walked across to the coffee machine. Alone for the first night in three, she had expected a better sleep, but neither Marker's mission nor the knowledge that the Blue Dragons still wanted her dead had been particularly conducive to a restful state of mind.

'You look awful,' Ormond said cheerily, appearing at her shoulder.

'You don't look so wonderful yourself,' she told him. And he didn't. The puffy face was redder than ever, reminding her of an article she had once read on spontaneous human combustion. Those people had burst into flame though; Ormond seemed more likely to simply explode.

'Any news of our SBS friends?' he asked.

'I haven't seen them since yesterday,' she said. 'They're probably working with the Marine Police on the latest hijacking.'

'Who knows?' Ormond said, pouring coffee into his Manchester United mug. 'No one tells me anything any more.' He smiled. 'Only two more years,' he murmured.

'And then what?' she asked.

'Then I go home, buy a semi-detached and sit in it, wondering why I was so damned honest out here,' he said. 'I'll probably take some security job. But it'll be strange going back. I've been out here for almost thirty years now, which is longer than I lived in England. And when I went back for my mother's funeral last year I couldn't stand the place.' He laughed, and walked away across the office towards his desk.

She went back to hers and sat there sipping at the strong coffee. Li was visiting the rest of the adoption agency offices, motivated more by a desire to be thorough than any expectation of a breakthrough. The baby-smuggling investigation had turned into a cul-de-sac: only the Blue Dragons knew where the babies were coming from, and the Triad vow of silence precluded any possibility that the relevant information would be shared with the police.

The cross-border connection was the key. In the hope that something might jog a memory or reveal a connection, she went back through her notes on the life and times of Wang Xiao-bo. Reaching the 'missing' mid-eighties years of his career, she stopped at her note in the margin: 'penal system director?' That struck a chord, but what was the tune?

The dissident. Two or three years ago, soon after Marker had left. She couldn't remember the man's name, but she remembered him talking on TV about the months he had spent in detention on the mainland. He had been held either in or near the Shenzhen Zone, and he had been part of a forced-labour crew working on the construction of a dock.

She reached for the phone, punched out the number for the *South China Morning Post*, and asked for Gu Yao-bang. He had no trouble remembering the dissident's name – Lin Chun.

'And he's still across the border?' she asked.

'Last I heard he still lives in Shenzhen.'

'If I remember right, he went back voluntarily when the Immigration Department told him he couldn't bring his whole family out.'

'He was too much of a Commie for them, and they

made a deal with the Communists. He went back, but not to prison.'

'I don't suppose you have an address?'

'No, but someone on the political desk might have. I can ask.'

'Thanks. And while you're at it, can you ask about Wang Xiao-bo? I need to know what he was doing in the early to mid-eighties.'

'I'll get back to you in a few minutes,' Gu said, and hung up.

She sat at her desk, feeling more than a little excited, waiting for him to call back. Eight minutes and twenty-three seconds had passed when the phone rang.

'Lin Chun lives on the city outskirts, in Baguling, in a block of flats on Nigang Road. Block 17, flat 43. He lives with his wife and daughter and his wife's parents, all in a two-room flat. One of the journalists went up to see him a few months ago hoping for a follow-up story and was told to take a running jump. He doesn't have many fond memories of Hong Kong, apparently.'

'That's no great surprise,' she said. 'What does he do now? Does he have a job?'

'Something very menial, I should think, but I don't know. As for your friend Wang, from 1982 to 1987 he was in charge of Guangdong's prisons and their labour force. And I'm told everyone remembers that – everyone but you and I apparently – because there was a big row when he appointed a completely unqualified brother to run the Shenzhen sector.' Gu grunted. 'The brother must have been busy – most of Shenzhen City was built by forced labour.'

She thanked him profusely, hung up, and drained the last of her coffee, thinking that the Immigration

Department should still have Lin Chun's original interviews on file. Its headquarters were only a short tram ride away on the other side of Wan Chai. She alighted at the southern end of Gloucester Road, and walked beside Victoria Park to the entrance.

After ten minutes of bureaucratic tussling she won access to Lin Chun's file and a microfiche machine, but the sense of triumph soon faded. There was no more information here than she had remembered for herself. No location was given for the dock construction; it was not even clear whether it had been built on the mainland or on one of the hundreds of islands close to the southern coast. It could even have been Chuntao, she realized with a start, in which case she was no further ahead than she had been that morning.

The one new fact concerned timing – Lin Chun had worked on the dock in the weeks immediately preceding his escape to Hong Kong. Seeing that the records of illegal entrants were chronologically arranged, Rosalie read through the interrogation reports on others who had been smuggled across the border in the following month, and struck gold with a young woman named Sung Mei-ling. She had also been an unwilling visitor to the dock construction site, and mostly in the same labouring capacity as Lin. But Sung had also, on several occasions, been taken away from her labouring duties to look after a roomful of babies.

She, according to Immigration, had been allowed to stay. And she was still living in Hong Kong.

Rosalie took the MRT and a taxi to the address in Sham Shui Po, and got directions from a neighbour to the hairdressing salon where Sung worked. There she spent the first ten minutes reassuring the woman that she wasn't about to be sent back, while inwardly thinking that in two years' time it would all be academic in any case.

She asked her about the times she had been taken to look after the babies.

'It was terrible. Very sad. Some of them were ill, and they cried a lot.'

'Were they all girls?'

'Of course,' she said, surprised, as if the improbability of unwanted male babies had never occurred to her.

'Where was this place? Have you any idea?'

'Not really. We always arrived after dark and we left before dawn. But it must have been in the Zone, or close by. The journey in the lorry only took about an hour.'

'They were building a dock?'

'Yes. They were breaking up rocks and mixing up the concrete, putting up new buildings. Hundreds of prisoners were there. It was a big project.'

'Was it on a river or the sea?'

'It was both. It looked like a river but the water was salt.'

More questions failed to elicit any other useful information. As she travelled back to Wan Chai on the MRT Rosalie came to the reluctant conclusion that a trip across the border was her only way forward. Reading his interview with Immigration, she had been struck by Lin Chun's obvious intelligence. And who knew, maybe he was also one of the human race's more observant members.

Through the hours of morning, as the rain beat down out of a leaden sky, Cafell and Dubery took turns keeping watch on the port below. The coming of daylight had brought little activity, and not much changed in the hours thereafter. An occasional figure scurried between buildings, but the jetties remained empty, and no ship hove into view across the rain-swept sea.

They made notes of every movement, drawing lines on Cafell's map like cricket scorers plotting the record of a batsman's innings. It was boring, Cafell thought. Anti-climactic. Frustrating. If they'd only had the camcorder with them on their last visit . . .

Still, he supposed he should be happy. The chances of their being caught seemed about a million to one. The Chinese were apparently every bit as arrogant as everyone said they were – the possibility of intruders on their soil didn't seem to have occurred to them.

At noon he woke Marker and Finn and told them the bad news. 'There's only about fifteen men down there. And one old woman, who washed the clothes you can see on that line.' He pointed towards the palm grove beyond the line of cabins. 'There's a regular two-man patrol which leaves the building down there on the hour. They walk down to the end of the main jetty and back, come up to inspect the washing – or maybe the cabins – and then go back to where they started. I can't imagine why they bother.'

'People with things to guard always like security systems,' Marker said, 'but if they don't really expect any intruders they can never work up the energy to care whether the system works or not. It's classic.' He smiled. 'And very convenient.'

Cafell sighed. 'I had a horrible feeling you wouldn't be happy just watching from a distance.'

*　　*　　*

It was mid-afternoon when Rosalie finally set off, taking the MRT to Kowloon Tong and there changing to a Kowloon–Canton Railway train for the forty-minute trip to the border. Several years had passed since her last visit to the People's Republic, and she was shocked by how much of the New Territories' countryside had disappeared beneath a succession of ugly new towns and the new motorway. For a moment she felt almost nostalgic for a rural China she had only ever known in pictures and films, and then shook her head at her own absurdity.

At the border she stuck close to a group of Americans, presented the tourist visa which she had acquired not two hours before, and passed inspection without any problem. The train inched forward across the river bridge and into Shenzhen Station. She joined the scrum heading for the exit and managed to commandeer a cab on Jianshe Road. The fare negotiations took almost as long as the train ride, but only because she was reluctant to bankrupt the RHKP.

It was about a four-mile ride, and not particularly scenic. Shenzhen looked like a poor cousin of Hong Kong, which she supposed was a fair description in more ways than one. The block of flats in which Lin Chun and his family lived had that old-before-its-time look of shoddy construction work.

At least the lift worked. She went up to the fourth floor and threaded her way through children and mothers to the Lins' door, conscious of the stares examining her clothes and unusual face. In the background she could hear the familiar voices of a well-known Hong Kong soap.

Lin Na-wen opened the door, her young daughter just behind her. 'He is not here,' she said immediately.

Rosalie did her best to seem vulnerable. 'I'd like to wait,' she said. 'I have had a long journey,' she added, not very truthfully. It had taken all of an hour to get from Kowloon Tong to this door.

Lin Na-wen sighed, and opened the door. 'You must have some tea before you go back,' she said.

The Lins' kitchen was as badly stocked as hers, and she doubted whether they ate out all the time. From the glimpses she had of the other room, they seemed to have precious few material possessions and, one shelf of books excepted, only each other for entertainment. She couldn't see even a radio, let alone a television, and this was Shenzhen.

'He will not speak to outsiders,' Lin Na-wen said, pouring the tea from a cracked porcelain pot. She didn't add 'and especially not half-*gweilos*', but then she didn't have to.

Rosalie sat there, conscious of the daughter's stare. 'You love your daughter, don't you?' she asked Lin Na-wen.

'Of course!' the woman said, uncertain whether to be surprised or angry.

Rosalie told her about the baby-smuggling, about the ones found suffocated in the boats, the one thrown overboard, the ones left dead on hospital steps in Hong Kong. 'They are brought from somewhere in Shenzhen,' she concluded, 'and I think it is the port where your husband worked as a political prisoner. I just want to ask him where that was.'

Lin Na-wen examined the surface of the table for several moments and then raised her eyes. There were traces of tears, Rosalie noticed. 'You can wait here for my husband to come home,' she said.

By six-thirty night had fallen on Chuntao. The brisk wind had swept the clouds into the east, leaving a clear, star-laden sky above, and as Dubery crouched on the hillside with a sandwich in one hand and the nightscope in the other, his three comrades were sharing a communal supper inside the hide.

'Know what I could do with?' Finn asked. 'Egg, bacon, sausage, chips, beans, mushrooms and a couple of fried slices,' he answered before anyone else could. 'Followed by a full trough of my mum's strawberry trifle.'

'And washed down with what?' Cafell enquired. 'A pint of *crème de menthe*?'

'I was thinking of an Australian Semillon Chardonnay,' Finn articulated with exaggerated precision. 'Eighty-five was a good year, I believe.'

'Not for me – I got married,' Marker said, and instantly wished he hadn't. Why had he said that? At the time he couldn't have been happier. 'OK,' he said, 'since we've come this far, I'd like to take a closer look at what they have down there.' He grinned. 'And like any reporter, I need my trusty cameraman. Finn, you're volunteered.'

Finn waved his sandwich in the air. 'Suits me. When do we leave?'

'I'd say midnight. That should give us time to have a good look, and still get back to the Kleppers by three at the latest. I'd like to be well outside Chinese waters when the sun comes up.'

'I'll second that,' Cafell muttered.

'You and Ian can follow us with the nightscope,' Marker continued. He went through the itinerary he planned to follow. 'If we run into any trouble we'll head straight for the boats, and meet you there. OK?'

'OK,' Cafell agreed, just as Dubery's head appeared in the gap beneath the raised corner of the tarpaulin. 'Boat coming in, boss,' he whispered, and disappeared again.

The other three slipped out on to the dark slope and watched the large sampan as it rounded the near end of the main jetty and headed slowly in towards the smaller wooden quay. Through the nightscope Marker could make out a foredeck crowded with passengers, all of whom seemed strangely silent. If it hadn't been for the gentle swish of the waves on the shore below and the steady put-put of the boat's engine they might have been watching a silent film.

As soon as the sampan was berthed, a single voice did ring out, and as if in response the passengers streamed on to the jetty. There were women as well as men, Marker realized.

Cafell tapped him on the shoulder and pointed a finger in the direction of the cabins below. More people were emerging from these, and walking down the path towards the small bay. Marker counted fourteen of them, and something like twenty-five more on the jetty. This latter group was now being divided between the waiting speedboats.

'Illegals,' Finn murmured unnecessarily, readjusting the quietly whirring camcorder on his shoulder.

Five minutes later the first twin outboards sprang into life, shattering the relative calm, and the first boat accelerated away past the empty main jetty. 'I'm going to arrange a reception committee,' Marker told Cafell. He went back into the hide for the PRC-319 satellite radio, and carried it across the brow of the headland to the open expanse of rocky ground he had noticed on their way in. Another speedboat burst noisily into action as he set up the tuning antennae and sorted out the correct frequency. He unfolded the keypad, typed out his identification code, and sent it. Liquid-crystal letters flowed across the tiny screen, acknowledging him. 'Five bandits carrying approx forty illegals leaving Chuntao nineteen-twenty hours. Route unknown. Out.'

He repacked the radio and sat there for a moment, listening to the sound of the speedboats fading into the distance. He had never felt good in the role of a border guard; it was the sort of job which seemed much more reasonable in theory than in practice. During his last stint in Hong Kong he had been present at several intercepts, and each time he had been left with the feeling that an Englishman could never begin to understand what drove people like that to leave behind the only country they had ever known.

He walked back through the trees to the other side of the hill. The port below was as empty of activity as it had been half an hour earlier – it was like one of those memory games where you had to point out what had changed. Plus one sampan, minus five speedboats, Marker muttered to himself.

Lin Chun arrived home shortly after half-past eight, a thin man with intelligent eyes and too many worry lines for his age. He took one look at Rosalie and said: 'I do not give interviews to journalists.'

'I am a police officer, not a journalist.'

He grunted in surprise. 'And I certainly do not give interviews to foreign police officers.'

Rosalie looked beseechingly at his wife.

'She has only one question,' Lin Na-wen said.

He said nothing.

'Before you came to Hong Kong you worked on a dock construction project,' Rosalie said quietly. 'I just need to know exactly where this was.'

She had at least piqued his curiosity, she thought. But whether that would be enough . . . He was living on bitterness, and she supposed she could understand why. The idealistic Communism which he had embraced as a young man had made him an enemy in his own country and an unacceptable risk in others.

'Why?' he asked, the single syllable hanging in the air.

She went through the history of her investigation for the second time.

He shook his head. 'No one would build a large dock just for that.'

'It wasn't just for that.' She told him about the piracy angle, and the suspicion that stolen cargoes were being brought back to Shenzhen for resale.

That made him laugh. 'I am sorry,' he said, sounding anything but. 'You have taught us too well.' He laughed again.

'My father once told me unregulated capitalism and organized crime were pretty much the same thing.'

He liked that. 'Was your father a policeman too?'

'Yes. An English policeman.'

'Ah.' He regarded her almost with pity, and for a moment there was silence in the room. Through the open window they could hear the children at play below. 'I will tell you,' he said at last, nodding to himself. He stood and pulled down a map from the bookshelf. It showed Shenzhen County in its entirety: the southern portion designated as the Special Economic Zone and the northern portion across the electrified fence in still officially socialist Guangdong.

'Our camp was here,' he said, indicating a spot some ten miles into the latter. 'And each day we drove along this road' – he followed it with his fingertip – 'to the zone border just here. Then we took this road to the coast. We built the dock near the mouth of this little estuary. It was only about a mile from Nantou, but in a military area.'

She took down the names and did her best to memorize the map. 'Thank you,' she said.

'I never heard any babies crying,' he said.

She nodded and got up to go. 'How can I get a taxi back to the border?' she asked.

'You can't,' he said. 'They won't come out here this late in the evening. But you can get a bus on Hongling Road.'

'Which way is that?'

'I'll show you,' he said.

It was not much past nine o'clock but the walkways outside were deserted, the street below eerily empty of traffic. He walked her to the intersection with Hongling Road, pointed out the concrete shelter where the bus stopped, and looked briefly into her eyes before turning back towards his home and family. She walked across to the stop, where two teenage girls were bitterly lamenting their parents' archaic attitudes towards make-up.

The bus arrived about twenty minutes later, by which time a small crowd had gathered to squeeze aboard.

The four-mile trip back to the city centre took another half an hour, which gave the other passengers ample opportunity to study every aspect of Rosalie's face, figure and clothing. She couldn't remember ever feeling more conscious of her bi-racial heritage. Post-1997 Hong Kong was going to be like a zoo, she thought: the pure Chinese would come and gawk at how their genes had been corrupted.

At the central bus station her heart sank with the discovery that the border had already been closed for half an hour. Look on the bright side, she told herself – at least the Blue Dragons would have trouble finding her.

She walked back out on to Jianshe Road and in through the doors of the first hotel she came to. The price of a room was staggering, but she was past caring. Her credit card would cover the cost for now, and with any luck she could convince the OSCG Accounts Department that it had been a necessary expense.

The room was at least comfortable. She took a shower, going back over what Lin Chun had told her as the water washed off Shenzhen's patina of dust.

Her stomach rumbled, reminding her she hadn't eaten since breakfast. The noisy hotel bar charged almost as much for a snack as it did for a room, so she went back out, and walked up the brightly lit Jianshe Road in search of a restaurant that was both cheap and lacking a karaoke machine. Eventually she found one which offered Hong Kong-style fast food in exchange for Hong Kong dollars.

On the way back to the hotel a crawling sensation in her back made her wonder whether she was being followed, but after a rigorous programme of checks she decided she was simply being stared at. Back in her hotel room, with the door wedged firmly shut, she wondered how Marker and his friends were doing. They would be back before her, she realized, and if he tried to contact her . . .

She reached for the phone, thought for a moment, then took her hand away again. Shenzhen might have two McDonald's and International Direct Dialling but it was still part of the People's Republic. If the PSB were listening in, a call to a British military base would ring all sorts of alarm bells. And whomever she talked to, she would have to be careful what she said.

Li would be best, she decided. A message for him on their work number.

She dialled, listened to her own voice answer, and said: 'Li, this is Rosalie. It's ten o'clock on Monday evening and I'm in Shenzhen, staying at the Shangri-La Hotel. I should be back by tomorrow afternoon at the latest.'

She hung up, thinking that the message would offer a modicum of insurance. If something went badly wrong, and she couldn't make it back to Hong Kong, then at least the search party would have somewhere to start.

It was twenty minutes past midnight when Marker and Finn started down the slope towards the nearest of the cabins below. Both men were carrying silenced MP5s, and Finn also had the camcorder. The two-man patrols had continued in their set pattern all evening, and the latest had just returned to the usual building, which was the only one still showing a light. It would be forty minutes before another patrol set out.

The cabins were all in darkness, and all the doors

seemed to be hanging open. Marker went into the first two, and found them bare but for a carpeting of tattered mattresses. It was a way-station for illegals.

The next few cabins were the same, and he was halfway to assuming that they all were when a different arrangement caught his eye. Two rows of cheap tables lined either side of the penultimate cabin, and on each row there was a line of cardboard boxes. A faint smell of shit and vomit hung in the air. It was a cut-price crèche. Built by cutthroats.

'Jesus,' Finn murmured as the camcorder whirred.

The door to the last cabin was shut, but they could hear snoring inside. It was a woman, presumably the old one they had seen doing the laundry. Finn had a mental picture of her at the Social Security office, explaining that her last job had been as a day-care attendant in a pirates' crèche. 'And why did you leave that job?' the man behind the glass screen would ask.

They moved on through the grove of palms, and crouched for a couple of minutes in the shadow of a ruined watch-tower. Satisfied that there was no movement among the buildings a hundred yards ahead, they continued advancing until they reached the corner of the first building. A glance through the window showed it was empty, and had been for years.

Marker led the way round the back of the other old buildings, and from the corner of the last they could see in through the lighted window of the new structure beside the small modern warehouses. Two Chinese men were facing each other across a table, playing some sort of game. Both were smoking cigarettes and the cloud hanging between them looked almost poisonous in the yellow light.

The SBS men slipped across the gap, and Marker risked a quick glance through one of the side windows. He saw nothing to indicate the keeping of records. There was no telephone, let alone a fax machine. The communications radio which sat on a wooden table had been manufactured long before the days of miniaturization.

The other permanent staff were presumably asleep in the back.

They investigated the warehouses, and found both almost empty. One contained two boxes of computer software, the other a consignment of silk shirts and scarves. Hong Kong produce, Marker guessed. Brought out on the speedboats which took the illegals in, and probably destined for the mainland. Just a sideline.

As Finn dutifully pressed the camcorder button, Marker stood listening by the closed door, feeling profoundly disappointed. All they had was proof of illegals being transhipped by non-uniformed Chinese. There was nothing to connect anything to the authorities. The port facilities would be explained away as economic development for the future, and all knowledge of the rest denied.

They had seventeen minutes before the two men in the adjoining building set out on another meaningless patrol. Marker eased the door open, MP5 at the ready, and slipped out to one side. Finn followed him towards the narrow passage between warehouses, and the two men walked swiftly down towards the rear, with the intention of circling round behind the old settlement and climbing back up the hill.

The sudden shout put an end to all that.

The two men froze. The shout had seemed to come

from above them, from somewhere up on the sugar loaf, but the first sign of movement came from the rear of the lighted building to their right. Another shout was followed by gunfire, the bullets zipping into the plastic roof of the warehouse like a storm of hailstones.

With enemies in front and to the right, and a wide empty space behind them at the other end of the passage, it wasn't hard to pick a direction. Marker led the way at a fast jog towards the main jetty. More bullets ricocheted off the warehouse, and several raised voices were now competing with each other in what was presumably Cantonese.

As they raced out on to the short section of the T-shaped main jetty the whole structure was suddenly illuminated, and for a ludicrous second Marker wondered if the pressure of their running feet had tripped a touch-sensitive switch. More shouts were audible behind them, and a few seconds later another, deeper-throated gun opened up.

Marker swung right on to the longer arm of the four-hundred-yard jetty and put on an extra burst of speed to reach the cover offered by the huge wheels of the mobile gantry crane. Finn did the same and both men laid a line of silent fire across the water at the entrance to the jetty, toppling one man and forcing several others to think twice about a further advance.

He glanced up at the headland and wondered if Cafell and Dubery were enjoying the show. 'Have you got the camcorder stowed away?' he shouted to Finn.

'All dry and snug,' the Londoner replied, just as

several guns seemed to open up at once, sending bullets whining off the steel crane.

'Leap-frog,' Marker yelled, and as he fired a long burst from the MP5 Finn moved down past him from the first wheel of the crane to the third. A burst from the younger man, and Marker moved from the second to the fourth. A few seconds later they were both racing past the eighth and down the open jetty like Olympic sprinters hungry for gold. As the breath rasped in his lungs Marker counted off the seconds – five, six . . . ten, eleven . . . eighteen, nineteen . . . The gunfire sounded far behind them, almost a world away, and then they were sailing out into space off the end of the concrete pier, landing with twin splashes in the warm waters of the bay.

A couple of minutes later, as they eased themselves up on to the beach which Cafell and Finn had reached three nights before, they could see men peering down from the jetty, and a figure with a powerful torch hurrying past the crane. One gun opened up and then another, though what they were aiming at was impossible to say. The sea was apparently unharmed.

Marker and Finn quickly struck out inland, determined to be well away from the beach before anyone thought to send a search party. The journey across the centre of the island proved harder than expected, and it was almost two hours before they reached the other side, where Cafell and Dubery were waiting anxiously, crouched in the undergrowth close to the hidden Kleppers.

'Any sign of the enemy?' Marker asked.

'The sampan sailed past twenty minutes ago, heading

south. It doesn't look like they have anything else until the speedboats get back.'

'With any luck, they won't be.' Marker glanced at his watch. 'Looks like we'll be in time for our lift,' he said. 'Let's get the fuck out of here.'

11

It was twenty past three on the Tuesday morning when the weary SBS team arrived back at the Stonecutters' Island naval base. Marker sent the other three to their bunks and headed for the CO's telephone. Once ensconced in the office, he sat in the swivel chair and tried to organize his thoughts.

The excursion to Chuntao had achieved next to nothing. The Marines who had provided their lift home had been full of the news that three speedboats loaded with illegals had been successfully intercepted, but as far as Marker was concerned this was extremely small beer. At the rate the pirate organization was making profits the boats could be replaced out of petty cash.

On the plus side, there were unlikely to be any repercussions from the Chinese. He and Finn had been fired on, and maybe even identified as Europeans, but they had left no evidence behind. And in any case he doubted whether the villains would want to draw that much attention to themselves. Beijing would probably not even be informed of the incursion.

It was like a 0–0 draw, Marker thought. Defences had been dominant.

He picked up the phone and punched out Colhoun's home number. It would be twenty to eight in England, and he hoped Colhoun wasn't a *Coronation Street* fan.

Judging by the speed with which the telephone was answered, he wasn't.

'We're back,' Marker told his CO. 'No problems, but not much joy either.' He took Colhoun through the events of the previous thirty-six hours. 'Chuntao's obviously just a transhipment point,' he concluded. 'Another time we might have been luckier, and come back with some real dirt, but I'm not sure how much good it would do us. We really need to get some dirt on the people who matter.'

'And they're on the mainland,' Colhoun said resignedly.

'Probably right next door in the Shenzhen Special Economic Zone.' He gave the CO a thumbnail sketch of the connections Rosalie had been trying to unravel.

Colhoun's long sigh was eloquent.

I thought we might take a look at the Shenzhen coast later today,' Marker added. 'From our side of the border of course.'

'Of course. Be careful.'

Marker hung up and sat looking at the phone. Rosalie had told him she wanted to know the moment they got back, but he was tempted to let her sleep. Then, remembering how angry Penny used to get when he second-guessed her, he punched out the number of the apartment. Listening to her voice on the answerphone provided him with ridiculous pleasure, but it quickly gave way to anxiety when she failed to pick up at the sound of his voice.

He shook away a mental picture of her lying dead on the floor of the flat and called the OSCG number. Neither she, Li nor Ormond was there, and the man who answered refused to give him Li's home number.

But he already had Ormond's – the Scot had given it to him only a couple of days before.

It took only one ring for the Chief Inspector's irritated voice to answer.

Marker explained that he couldn't get through to Rosalie. 'After what happened the other night . . .'

'I'll get back to you,' Ormond interrupted him.

Marker sat in the Marine CO's chair and waited, trying not to imagine the worst. It wasn't easy, and as the minutes went by he felt himself trying to build mental defences against the inevitable blow.

It was more than half an hour later when Ormond called back. 'The locals took a look – the flat's empty,' he began. 'So I got hold of Li. He didn't know anything, but he called their answerphone at the OSCG, which both of them use to leave messages for each other. She called from a hotel in Shenzhen at around ten, saying she'd be back by tomorrow afternoon.'

The sense of relief, though enormous, soon wore off. 'What's she doing in Shenzhen?'

'A good question,' Ormond said drily. 'And it's probably no accident that she didn't say. In the People's Republic there's no such thing as a private phone call. I guess we'll find out tomorrow . . . or rather later today.'

'I appreciate the help,' Marker said. After hanging up he sat there in the darkened room, looking out at the night breeze whipping up the waters of the bay, feeling scared by how much he needed her.

Rosalie woke at her usual seven o'clock, showered again, and went down to the hotel dining room in search of breakfast. The *dim sum* trolleys were doing their rounds, much to the dismay of an American couple who wanted waffles. She loaded her plate with sweet coconut balls, water-chestnut cake and mango pudding, and then spoiled the impression by demanding coffee instead of tea. Over the resulting cup of instant sludge she considered her two options – return or further investigation – and decided that the latter required more research. The hotel reception provided her with a tourist map of the Zone, and from this she was able to work out that Lin Chun's dock was less than two miles from the road which connected Shenzhen City to the port of Shekou. And from the latter there was a regular hover-ferry service to Hong Kong.

There were other things to see on this road: 'Splendid China', which boasted models of famous areas and buildings, and 'China Folk Culture Villages', showing off the country's ethnic diversity through the re-creation of peoples and their homes. So there would be nothing suspicious about her going this way – the only problems would arise when she left the beaten tourist track.

A taxi probably wouldn't take her, she thought. And even if she found one that would, she could hardly ask the driver to wait while she investigated a closed military area.

She sounded out reception, and found that the fates were on her side, for further down Jianshe Road the country's first car-hire firm for tourists had recently opened for business. Back in her room she thought about leaving another telephone message, but could think of no way of conveying anything useful which didn't also betray her intentions. After checking out of the hotel she walked down the street to Shaolin Cars, picked out a shiny black Fiat Uno, and arranged, at an exorbitant extra cost, to leave the car at the ferry terminal in Shekou.

She was waiting at a traffic light on the wide Shennan Zonglu when she first noticed the black Renault some three cars behind her. There were two men in the front seat, and without really knowing why she knew they were from the PSB.

She drove out through the landscape of vast building sites which clung to the city's outskirts and followed the road west through several miles of flat countryside before passing under the new Canton to Hong Kong motorway. A mile further on the waters of Shenzhen Bay came into view, deep aquamarine beneath the clear blue sky.

The Renault was still fifty yards behind her.

The sign for 'Splendid China' hove into view, and without a second thought she turned the Fiat into the approach road. The Renault followed, and as she bought her entrance ticket she glanced back to catch the two men leaning against the bonnet of their car, lighting cigarettes.

She dutifully went round the exhibits, admiring shrunken versions of Guilin, the Great Wall, the Forbidden Palace in Beijing – just about everywhere a tourist might wish to tread. She stopped by the model of Lhasa's Potala Palace, listened to an English group lamenting the fate of Tibet, and restrained herself from pointing out that the Chinese had behaved no worse in that country than their own ancestors had done in Scotland, Wales and Ireland.

What was she going to do? There really didn't seem to be any choice – if the PSB men were still waiting she would have to go home.

But there was no sign of either them or their car in the parking lot. She strolled from one end to the other, checking behind the tourist buses and minibuses to make sure, and then climbed back into the rented car. Two miles down the road, approaching the crucial turn-off, she checked the rear-view mirror for one last time, took a deep breath, and aimed the Fiat into the unknown.

The road, freed of the need to impress foreigners, rapidly deteriorated. It passed through one oversize village, dipped to cross an area of flooded rice fields on a low embankment, and then climbed again to enter the small town of Nantou. Here the faces turned towards the car were full of curiosity, but when she stopped to ask for directions to Shekou her presence was satisfactorily explained – she was just another stupid foreigner lost in the immensity of the Middle Kingdom.

Not far outside the town the road crossed Lin Chun's river, but the view downstream was limited to little more than a hundred yards by a bend in the waterway. On the far side of the bridge a recently built side road forked off alongside the river, running through high gates and past an occupied gatehouse. Beyond the junction a high wire fence restricted all access to the area west of the main road, and the lie of the land ensured that the view through its mesh was limited to rocky slopes and blue sky. After several hundred yards of this she pulled the car over and climbed out, her sense of frustration winning out over her caution.

There was a hole at the bottom of the fence. In fact there were several of them: over the years erosion had washed away the top layers of soil, exposing the uneven rock in which the fence posts had been concreted. She would have no difficulty in crawling through.

Could she leave the car like this on an open road? The ridge line seemed no more than fifty yards away, and from there she should have a view of the estuary. She hadn't seen another vehicle since she left the tourists' beaten track. And it would only take five minutes.

She squeezed through and started clambering up the slope, her heart pounding. Two ridge lines later she was looking out and down at what she had come to see.

The land fell away across empty fields to the shoreline of the wide Pearl River estuary, and a faint line on the horizon marked the opposite coast some thirty miles into the distance. Almost directly in front of her, Lin Chun's river, now more than two hundred yards wide, flowed lazily into the Pearl. And a few hundred yards upstream, hidden from the estuary by a long bend and a tree-covered headland, a clutch of low buildings marked the small roadstead. A couple of short-sea traders were anchored in mid-river, and a third, which stood close behind the buildings, was presumably tied up at the invisible dock. Two container lorries were visible through the trees on the near side of the river.

It occurred to her that with binoculars she could have identified the ships.

But it didn't really matter – this was the place. The babies were sent south from here, the pirated cargoes unloaded and taken by lorry to other ports for their second sale.

And there was nothing more she needed to know.

She was halfway back to the fence when she heard the approaching cars, with no chance of making it forward to the road or back to the dubious safety of the ridge. Five PSB men climbed out in leisurely fashion, and watched as she scrambled back through the hole in the fence. They seemed more amused than anything else.

She smiled at them. 'I just went up to see the view,' she said apologetically.

Two arms grabbed hers and rammed her against the side of the Fiat. Hands roughly probed her body for any concealed weapons. Once the searcher was satisfied she was bundled into the back of a familiar-looking Renault, where she was immediately sandwiched by two men. As the driver turned the car she saw one of the other men climbing into her rented Fiat.

At the bottom of the hill they turned left through the now-open gates and on to the road which ran along beside the swiftly widening river. After a mile or so she could see the ships in mid-stream, and shortly after that the structures gathered behind the dock.

The first building looked neglected, and it was towards this that she was half led, half pulled by two of the PSB men. Once through the entrance she had a momentary glimpse of several doorways before she was pushed into an empty room. She looked up to see two lines of rusted hooks suspended from the ceiling – her new home had once been a cold store. And then the door slammed behind her, flooding the room with darkness.

She leant against a wall and let her weight take her down on her haunches, wondering how she would be rewarded for her stupidity.

* * *

It was noon when the SBS team reassembled for brunch in the Stonecutters' Island canteen, and after each of them had made up for lost cholesterol Marker outlined his plan for the day. 'Everything points to Shenzhen,' he said, spreading a large-scale map of the area out across the cleared table. 'By my reckoning the Zone has about thirty-five miles of coastline – ten around Mirs Bay in the east, and about twenty-five in the west around Deep Bay and along the Pearl estuary. And with the exception of the seven or so miles along the Pearl, it's all viewable from British waters. So Rob, you and Ian take Mirs Bay. Finn and I will take the west. The first things we're looking for are the two short-sea traders Rob and Finn saw on Chuntao – I'm sure we've all committed the Chinese characters to memory by this time . . .'

The others groaned.

'And the second thing is a likely port. It won't be that big, or there wouldn't have been any need to tranship cargoes, but it has to have enough water to take fully laden short-sea traders.'

'There's always a chance they're using several small ports,' Cafell said gloomily.

'Maybe, but if I were the Big Cheese I'd want more control than that.'

'I hope you're right,' Cafell agreed.

The four men scattered to collect the necessary gear, and Marker took the time to phone the OSCG office. She hadn't yet returned, her partner said. But there was no reason to worry, Li added, sounding less than convinced by his own words.

Ten minutes later Marker was watching Stonecutters' Island and the towers of Kowloon fall away behind them as Finn steered the Rigid Raider at a steady thirty knots towards the Kap Shui Mun channel. The sea had never yet failed Marker, but on this particular afternoon the uplift he always felt in its swaying grip had a hard time competing with the sinking feeling which the conversation with Li had left in his stomach.

It took them most of an hour to reach a point astride the maritime boundary some two miles off the mountainous Shekou peninsula, and from there they slowly followed the Chinese coast eastwards, taking turns with the high-powered binoculars. They passed the Shekou hover-ferry terminal, and then, a mile further on, Shekou itself, with its port capable of handling ocean-going ships. Two short-sea traders were riding at anchor offshore but neither bore the characters Cafell had so painstakingly copied down.

The coast receded somewhat after that, but never beyond the reach of the binoculars. The two men watched a succession of tiny fishing villages give way, somewhat incongruously, to the distant silhouettes of a roller-coaster and Ferris wheel.

The coast drew nearer once more as they approached the head of the bay, but there was no sign of any port facility, only flat fields receding towards a raised highway. Finn turned the boat round and headed them back towards Shekou.

'What about the estuary coast?' he asked.

'Not this time,' Marker said. 'If Rob and Ian come up empty then maybe we'll risk it after dark.'

'You'd think it would be too public,' Finn observed. 'The Canton ferry would go straight past it.'

'About five miles offshore,' Marker corrected him. 'I checked before we left.'

'Ah. Possible, then. But what are the chances of Whitehall OK'ing another venture into the unknown?'

'They'll only get the chance to say no if we ask them. As far as I'm concerned we've already been given the green light to trespass in Chinese waters.'

Finn smiled. 'The politicos might make a distinction between the waters around an uninhabited island and the waters off the mainland.'

'Yeah,' Marker agreed. 'They might.'

From the window of his Shenzhen City office Wang Shao-qu could see across the border into Hong Kong's New Territories, and he often sat watching the Canton–Kowloon Railway trains disappear into the hills on their way to the centre of the British colony. In a little over two years he hoped to be making the same journey himself, rather in the manner of a conquering general come to claim his prize.

And there was no reason why Hong Kong should not be his. He had made Shenzhen prosperous enough, and he shared that prosperity with all the right people. The PSB were loyal to a man, as were most of the local Party functionaries. The local PLA commanders were all in his pocket, and with good reason. They knew Mao's old army had a doubtful future in the new China, and there was no better hedge against uncertainty than money.

He heard his secretary's footsteps, listened for the sound of the tea being placed on his desk, but didn't bother to turn round. In Hong Kong he would have a *gweilo* secretary, a blonde with long legs and heavy breasts. He would live in a truly cosmopolitan world at last. He could hardly wait.

Sometimes he was almost tempted not to. The $200 million already on deposit in Zurich would buy a cosmopolitan life anywhere on the planet, and he could indulge his hunger for blondes until the urge – which even he found perverse – finally faded. But opting for a life like that would cut him off from that unrestrained exercise of real power, both in the office and the bedroom, to which he had grown accustomed over the years. And he didn't want to give that up. He liked the way the women prisoners wept beneath him – that was the way relationships between men and women were supposed to be. No wonder they were so obsessed with sex in the West – there was no satisfaction to be had from a pretence of equality.

His phone rang, and he turned to pick it up.

'Comrade Hua for you,' the secretary announced, making him smile. Her use of the word always amused him.

'We caught the woman snooping around,' Hua said without preamble.

'Good,' Wang said, taking a Winston from the silver cigarette box and flicking open his Zippo lighter.

'What do you want done with her?' Hua asked.

Wang expelled smoke. 'She made no further contact with Hong Kong?'

'None.'

That was good, Wang thought. She would be just another mysterious disappearance, just one more victim of the crime wave engulfing the Zone. Deng might trumpet his 'Four Modernizations' – agriculture, industry, defence and technology – but in Shenzhen everyone knew there were five, and crime was the one with the highest growth rate. 'So send her back to the camp with the rest after the night shift. How old is she?'

'About thirty, I should think.'

'And three times as healthy as one of our people,' Wang said. 'If one of our illustrious leaders has a sudden need she'll be very useful.' There was, after all, nothing quite so gratitude-inducing as an immediately available life-saving organ. There were already four men on the Guangdong politburo, and one on the all-nation body, who had Wang's prison population to thank for their continued existences.

'She's attractive too,' Hua said ingratiatingly. 'She's half-English.'

'Is she?' Wang was interested in spite of himself.

'I can keep her here for you.'

He had nothing else on that evening. 'I may come down to the villa later,' he said.

Marker and Finn arrived back to find the other two enjoying mugs of tea on the end of the dock. Cafell was looking pleased with himself.

'Any joy?' Marker yelled out.

'Nope, but I've had two brainwaves . . .'

'A year's supply in one afternoon,' Finn observed.

Cafell ignored him. 'The stuff's in my room,' he said, getting up. 'You didn't check the estuary coastline?' he asked Marker, as the four men walked across to the barracks entrance.

'No, why?'

'All will be revealed. First brainwave – since we're assuming that the *Ocean Carousel* cargo is going to be re-exported why not check the insurance companies' register of cargoes?'

'Which would tell us what?' Finn asked.

'Where our cargo is going to be picked up the second time round,' Marker told him.

'And the answer is Shekou,' Cafell said. 'I phoned the boss in Poole when we got back and asked him to find out. He called back half an hour later. Ships will be calling at Shekou tomorrow and next Monday to load the exact same cargoes which were taken off the *Ocean Carousel* and *Indian Sun*.'

They had reached Cafell's room.

'Which leaves us with two possibilities,' he went on, after they had all crammed in. 'Either they're using Shekou for everything, which seems unlikely – it's too visible – or they're being really cunning, and bringing the stuff overland from its port of re-entry. If they're doing that then the people at Shekou would assume it was coming straight from the factory.'

It made sense, Marker thought. 'And where is the port of re-entry?' he asked.

Cafell reached back for the aerial photograph which they had looked at several days earlier. 'I'd put money on here,' he said, indicating the river estuary just below Nantou on the Pearl estuary coast.

'Why?' Marker asked, disappointed.

'Look at the bend in the river,' Cafell said. 'It would mask any view from the estuary, and the river looks wide enough to take short-sea traders.'

Marker shrugged. 'It may be a good guess, but . . .'

'We'll soon know,' Cafell interrupted, a wide grin on his face. 'This picture was taken in 1978. I asked the boss if there was any chance of getting a more recent photo, and he said he'd try. When he called back he said the Yanks had agreed. Apparently they're feeling sufficiently pissed off with the Chinese to do us a favour. And a 1993 vintage photo is on its way from the Pentagon, via the US Embassy. It should be here in the next hour or so.'

Finn was less than impressed. 'OK, I get all that,' he said, 'but what about the brainwaves?'

Marker gave Cafell a playful pat on the head and went off in search of a phone. Rosalie still wasn't back, Li told him, and according to the Lo Wu border officials, whom the detective had alerted late that morning, she had not yet re-entered the colony. 'If she has not appeared by six o'clock,' Li said, 'I shall take the matter to our superior. He will ask the Shenzhen police to start an investigation.'

Marker hung up the phone and stood beside it, his eyes closed. He knew in his bones that something had gone badly wrong, and could only pray that the situation was still retrievable.

He walked back towards Cafell's room, wanting to take off for Shenzhen himself, but knowing that for all the good such a gesture would do, he might just as well hit his head against a wall. A messenger arrived at the same time he did, large envelope in hand. Marker took it in and ceremoniously handed it to Cafell, who was already armed with his magnifying lens.

He took out a large contact sheet and a wad of prints, sorted through for the one he wanted, and applied the lens. A few seconds later he said 'Bingo' softly, and invited Marker to look. It was all there: the dock, the dredger in mid-river, the warehouses and the access road.

'This is the adjoining photo,' Cafell said, putting it alongside the first. The access road continued on beside the river for half a mile, then cut across behind the hilly headland which stood sentry at the river's mouth, to end among a cluster of buildings on the shore of the wide Pearl estuary. 'It's a small naval base,' Cafell explained. 'It's been there since at least '78. But this' – he pointed out a single large building on the estuary side of the headland – 'is new. And so's the track to it.'

'If it was built at the same time as the port, then maybe it belongs to Mr Big,' Finn suggested.

'Maybe,' Marker said. Looking at the photos he felt strangely certain that this was where she was. 'OK,' he said, 'before I make any suggestions there's something I have to tell you all. You all know that Rosalie Kai is involved in this business, and you've probably noticed that she and I have been spending a lot of time together . . .'

'We get the picture, boss,' Finn said. 'It was the spring in your step which gave you away.'

Marker smiled in spite of himself, but only for a second. 'What you don't know is that she's gone missing in Shenzhen, as of yesterday afternoon.'

There was a silence as that sank in.

'What was she doing there?' Cafell asked eventually.

'No one knows,' Marker said. He felt angry with her about that, and wished he didn't. 'The reason I'm bringing it up is that I really feel the need to *do* something, and there's always the chance it's warping my judgement.' He did the rounds of the others' faces. 'That said, I'd like to pay this place a visit tonight. We've followed the trail of these bastards all the way from Singapore, and I don't see any point in giving up now.' He looked at Cafell, who had as much common sense as himself and Finn put together. 'Rob?'

'What are our objectives?' Cafell asked in a neutral voice.

'Same as on Chuntao – we gather evidence. Finn can do his Spielberg impersonation. And this may be the place they keep their records – an organization operating on this sort of scale must keep some somewhere, and it's hard to imagine anywhere safer.'

'What sort of records?' Finn wanted to know.

'Cargo inventories. Accounts. Lists of pay-outs to all the different groups involved. Receipts from dock handlers and shipping lines. That sort of thing.'

'Makes sense,' Cafell agreed.

'And what else are we going to do?' Finn asked rhetorically. 'Like the boss says, we're following a trail. And if all else fails there's always the grand old SBS tradition of making up objectives as you go along.'

Cafell didn't look completely convinced. 'There's always the chance that this bunch have got the thing really well sussed, that none of their facilities are vital, and that all of them are replaceable . . .'

'So we don't bother?' Finn asked.

'If you'd wait until I finished . . . I was going to say that maybe the best we can do is put a spoke in the bastards' wheel, and if so we should make it as big a spoke as we can manage, and take some C4 along.'

'Sounds good to me,' Marker said, smiling. 'Ian, what do you do think?'

Dubery looked surprised to be asked. 'If we use the Kleppers then getting in shouldn't be a problem,' he said slowly, 'but getting out might be. If we run into any trouble at all, and someone alerts the naval base . . .'

'We'll have a hell of a job getting home in the Kleppers,' said Cafell, completing his thought for him.

'These guys are usually considerate enough to leave us a speedboat,' Finn said optimistically.

'And if they don't?'

'Then we're up the Pearl estuary without a paddle.'

Rosalie sat on the floor of the dark, empty cold store, her back against the mould-encrusted wall. The jade-green trouser suit she had been wearing for thirty-six hours was covered in dirt, and the smell of her own waste hung in the trapped air. The luminous dial on her watch told her that she had been here for eight hours, but it felt a lot longer.

Outside it would soon be getting dark, and in Hong Kong Marker and Li would be beginning to worry in earnest. And also in vain. Only Lin Chun could point them in this direction, and they had no earthly reason to ask him.

It was greed, she thought. Her father had never known when to stop, and neither had she. He had always wanted a little bit more, had never been satisfied, and when the bridge burnt down behind him there had been no way back across the river. And now she had done the same: kept on pushing and pushing until it was too late. She could have gone back to Hong Kong with her knowledge of the location, or simply satisfied herself with seeing the tell-tale gates and fence. But no, she had needed to climb under it, see for herself, have it all. It was the same greed, and the fact that she and her father had been on different sides of the law seemed almost irrelevant. Neither of them had found the balance, the inner harmony, which the Buddhists knew was central to both happiness and effectiveness in this world.

She stared into the darkness, thinking that it was probably a little late to be worrying about this world. No doubt the Wangs could arrange to have her tried for espionage if they wished, but there didn't seem any reason why they should. There was no way they could risk her simple imprisonment – no one in China, no matter how powerful, could guarantee that the political winds would blow their way for ever. The puritan left might one day regain power, and the prisoners of today would become the witnesses of tomorrow. It had happened before, and not so long ago. They could not afford to let her live.

So why was she still alive?

She could think of no comforting answer.

12

The Rigid Raider dropped off the four men and their two Kleppers near the north-western corner of British waters, some two miles to the south of the mountainous Shekou peninsula. Normally each man would have relished the beauty of the star-strewn sky and moon-washed waters, but the clarity of the night only increased their chances of being seen. The four of them paddled swiftly in towards the sheltering silhouette of the Chinese coast, each engrossed by the needs of the moment.

When they had drawn to within a few hundred yards of the shore Marker slowed the pace, conserving energy for the night ahead. He was trying not to think about Rosalie, and wondering how anyone could have come to seem so important, so central to his life, in such a short space of time.

In the seat behind him Finn was pondering the same subject. He had watched as Marker explained the thing about the woman, and he had seen something in the boss's eyes which he was sure no one had ever seen in his own. That was kind of sad, he thought, and maybe he was being given nights like this so that he could tell his children about them. It was a frightening thought, but maybe his mother had been right about something.

The coastline floated by, and not much more than

half an hour had elapsed when Marker judged it time to steer further out into the estuary, and so draw a wide half-circle around the naval base. There was no activity on the several jetties, but lights shone in several windows and the distant sounds of a TV show carried across the water. A quarter of a mile further up the coast the villa nestling at the foot of the small wooded headland showed no obvious signs of life, but a motor launch lay alongside the small private dock.

The mouth of the river appeared, but as expected the view was foreshortened by the tight bend, and there was no visible clue to the fact that a port facility had been constructed only half a mile upstream. The SBS men paddled across the river mouth towards the northern shore, pulled the Kleppers up out of the water, and carried them quickly across the rocks and up a short slope into the shelter of the trees. This headland, bordered on three sides by the twisting river, was mostly wooded, around two hundred yards wide, and rose to a fifty-foot ridge. The satellite photos had shown no trace of a human presence.

Having hidden the Kleppers, the four men pushed their way up through the tropical vegetation, stopping a few yards short of the crest to listen for movement on the other side. Behind them the moon rode high in the southern sky and the gleaming black waters of the wide estuary stretched away towards the pinpricks of light which marked its farther shore. Myriad boats dotted the water, the closest a princely-looking junk with latticed sails that shone pale gold in the moonlight. The four of them were behind enemy lines, a hell of a long way from home, and hopefully on their way to smite the wicked. It was one of those brief moments in which Marker felt blessed, both to be alive and to be a member of the SBS.

An engine of some sort started to grind in the distance, but the headland seemed locked in silence. Marker moved forward on his stomach to the crest, and looked out through a dense mesh of foliage at the wide river below. A few yards to the left he found a better window on the scene, one which also framed the buildings on the bank beyond.

The four men hunkered down, draped the anti-reflective gauze veils across their binoculars and started exploring the view. On the far side of the two-hundred-yard-wide river a single concrete jetty had been built out from the bank. It was about twenty yards wide and five times as long, offering room to spare for the three-thousand-ton short-sea trader which was tied up against it. This was in the process of being unloaded, and the grinding noise they had heard was emanating from one of two derricks amidships.

Beyond the boat and the jetty, and half masked by the yellow floodlighting, several buildings crouched beneath a line of ailing coconut palms. Two covered lorries were parked off to the left, and as the four men watched a fork-lift truck emerged from behind the boat and hummed its way towards one of the buildings. Its driver was one of many dressed in what looked like light-blue pyjamas. They were from the local camp or prison, Marker guessed, for there was something painfully submissive about the way they moved. It was hard to count, with all the moving to and fro, but there were at least twenty-five of them, mostly men but with a scattering of women, none of whom was Rosalie.

There were another ten or eleven men engaged in the

unloading, most or all of whom were in supervisory mode. They were the ship's crew, he decided, and they weren't carrying weapons. They didn't need to – a third group, noticeably younger and more smartly dressed, was doing that for them. Marker counted eight spread out around the jetty, and every one of them was either carrying or sitting within easy reach of a Kalashnikov AK47.

After fifteen minutes of observation the team slipped back across the crest and crouched down among the trees for a tactical conference.

'Suggestions?' Marker asked quietly.

Cafell spoke first. 'They've almost finished unloading the ship, and if we wait till they have, then there's a good chance the labour force and most of the guards will be driven back to wherever it is they come from. That'll leave us with only the ship's crew to deal with . . .'

'The ship may sail,' Finn interjected.

Cafell shrugged. 'All the better. We can wander across, turn the place upside down and leave our calling cards on a one-hour fuse.'

'Sounds good,' Marker agreed.

'Yeah,' Finn agreed. 'Since the bastards haven't left us a speedboat, a quiet exit seems kind of essential.'

She would not have believed it possible, but with the coming of night it had grown even darker inside the cold store. The temperature had seemed to rise too, but perhaps that had something to do with the staleness of the air. She still didn't feel hungry, but thirst was becoming a real problem, and it was no great consolation that the sweat which dripped from her forehead offered a modicum of relief to her parched lips.

Soon after half-past seven the silence outside was broken by the arrival of vehicles. Heavy lorries, she guessed from the sound – probably two of them. The engines had no sooner been switched off than she heard voices raised in shouts of command: 'Hurry up!', 'Keep quiet!', 'Move!' And then, a few moments later, she was sure she heard a baby crying.

She put her ears against the door but the sound was not repeated, and she found herself wondering whether she had imagined it, whether the darkness and the fear had magnified her work of the last few months into an obsession. And then, all of a sudden, she found there were tears streaming down her cheeks, sobs racking her body.

She sank to the floor once more, buried her head in her hands, and let the inner storm slowly blow itself out.

Raising her head several minutes later, she could hear machinery. It had to be the ship's derrick. The shouts of command had been for the forced labourers who were now unloading the cargo.

It crossed her mind that she might be sent back with them, and that that was why she had been kept in this room all day. The thought of companionship made her smile inside, and took her back through the encounters of the last few days, listening to Hu Guang-fu talk about the Triads, sitting on the edge of Gu Yao-bang's desk in the picture library, the daily enjoyment of working with Li.

She liked being with people. So why had she spent so much of her life alone?

In the observation point on the other side of the river Marker was beginning to feel his frustration mount. As expected, the unloading of the ship had been completed, the blue-pyjama-clad labour force had been led back to the lorries, and the crew had disappeared inside the superstructure. But another half an hour had brought no further advance. There was no sign of the lorries leaving, and the eight armed guards were standing around beside them, talking and smoking, as if the whole night was theirs to waste.

Nor was the ship giving any indication of an early departure, though they had been given one strong hint that it would leave that night. Shortly after the unloading was finished the fork-lift had returned with a teetering pile of cardboard boxes, each of which was then passed from hand to hand over the freighter's side. The sounds of babies crying had easily carried across the wide river.

With such a cargo, Marker reasoned, the captain would probably wait for the early hours before setting off downstream towards Chuntao. But that wasn't really a problem – if need be they could cope with the ship's crew. He wanted to know what the armed guards were waiting for.

'Boss, I've had an idea,' Finn whispered at his side.

'Tell me.'

'They forgot to leave us a speedboat, but they have left us a ship. Why don't we take it home?'

Marker thought about it. The jetty was empty. The ship's crew had not looked armed. If they could get aboard unseen and unheard . . . Jesus, he thought suddenly, they could take the prisoners with them. Those men and women would have loaded and unloaded any number of pirated cargoes – their evidence would be damning.

'I like it,' he murmured, as much to himself as to Finn.

'I was afraid you would,' Cafell said mournfully in his other ear. 'The last time you liked one of his ideas I spent six days sitting on a container.'

'Ah, but this time we get to drive the boat,' Finn said.

Cafell sighed. 'OK, so what's the plan?'

Marker told them. 'And once we're on board,' he concluded, 'don't let your better natures get the better of you. One audible gunshot and we're in trouble.'

It took them ten minutes to reach the edge of the river. The bulk of the boat lay between the jetty lights and the water, casting the starboard side and a twenty-yard swath of river into shadow, but that still left a large stretch bathed in moonlight to traverse undetected. The shifting patterns of light in the tidal swell would help, but if anyone applied binoculars to the centre of the river, or even a keen naked eye, then they would probably be seen.

Sink or swim, Marker thought. He looked around at the other blackened faces. They had wasted enough time.

The four men crawled head first into the water and struck out in the direction of the black freighter's bow. Each knew that these would be the crucial moments – if the alarm was raised they might regain the headland but their chances of getting back to Hong Kong would be remote indeed.

Twenty yards, thirty yards . . . fifty, sixty . . . they were in mid-stream now, swimming as fast as the packs allowed, concentrating on keeping each stroke as silent as was humanly possible. It seemed to take an eternity, but at last they were in the shadows, the freighter's side looming above them. The grab-hook snaked up out of the water, catching on the rail with a noisy thunk, and after a minute's wait had produced no sound of movement on the deck above Finn shinned up the rope and slipped aboard. A tug on the rope announced the all-clear, and the other three followed him up on to the deck. The four men crouched down by the rail, the silenced MP5s now cradled in their arms, and took stock of where they were.

The ship's working lights were off, but those on the jetty were still on, casting a bright yellow glow across the sixty yards of deck which stretched between them and the superstructure. The two figures visible on the illuminated bridge would have a hard job seeing out, but Marker still didn't fancy the odds on their running the length of the deck without being spotted, even with the cover offered by the derricks and several casually strewn packing cases.

As if in answer to a prayer, the jetty lights suddenly went out, casting the deck in deep shadow.

Someone up there liked them, Marker decided. 'Let's go,' he said, and the four men set off at a swift jog along the starboard rail. Neither of the two silhouetted heads on the brightly glowing bridge turned towards them, and within twenty seconds the four men had their backs to the wall of the superstructure beside an open doorway. The smell of food and the sound of conversation came floating up the stairway inside.

On the bridge above them one of the two men made a clapping sound.

Marker made a downward gesture with his thumb, and moved through the door just as a young man – a boy, really – appeared at the bottom of the stairway. He had a brimming bowl of noodle soup in each hand, his eyes were guiding his feet, and he didn't see Marker until he was only a few steps from the top of the stairway.

The eyes widened, the hands shook violently, slopping the soup down the steps, but he didn't drop either bowl.

Marker gestured that he should put down the bowls, and the boy obeyed. Another hand signal put him in Dubery's custody.

Marker went carefully down the steps, stopping at the bottom, where a passage led aft towards the source of food and conversation. Then, with Cafell and Finn close behind him, he walked stealthily down the corridor towards the open door of the ship's galley.

He took a deep breath, stepped through the door and moved to the right, the MP5 held loosely in firing position. Behind him Cafell moved to the left, leaving the space between them for Finn.

The male voices died away in a second, leaving only the sound of a woman talking on the radio. There were eight men in the room, eight faces expressing surprise. No one made a move.

Finn turned away to cover the corridor, and ushered Dubery forward with the boy.

That made nine, Marker thought, and they had estimated ten or eleven. The two on the bridge should be the only ones left. 'Rob, you and Finn keep this lot happy. Ian, let's take the bridge.'

He led the way up the first flight of stairs and paused at the bottom of the second. 'I'll go in first,' he whispered. 'They'll be expecting one pair of feet with their supper. You follow me in, but be careful to keep to the back wall – we don't want to be seen from outside.'

The two Chinese men on the bridge, one of whom was wearing a captain's hat, looked up from their mah-jong board as Marker opened the door and stepped inside with the levelled MP5. The man without the hat barked out what sounded like a question, and was halfway out of his chair before common sense took hold. He sank back looking angry as the captain took a leisurely pull on a thick cigarette. The bridge air, Marker realized, smelled of opium.

Dubery moved in behind him, and he gestured the two men to their feet.

They just sat there, as if they didn't understand.

Marker pulled his finger on the trigger, and sent a three-tap burst between them, scattering the mah-jong tiles against the cushioned bulkhead.

They allowed themselves to be escorted down to the galley, where the captain walked into a sudden barrage of questions from his own men.

Finn raised an eyebrow at Marker, who told him to let them talk. 'Go and find somewhere we can put them, preferably somewhere escape and sound-proof. If we have to tie and gag this lot it'll take till Christmas. And be careful,' he added, as Finn started off, 'we're not sure we've got them all.'

For the next few minutes captors and captives stared at each other, the Chinese no doubt wondering who these crazy *gweilos* were and what they wanted, the Brits hoping that none of the guards outside had noticed anything different about the ship at the jetty.

Finn came back with two pieces of good news: the babies they had seen carried aboard were all sleeping in a cabin further down the passage, and down near the engine room he had found a windowless storeroom which would serve as a temporary brig. As he and Dubery escorted the eleven crew members down in batches, Marker went back aloft, finding a spot behind the bridge from which he could look out across the jetty to where the guards were still idly chatting beside the lorries.

He had not been watching for much more than a minute when the headlights of a car suddenly appeared in the distance. It was coming down the access road beside the river. The armed guards heard it too, and Marker wondered if this was what they were waiting for.

It was a big car, the sort he had seen on news film of Party bosses driving down roads lined with adoring masses. There were two men in the front and one in the back, and it quickly became apparent where the power lay. As the car stopped one of the armed guards went up to the back window, listened for a moment, and then ran off to do his master's bidding. Marker strained his eyes to see the face of the man in the back, and then remembered the nightscope. He was in the act of putting it to his eye when the guard returned, dragging someone along with him. Someone barefoot, with a dirt-streaked face and clothes.

It was her.

When she had first heard the hands on the cold store door Rosalie's heart had leapt with the hope that her guess had been right, and that she was about to be sent back with the others to a prison camp. But the hope lasted no longer than the time it took her eyes to readjust to the gloomy light. The lorries were parked away to her right, and the two men grasping her by the upper arms were leading her straight towards a car that was stopped on the road.

Her foot struck something sharp and she realized she had left her shoes behind. Then her two captors stopped and she was suddenly conscious of eyes looking out at her from the back seat.

'This is her, Comrade Wang.'

The man nodded. 'Yes,' he said in Cantonese.

She was bundled into the front seat, where the driver sniffed and made a face before putting the car into gear. One of the two men who had collected her from the cold store had climbed into the back, and was now almost caressing her neck with the barrel of a revolver. The whole car stank of aftershave.

They moved forward, passing between the still-berthed ship and a clutch of buildings before venturing back on to the road which ran along the river bank. A few moments more and she could see where the river flowed out between two low promontories into the wide Pearl estuary.

The road divided, and the driver took the right fork, continuing on around the headland to where a large white villa with a pagoda-style roof looked out across the sea. As she was bundled out of the car and up the steps towards the front door, Rosalie had a momentary glimpse of a small private dock and the boat which was berthed alongside it.

The driver and the man with the gun took her into a luxurious living room with a large picture window, and held her by the arms until the other man returned. Then her arms were wrenched behind her back, and something strong but supple was looped around her wrists. She squirmed violently but it was too late. The hands that had held her arms were now grasping her by the calves, and she felt the same material tighten around her ankles. It was a length of leather thong, and she had been hobbled like a member of a chain-gang.

Now, for the first time, the man in charge came round in front of her. He was about forty, slightly plump, no taller than her. He had cold, intelligent eyes, vestigial lips and closely cropped hair; beads of sweat were glistening on his brow and forearms. He was wearing dark-blue slacks and a striped shirt open at the collar.

He told the other two men they could go.

They went, licking their lips with someone else's anticipation.

Wang walked across to a desk, came back with a pair of scissors, and began cutting her clothes from her body. First the blouse, then the bra, the trousers and the knickers. Having peeled away the pieces caught by the leather restraints he stepped back to admire what a thorough job he had done.

She stood there, naked and bound, feeling more frightened than she thought it possible to feel.

'You need a wash,' he said.

After the car had disappeared from sight behind the headland at the river's mouth, Marker had stared at the empty road for several seconds, as if reluctant to accept the fact that it was gone. The temptation to take off in pursuit was strong, but the responsibilities of command could not be shaken off so easily. He had to balance the interests of everyone involved – Rosalie's and the team's, the prisoners' and the babies', even those of the pirates' victims, both past and future.

A hundred yards up the road in the opposite direction the posse of armed guards had resumed their waiting game. Matches flared as they lit cigarettes, and the smiles on the illuminated faces looked like an adman's dream. Marker found himself remembering reading that the tobacco companies' rising profits in the Third World had more than made up for the downswing in Europe and America.

He still didn't know what the guards were waiting for, but he suspected the time for finding out had passed.

The other three were waiting in the galley, Finn with spoon in hand. 'It's good soup,' he said.

Marker told them what he had just witnessed, and brushed aside the others' concern. 'First, we'll complete the round-up,' he said curtly. 'Once we have the area secure we can start thinking about getting everyone home. OK?'

The others nodded soberly.

Marker smiled grimly, and led the way back up the stairs and on to the deck. A raft of planks took him across on to the darkened jetty, and he jogged towards the nearest building, the others in a line behind him, their running feet making only a soft slapping sound on the concrete.

They passed down the side of one warehouse and along the back of another, emerging into a grove of palm trees some fifty yards inland from the road. Two grounded containers had been left in the intervening stretch of flattened grass, and these, while blocking the lorries from sight, also provided excellent cover for the four men's advance.

They moved stealthily forward through the grass, circumventing a discarded Coke can as if it were a mine. Behind the first container they stopped and listened for movement beyond, but all they could hear were the overlapping conversations of guards and prisoners. They had just reached the shelter of the second when a loud banging noise erupted away to their left, from the general direction of the jetty. It took several seconds before they realized what it was – the imprisoned crew had started drumming on the inside of the ship's hull.

The conversations in and around the lorries had stopped. Then a lone voice uttered something in Cantonese which Marker would have bet money meant 'what the fuck?', and footsteps sounded on the road.

They could not allow the guards to disperse. Marker gestured Finn and Cafell to take one end of the container, and Dubery to join him at the other. Then, without preamble, the four men stepped out into the open, their eyes taking in the scene, their minds calculating angles, their fingers ready on the triggers of their MP5s. Marker thought about shouting a warning, but decided that the guards would understand the levelled guns a lot better than his English.

And for a moment he thought it had worked. The four men standing together by the nearest lorry still had their Kalashnikovs slung across their backs, and they knew at once that there was no contest. The other four, who had just started off down the road to investigate the hammering noise, had pulled their guns round into a cradling position, and one of them took an impulsive decision to fight it out. His gun was still swivelling when the silenced MP5s opened up, throwing both him and the man next to him back across the road. It was as if a sudden gust of wind had suddenly plucked the men from their feet and thrown them down violently.

Having seen death pass so swiftly between them, the other two threw up their hands, leaving the Kalashnikovs to hang loose across their stomachs. The group of four by the lorry looked like they were auditioning for Madame Tussaud's, mouths hanging open, all the better to display their golden teeth. All six men were disarmed, persuaded to sit in a group on the grass, and watched over by Finn.

Marker closed the dead men's eyes, sighed, and walked over to the back of the first lorry. Several curious faces stared out of the gloom at him. 'Does anyone hear speak English?' he asked.

'Yes, I speak,' a voice said from the back. A few moments later a young woman was standing beside Marker, listening to him explain the situation. She didn't think any of her fellow prisoners would object to a life in Hong Kong.

While she passed on the good news to the others Marker rapped out orders. 'Rob, you and Ian get this lot on board, the guards first and then the prisoners. The ex-prisoners,' he corrected himself. 'And then see if you can work out how to get the ship underway. If you have to get help from the captain or first mate you can use the girl as an interpreter. And get one of the women to check on the babies. And stop that fucking drumming,' he added, staring in the direction of the ship. 'Shoot one of the bastards in the foot if you have to.' He turned to Finn. 'You and I are going to take a look round.'

*　　*　　*

Wang had ushered her towards the bathroom, pulled back the plastic curtain to reveal a separate shower stall, and spent several seconds adjusting the water temperature. Satisfied, he stepped aside and gestured to her to step in. She did so, and for a split second the pleasurable sensation of the water on her skin almost blocked out the sense of terror which was throbbing in her brain.

Then he was rubbing her with the bar of soap, lathering it across her breasts and stomach, down her back, and up between her legs. She could hear a voice screaming inside her head, but only a whimper came out of her mouth, and deep down inside, almost too far away for her to hear, another voice was saying: 'Your fear will make him stronger.'

She closed her eyes and let his hands have her physical self. She remembered the biology teacher at school telling the class how human skin was continually being sloughed off. The skin he was touching would be dust in a few days. She felt the water on her face and remembered the joy of making love with Marker. She felt the tears well up in her eyes, and knew from the look in his eyes that he had seen them, even through the streaming water.

He pulled her from the shower, reached for a towel, and then seemed to think better of the idea, bending to lick a drop of water from her right nipple with his tongue. She shuddered, which he took as an invitation to do the same with the left nipple.

Then, with her body still dripping water, her hair a wet curtain across her face, she was pushed out of the bathroom, across a passage and into a room she hadn't yet seen. A large bed occupied most of the space, and he shoved her roughly across it. She instinctively curled up like a foetus, but he was already on his way out of the door. She lifted her head and frantically looked round for something to help her – a way out, a weapon of some sort.

There was nothing.

Marker and Finn started with the nearest warehouse, which proved as empty as those on Chuntao had been. The next one was more than half full, the third crammed from floor to ceiling – these had received the cargo unloaded that evening from the short-sea trader. A fourth warehouse was as empty as the first, leaving only the low, sprawling building which housed the office and social accommodation. Marker tackled the office room while Finn went through the rest, and the first thing which caught his attention was a computer terminal.

He turned it on, and watched the monitor spring into life.

'This is no time for computer games, boss,' Finn said behind him.

They both stared at the first screen. 'Is there any way we can get at what's stored in this?' Marker asked.

'Why don't we just take the whole thing with us?' Finn asked. 'If there's anything on the hard disk we can read it in Hong Kong.'

Marker looked at him with admiration. 'I'd never have thought of that,' he said. 'And I guess the same goes for these records,' he added, scooping up an armful of papers and looking for something to carry them in. On the desk there was a wooden in-tray which probably dated back to the Ming dynasty.

He was reaching for it when the burst of gunfire erupted.

When Wang came back he was wearing nothing but a loincloth. It was probably the ritual uniform of some esoteric martial arts group, but it looked like a giant nappy, and Rosalie felt her spirits boosted by the sight. He had a small glass in one hand, which he sipped at carefully as he looked at her.

She suddenly remembered the film Marker had taken her to three years before. She couldn't remember its name, or even the crucial scene in detail – only that the mother had unintentionally killed her son with a wine glass. She had tried to hit him, the glass had got in the way, and his throat had been cut.

'Can I have some water?' she asked, and was pleasantly surprised to find her voice was steady.

'No,' he said instinctively, and then his lipless mouth broke into a grin. 'All right,' he said. 'It won't be in anyone's interest for you to have a dry mouth.'

He left his own glass on the floor and went out again.

She stared at it, knowing she would only have one chance, her mind running through all the possibilities and finding that most of them ended in failure.

Marker's orders had been simple enough, but it soon became apparent that carrying them out was easier said than done. Cafell and Dubery had six new prisoners and more than twenty ex-prisoners to look after, and getting both groups on to the freighter in an orderly fashion was likely to be about as simple as boarding English football fans on their way home from the latest Continental skirmish.

This was also obvious to the lone English-speaker. 'We help?' she asked.

Cafell couldn't see how. 'Just wait a few minutes and then get your people on the ship,' he said, and then noticed that two of them had already picked up discarded Kalashnikovs. It occurred to the SBS man that for all he and the others knew, these people were murderers and child molesters, and not political prisoners at all. But they didn't seem so, and Cafell didn't think that was because they were better at looking inscrutable. As far as he could tell, they seemed genuinely grateful, and eager to help.

'Just these two,' he told the woman, pointing at the men who had picked up the guns. 'No more.'

She spoke quickly to the others, some of whom were still emerging from the back of the lorries. No one else reached down to pick a weapon from the pile of Kalashnikovs. Cafell breathed a sigh of relief, and gestured to one of the two armed men to join Dubery at the head of the guard detail, the other himself at the rear.

They set off on the two-hundred-yard walk to the ship, their pace slowed by the obvious reluctance of their prisoners. The ex-prisoners, who had started off in the rear, were soon walking a parallel path, leaving the width of the road between the two columns. This worked fine until they were on the jetty, when the need to take the gangplank caused the gap between the two groups to shrink. Realizing what was happening, Cafell looked desperately round for the English-speaking woman.

He couldn't see her. 'Stop,' he yelled, hoping that she would hear and translate, but it was already too late. The armed prisoner who had accompanied Dubery, and who had been walking backwards to keep the guards under his gun, suddenly tripped on the end of the gangplank, and dropped the Kalashnikov as he fell.

The nearest prisoner took what he thought was his chance, grabbing for the gun and half falling into the line of his previous charges.

Cafell's finger waited on the trigger for a clear target.

The Kalashnikov opened up, the sound of its fire mingling with screams and the hailstone effect of bullets hitting the side of the ship.

And suddenly the gunman was rising as those around him sank to the ground, and Cafell took his chance, firing a triple tap through the man's upper trunk. The Kalashnikov flew up in the air and the man fell backwards with a rattle in his throat, down into the narrow gap between freighter and quay, crashing into the water with a splash which seemed to echo in the sudden silence.

Cafell walked forward and kicked the gun off the quay, keeping his eye on the five surviving prisoners. A single glance to his left took in the two men spread-eagled on the gangplank – one of the Chinese prisoners and Dubery. The former had half his head blown away, the latter blood steadily seeping from a hole in his chest.

'Oh shit,' Cafell murmured, his attention back on the still prone prisoners.

Running feet on the jetty told him the other two were on their way.

Marker bent down to look at Dubery's wound, his mind racing with the choices still to be made. The youngster's eyes seemed locked in surprise – as well they might be. His chances of survival would be better than even if there was a hospital next door, but as it was . . .

He looked round for the English-speaking woman, and found her at his shoulder. 'Is there a doctor here?' he asked.

'No,' she said.

Marker stood up. 'Get these bastards below,' he told Finn and Cafell, 'and bring up our medical kit from the galley.' He asked the woman to get him help to carry Dubery aboard; she spoke, several arms reached out, and the young Scot was carried along to a cabin on the boat deck. Marker walked alongside, ears and eyes straining for sounds of trouble. Had the sound of the Kalashnikov burst carried? And if it had would anyone come to investigate, or would they just assume one of their forced labourers had been cut down trying to escape?

He looked at his watch. Almost twenty minutes had passed since the car had vanished round the headland.

Finn arrived with the medical kit and a bowl of water. 'Rob's seeing about getting the boat underway,' he said.

Marker carefully washed and disinfected the entry wound, then told Finn to turn Dubery around and followed the same procedure with the exit wound. The bleeding had almost stopped.

There was nothing else he could do but put on a bandage.

'I do bandage,' the woman said, as if she could hear the seconds ticking away in Marker's head.

'Is everything secure down below?' he asked Finn.

'Yep.'

'Then go and get the computer and papers.'

Finn went out through the door as Cafell came in. Marker took his second in command back out on to the deck. 'Can you get this lot back to Hong Kong?' he asked.

'I'll do my best,' Cafell said.

'I sent Finn for the records we found. When he comes back, get the ship underway as quickly as you can. I'm going after Rosalie. With any luck she's in that villa, and the boat we saw at the dock will still be there. If so I'll join you at sea. But don't wait around. If I have to I can always go to ground and use one of the Kleppers once the fuss has died down.'

Cafell nodded. It hardly seemed worth pointing out that this wasn't a fuss which would die down very quickly. 'Good luck,' he said.

'Thanks,' Marker said. He picked up the MP5 and walked swiftly towards the gangplank, passing Finn groaning beneath the weight of the computer. 'See you later,' he told the surprised Londoner, and broke into a run as his feet hit the gangplank. As he sped along beside the darkened river the relief of a single purpose warred with the fear of what he might find at the end of the road.

Wang came back, glass of water in hand, and pushed it against her mouth. She drank, not knowing what else to do. With her hands tied how could she . . . ?

He took the glass away and stood up, let the loincloth

fall to the floor, and took hold of his half-erect penis. For a moment she thought he was going to piss on her, but he didn't. Instead he coaxed himself with one hand, and reached down with the other for the glass he had left on the floor.

Without – or so it seemed – taking any conscious decision, she jerked violently backwards, uncurled her body and struck out with the two hobbled feet, all in the one explosive movement. The feet struck the glass in front of his mouth, and he was thrown backwards, his head striking the partition wall with a solid thump.

She rolled off the bed, and knelt down beside him. There were cuts around his mouth, but none of them serious. He seemed to be unconscious, but for how long?

His body twitched, as if to remind her he was still alive.

She looked round and her eyes fell on the broken glass, just as a low groan escaped from his lips.

There didn't seem to be any other choice . . .

She conjured up the picture of the infant bodies between the sampan's decks, the baby tossed up and out into the speedboat's slipstream . . .

He groaned again.

She twisted round to pick up the broken glass with one of the hands tied behind her back, knelt down on the carpet beside his upper body, and blindly reached back with her knuckles for the open throat. Finding it, she took a deep breath, grasped the jagged glass between her fingers and tried to slice the skin. The first time she cut only air, the second time flesh, and a wash of warm blood flowed between her fingers.

She leaned forward, still kneeling, reluctant to turn

and see what she had done. His flaccid penis lay across his leg and for one raging instant she wanted to cut that off too.

For several moments she didn't move, and then the raised voices suddenly reminded her of the two men outside. Cursing herself, she started sawing at the leather thong which bound her ankles.

Nearing the villa, Marker had left the road for the bordering trees and reluctantly slowed his pace to a walk. He could see the car parked in the circle of gravel where the road ended, the motor launch bobbing in the water by the small dock, but the villa itself was still hidden in the trees to his left.

Then the flare of a cigarette showed him the two men sitting on the steps, facing out to sea. They made him think of fathers waiting outside a hospital ward for their wives to give birth.

The other man was alone with her, inside.

He forced himself to look, to think, to plan. A few seconds were enough. There might be another way up through the trees to the villa, but a silent approach would take far too long.

His mind made up, Marker slipped back down to the road and walked towards the two men, the MP5 up against his chest, hidden in the darkness of his silhouette. In his mind he went over the pronunciation she had taught him three years before, and at the moment it became clear that his approach had been noticed he lifted an arm and waved. 'Nei ho ma,' he shouted. 'Hello.'

One of the men returned the greeting as he got to his feet, and then added what sounded like a question.

Marker offered an exaggerated shrug. The distance had now shrunk to thirty yards, and even in this light . . . Half of him wanted them to buy his bluff, to let him reach the point at which their only choice was surrender, to take the burden of killing away from him, but the other half wanted blood, wanted vengeance for whatever it was they had done to her.

The standing man reached for his belt, setting the avenger loose. Marker smoothly pulled the MP5 into the firing position, squeezed down on the trigger, and some twenty-five 9mm bullets did their silent work, shattering the skull of the sitting man and almost cutting his companion in half at the waist.

Marker sped up the steps, scattering sparks from the posthumously discarded cigarettes. Lights were shining from all the villa windows, and the door stood slightly ajar, as if someone hadn't bothered to close it properly. He paused only for an instant, then shouldered his way through, shouting 'Rosalie' at the top of his voice.

No one answered.

He looked in the first room, saw the pieces of cloth strewn across the floor, and knew they had once been her clothes. His stomach knotted in fear.

He turned and there she was, standing in the doorway, naked, her hands and wrists red with blood.

'Callum?' she said, as if she couldn't believe it.

He found her a shirt and a pair of cotton trousers, dressed her, and carried her down to the small dock. There was no key in the ignition, but it took him only a few seconds to hot-wire the engine. She climbed aboard without help and sat beside him as he made sure of the controls.

'We're going to be OK,' he told her.

'I know,' she said simply, and the ghost of a smile was in her eyes.

The sound of another engine suddenly invaded his consciousness, coming from the other side of the headland. It had to be the freighter. Cafell and Finn had got it underway.

Marker eased forward on the throttle and they pulled out into the estuary. A hundred yards and they could see the short-sea trader gliding out of the river mouth, showing all the correct lights for a vessel under steam. It looked like a freighter in search of a cargo, not a ship on loan to the SBS for transporting babies for sale, political prisoners and foreign-devil trespassers back to Hong Kong.

Ten minutes more and Marker was manoeuvring the launch alongside as Rosalie grasped for the rope ladder which Finn had thrown down.

'Can you make it?' he asked.

'I think so,' she said. The exhaustion born of shock seemed to be fading like a nightmare, leaving only fragments of irrelevant despair.

He watched her go up, her movements surer with each rung, and then followed, leaving the launch to drift with the tide. Scrambling across the rail, he asked Finn how Dubery was.

'He'll make it,' was the answer.

'Thank Christ. Where's Rob?'

Finn grinned. 'On the bridge, of course. He's always wanted to be a captain.'

'He's welcome. Go and tell him to keep up the good work. I'm . . .' He gestured towards Rosalie, who was leaning against the rail, looking out to sea.

Finn smiled and disappeared through the doorway.

Marker walked over to her. 'Do you want to go inside?' he asked.

'I want to be held,' she said.

He held her, feeling the warmth of her body through the thin cloth, the warm breeze flicking her still-wet hair across his face. Over her shoulder, in the far distance, he could see the faint yellow glow of Hong Kong's gaudy halo hanging in the southern sky.

OTHER TITLES IN SERIES FROM 22 BOOKS

Available now at newsagents and booksellers
or use the order form provided

SOLDIER A SAS:	Behind Iraqi Lines
SOLDIER B SAS:	Heroes of the South Atlantic
SOLDIER C SAS:	Secret War in Arabia
SOLDIER D SAS:	The Colombian Cocaine War
SOLDIER E SAS:	Sniper Fire in Belfast
SOLDIER F SAS:	Guerrillas in the Jungle
SOLDIER G SAS:	The Desert Raiders
SOLDIER H SAS:	The Headhunters of Borneo
SOLDIER I SAS:	Eighteen Years in the Elite Force
SOLDIER J SAS:	Counter-insurgency in Aden
SOLDIER K SAS:	Mission to Argentina
SOLDIER L SAS:	The Embassy Siege
SOLDIER M SAS:	Invisible Enemy in Kazakhstan
SOLDIER N SAS:	The Gambian Bluff
SOLDIER O SAS:	The Bosnian Inferno
SOLDIER P SAS:	Night Fighters in France
SOLDIER Q SAS:	Kidnap the Emperor!
SOLDIER R SAS:	Death on Gibraltar
SOLDIER S SAS:	The Samarkand Hijack
SOLDIER T SAS:	War on the Streets
SOLDIER U SAS:	Bandit Country
SOLDIER V SAS:	Into Vietnam
SOLDIER W SAS:	Guatemala – Journey into Evil

continued overleaf . . .

SOLDIER OF FORTUNE 1:   Valin's Raiders
SOLDIER OF FORTUNE 2:   The Korean Contract
SOLDIER OF FORTUNE 3:   The Vatican Assignment
SOLDIER OF FORTUNE 4:   Operation Nicaragua
SOLDIER OF FORTUNE 5:   Action in the Arctic
SOLDIER OF FORTUNE 6:   The Khmer Hit
SOLDIER OF FORTUNE 7:   Blue on Blue
SOLDIER OF FORTUNE 8:   Target the Death-dealer
SOLDIER OF FORTUNE 9:   The Berlin Alternative
MERCENARY 10: The Blue-eyed Boy
MERCENARY 11: Oliver's Army

*   *   *   *   *

MARINE A SBS: Terrorism on the North Sea
MARINE B SBS: The Aegean Campaign
MARINE C SBS: The Florida Run
MARINE D SBS: Windswept
MARINE E SBS: The Hong Kong Gambit
MARINE F SBS: Royal Target

*   *   *   *   *

WINGS 1: Typhoon Strike
WINGS 2: The MiG Lover

All at £4.99

All 22 Books are available at your bookshop, or can be ordered from:

22 Books
Mail Order Department
Little, Brown and Company
Brettenham House
Lancaster Place
London WC2E 7EN

Alternatively, you may fax your order to the above address. Fax number: 0171 911 8100.

Payments can be made by cheque or postal order, payable to Little, Brown and Company (UK), or by credit card (Visa/ Access). Do not send cash or currency. UK, BFPO and Eire customers, please allow 75p per item for postage and packing, to a maximum of £7.50. Overseas customers, please allow £1 per item.

While every effort is made to keep prices low, it is sometimes necessary to increase cover prices at short notice. 22 Books reserves the right to show new retail prices on covers which may differ from those previously advertised in the books or elsewhere.

NAME ....

ADDRESS ....

....

....

☐ I enclose my remittance for £_____
☐ I wish to pay by Access/Visa

Card number

☐☐☐☐ ☐☐☐☐ ☐☐☐☐ ☐☐☐☐

Card expiry date

☐☐ ☐☐

Please allow 28 days for delivery. Please tick box if you do not wish to receive any additional information ☐